Once Upon a Duke's Wish

The Duke's Lost Treasures
Book 1

LANA WILLIAMS

ARE YOU SIGNED UP FOR DRAGONBLADE'S BLOG?

You'll get the latest news and information on exclusive giveaways, exclusive excerpts, coming releases, sales, free books, cover reveals and more.

Check out our complete list of authors, too!

No spam, no junk. That's a promise!

Sign Up Here

www.dragonbladepublishing.com

Dearest Reader;

Thank you for your support of a small press. At Dragonblade Publishing, we strive to bring you the highest quality Historical Romance from some of the best authors in the business. Without your support, there is no 'us', so we sincerely hope you adore these stories and find some new favorite authors along the way.

Happy Reading!

CEO, Dragonblade Publishing

Dedication

To Dee and Steve for always believing in me
and for wondering, could it be?

Chapter One

London, England
April 1875

"I WISH..."

Leo Stanton, the Earl of Marbury waited for the Duke of Rothwood, a man who was like a grandfather to him, to finish the thought, yet only the crackling fire echoed in the duke's quiet study.

The two men had enjoyed dinner together, something Leo tried to do every week or two in order to help assuage the duke's obvious loneliness. They now sat in massive wingback leather chairs before the fire, brandies in hand.

Rothwood's melancholy this evening suited Leo. They both knew what the date was—the fourth of April. A day that had affected them both deeply. The thirtieth anniversary of the duke's daughter's wedding day and the last time he'd seen her.

It had been the last day of happiness for Leo's late father, as well. He was the groom she'd left standing at the altar, waiting for the love of his life, who had never come.

Lady Bethany, the duke's daughter, had chosen to elope with David Wright, an adventurer she'd met at a garden party a month prior. The pair had married in Scotland, then soon after, sailed to the wilds of Nova Scotia to a little-known place called Oak Island in search of buried treasure.

"I wish my life had turned out differently." Rothwood at last finished his thought as he stared into the flames.

"I know, Your Grace." All Leo could offer was understanding and sympathy. He couldn't change the past any more than he could predict the future.

Leo's father had eventually married for convenience and been content at times but never happy. Something he made no effort to hide, even for the sake of his wife and son.

Lady Bethany's death had been reported to the duke some five years ago, though he'd never acknowledged her marriage. Oddly enough, Leo's father had passed away that same year. Whether the explorer with whom Lady Bethany had eloped still lived remained a mystery. The duke claimed not to care, but Leo wondered if he was as curious as Leo.

As a member of the Royal Geological Society and an expert on pirate lore, Leo had heard rumors of David Wright's efforts as recently as two years past, suggesting he was alive. It gave Leo great pleasure to advise the other interested members of the Society that Wright had dug in the wrong place. Discrediting the man seemed the least he could do both for the duke and for his own father.

"You might've been my grandson." The duke swirled the brandy before taking a drink, then meeting Leo's gaze.

Leo never knew what to say at moments like this. Regret served no purpose. Lady Bethany had departed years ago, and nothing could change that truth. Yet he knew how lonely the duke was. The difficult past had aged him. Did Rothwood wish he hadn't cut ties with his only child? He needed family and a purpose. Preferably both. Something to keep him from dwelling on the past.

"I would've been honored to call you grandfather," Leo spoke with sincerity for it was true.

He'd inherited his friendship with the duke from his father. The late earl had maintained a close relationship with the man he'd expected to become his father-in-law, even if that hadn't come to pass. Leo and the duke had deepened their ties through their shared interest in exploration. Leo's mother thought their friendship odd and was often exasperated by it.

Rothwood's brother, his only sibling, lived in the country and rarely visited London. The duke's nephew and heir apparent lived abroad and hadn't been heard from in years. But no purpose would be served in dwelling on the grim future of the duchy this evening when Rothwood was already in poor spirits.

Leo finished his brandy, searching for an uplifting thought to share before he took his leave. "Sometimes our wishes are fulfilled when we least expect it. And in unexpected ways."

"That sounds more like a curse than words of comfort," the duke countered, though he chuckled as Leo stood. "Thank you for coming by. I shall see you at the next Society meeting."

"I look forward to it."

Leo and Rothwood both served on the council of the Royal Geological Society, which concerned itself with exploration of all types, including treasure hunting.

Leo had dabbled in it himself in his earlier days but now preferred to sort through and analyze the information received from the comfort of his home. He enjoyed the challenge of investigating the various theories and lending his expertise, focusing on history to determine what was likely to be true or merely a rumor.

Inviting the duke to become a member of the council had been an excellent idea, as he had considerable resources, as well as knowledge to offer. It also had the added benefit of catching the duke's interest and easing his loneliness. Rothwood's passion for exploring the world might have been partially to blame for his daughter's interest in a treasure hunter, as she had shared that same interest, according to Leo's father.

Leo did indeed wish the Duke of Rothwood was his grandfather, as they had much in common. But as he'd said, regrets served no purpose. He intended to make certain his life held as few as possible. When he eventually married, it would be to a woman he respected and admired. Love was not a requirement. In fact, he hoped never to experience romantic love. That emotion only caused pain. His marriage would be more of a business partnership. Happiness was best pursued in his work, not in his personal life.

"I'm meeting Viscount Worley at the dock tomorrow morning. He's returning from Africa with several artifacts that will require study."

The light of interest that filled Rothwood's eyes comforted Leo. "I look forward to hearing more."

"As soon as I know the details, I'll be in touch. Thank you again for dinner." With that, Leo took his leave. He had to wonder if Lady Bethany and David Wright had any idea of the damage they'd left in their wake. Had the love they'd found been worth the hurt they'd caused others?

Leo shook his head. That was a question to which he'd never know the answer.

⊰⊱

ELLA WRIGHT GLANCED about the crowded, chaotic dock in London as she and her two sisters disembarked from the *Campania*, her breath hitching. She wondered not for the first time if she'd made a terrible mistake.

She had convinced her sisters to leave the only home they'd known, and for what?

A grandfather who had never acknowledged their existence.

A city that looked anything but welcoming.

A country that was not their own.

And a future that now seemed more uncertain than ever.

The harsh shriek of a steam whistle rent the air as if mocking her. The weight of it all caused her to stagger on the gangway, the world shifting beneath her feet. For once, the steamship that had traversed the Atlantic was not the cause.

"Are you well, Ella?" Norah, her younger sister by four years, asked. Trust Norah to notice her upset. As the middle child at one and twenty, she was the observant, even-tempered, peacemaker of the family.

Ella nodded, determined to keep a positive outlook, even if it was only a mask. After all, what choice did she have? Nothing remained for them on Oak Island in Nova Scotia. She could only hope there was something—anything—for them in London.

Their mother had died five years past of smallpox and their father six months, two weeks, and three days ago. The thought of them brought heavy grief she and her sisters continued to feel, made even worse by the unknown way their father had died. The worry over what his last minutes had been like in the shaft he'd dug kept Ella awake at night.

David Wright had been enamored with treasure hunting his entire life. When rumors of pirate gold buried on the small island in Nova Scotia had caught his notice, he'd become obsessed with discovering all he could. His excitement had piqued the interest of a lady he'd just met, Lady Bethany, the only child of the Duke of Rothwood.

According to the stories their mother had shared, it had been love at first sight.

Yet Ella could imagine how hard it must've been for her mother to leave behind her father, the duke, and his expectations—not to mention the man to whom she'd been betrothed, her friends, and the elegant life she'd led.

How brave her mother had been, though Ella knew many thought her foolhardy. London was not so distant from Nova Scotia that she'd escaped the notoriety that had followed her because of her actions.

Ella and her sisters had experienced some of that same speculation on the rare occasions they'd traveled to Montreal, Quebec, and other large towns in the area with their parents. The feeling of being watched with curiosity, as if they were an exhibit in a zoo was unpleasant, to say the least. Unfortunately, she feared they'd have to endure more of that in London.

"What's taking so long?" Lena, the youngest of the three sisters at the age of nineteen years, leaned back and forth, then lifted on her toes in an attempt to see over the heads of the passengers before them on the gangway.

"Patience, my dear," Ella responded, more out of habit than with the hope of placating her. "Everyone is as eager to set foot on land as we are."

Lena was rarely still—as if she couldn't contain the energy inside her. Though their journey on the ship had been only two weeks, it had felt much longer, especially to Lena. Ella knew the months leading up to it had also made her sister restless.

The decision to move to London had come soon after their father's death. It had taken a few months to settle their father's affairs, make the arrangements for the trip, sort through their belongings to determine what to take, sell what they could, then pack the rest.

Ella had managed to find an older woman to serve as a suitable chaperone. Mrs. Whitsome, a widow traveling to London to stay with her sister, had been a blessing.

The last evening on the ship had been a celebratory one with many of the passengers in high spirits. Ella had been happy, as well, until she and Mrs. Whitsome had returned to their room to find their belongings upended as if they'd been searched.

Had someone been hoping to find items of value? Or had they been looking for something specific? The latter thought had her clutching her reticule tighter, for hidden inside was her father's journal detailing his search for treasure, as well as a few artifacts he'd found. Thank goodness she'd kept it close since they'd begun their journey, or they'd have little left by which to remember him.

Luckily, nothing appeared to be missing. With Mrs. Whitsome's assistance, she'd managed to put their room back in place before her sisters saw the mess. They were worried enough about the move to London without making it worse. Ella had been relieved that Lena hadn't seen through her efforts as her sister sometimes had an extra sense. A kind of knowing that washed over her and provided insight not easily explained.

If Ella had received a reply to her letter from their grandfather, the journey would've been easier. But the worry that he'd simply refuse them entrance placed a knot in Ella's stomach that made it difficult to function. Between grief and fear, she felt terribly fragile.

Norah glanced back at her again, her bright blue eyes filled with worry. "Where will we stay if the duke won't see us?" She whispered the question to keep Lena from hearing.

"He'll see us," Ella promised. "We won't leave until he does."

Norah managed a small smile. "You think because we all look so much like Mother, he won't be able to deny our identity."

"Exactly." Ella was counting on that fact. They all had the same blonde hair and heart-shaped faces, even if their eye color varied. How could he possibly suggest they weren't their mother's daughters?

But from what little her mother had shared prior to her death, they would be better off not mentioning their father, as the duke had disapproved from the moment he'd met him. Father had not been a peer, merely the son of a wealthy merchant, and therefore, beneath the duke's notice.

Ella had difficulty understanding how any of that mattered. Shouldn't one's merit be based on one's actions and strength of character? She feared her opinion on the issue would make her fit in even less with their grandfather and the society in which he moved.

At last, they reached the end of the gangway and stepped onto solid land. But the chaos there was even worse than it had looked from the ship.

Wagons and carts piled high with timber, barrels, boxes, and bales moved past. Masses of people—mainly men—hurried by, some dressed in soldiers' uniforms, many sailors with their odd gait, and numerous clerks clutching papers.

One could barely move through the throng.

"What is that terrible smell?" Norah asked, pressing the back of her gloved hand against her nose.

"I believe it's London," Ella replied. A briny scent stung her nostrils, along with the smell of rotting fish, coal smoke, and a myriad of other odors that were foreign compared to the clean air in which they'd previously lived. A haze hung over the city like an old woman clutching a dirty shawl around her shoulders. Did it always look and smell like this? The thought was terribly depressing.

"This way to collect our baggage," Mrs. Whitsome said and led them to where it was being unloaded. Lena and Norah followed with Ella directly behind.

"Miss Wright."

Ella turned to see Julius Conway, a kind gentleman near her age who'd befriended them on the ship. "Mr. Conway, how nice to have the chance to bid you goodbye."

"Pray, do not tell me it will be goodbye." He offered the charming smile he so often wore. The handsome man, who seemed to have a far better and definitely brighter wardrobe than she, had been friendly during the journey and helped to keep them all in good spirits.

Ella smiled, resisting the urge to advise him that his attempt at charm was wasted on her. She had no intention of allowing anyone to sway her from her goal of seeing her sisters settled.

"I despair at the thought of not seeing you or your lovely sisters again soon," he continued. "I have grown rather attached to the three of you."

She easily dismissed the compliment, as he gave them so frequently. Did she dare ask whether his room had been searched? It was impossible to know who to trust. Perhaps it was best if she didn't trust anyone.

"It has been a pleasure traveling with you, sir. I hope our paths cross again soon." She glanced over her shoulder, realizing she'd lost sight of Norah and Lena, as well as Mrs. Whitsome. "But for now, I must find my sisters."

"Of course. Good luck with your new beginning." He tipped his hat and strode away.

A new beginning. Yes, that was what this was. But rather than greet it with excitement, only worry filled her.

She turned and searched the throng, hoping to see Norah or Lena. As she eased forward with no sight of them, panic clutched her chest. She craned her neck this way and that, to no avail, only to be jolted from behind, sending her tumbling into another.

"Pardon me." The deep voice, along with the steadying hands on her arms, had Ella stiffening in alarm.

"My apologies, sir." Filled with remorse at having plowed into him, she glanced up at the man, her attention immediately caught. He was striking—so tall and handsome, well dressed in a fine black wool suit with a close fit that emphasized his broad shoulders.

"The fault is mine." His hazel eyes with green and gold flecks regarded her with a cool reserve.

"I was looking for someone." They both said the phrase at the same time.

Ella smiled, as did the man, which warmed his expression along with his eyes.

"It appears you dropped this." He reached behind her to retrieve her reticule, then brushed it off before handing it to her. "Have you just arrived?"

Her heart thudded at the idea of nearly having lost it. "Yes. On the *Campania*."

"Ah." He nodded. "My friend is arriving on a different ship." He looked to the side, giving her a view of his profile. Black eyebrows arched over wide eyes. A straight nose and high cheekbones lent a chiseled appearance to his features. His dark hair was clipped short and just visible beneath his hat. Broad shoulders and a thick chest were at odds with his fine attire. The white linen of his shirt was starched perfectly, his tie knotted with precision.

All of which made her even more aware of her rather bedraggled appearance.

"Did you have a good voyage from…" His voice trailed off as if he waited for her to assist him.

"Nova Scotia."

A light of interest sparkled in those intriguing eyes. "That must've been quite the journey."

"It was indeed." The urge to share a few details took her by surprise. The man was a stranger, albeit a handsome, well-attired one. Yet he looked so capable and confident. How lovely it would be to share her burden with someone who looked as if he could deal with any adversity that came his way.

"Who are you in search of?" He studied her, making her feel as if she had his undivided attention and causing a shiver of awareness to run along her skin.

Ella blinked, annoyed with herself for having forgotten for even a moment what she was about. "My sisters who traveled with me."

"Allow me to assist you. My height is occasionally good for something." He glanced around, then smiled. "I can see two rather worried young ladies who share your beauty standing beside several bags. Might that be them?"

Ella's face heated with his casual compliment. "More than likely."

He offered his arm. "After running you over, the least I can do is assist you in wading through this crowd to reach them."

Touched by his kindness, she took his arm. "Thank you so much. How nice to be welcomed to London with such gallantry."

"Is this your first time here?"

"Yes."

"I do hope you won't judge the city by the chaos of the dock." He paused his stride to allow a dockworker hauling crates to pass before continuing forward.

"If you're suggesting it becomes better, I would be pleased to believe you." She tucked her reticule more securely under her arm, reassured by the weight of her father's journal and the other items it held.

"It does. I promise." He offered a smile with his pledge, his teeth as perfect as the rest of him.

"We shall see. In all honesty, I'm not certain of our welcome here."

"Oh?" He lifted one of those elegant brows as he glanced at her.

She shook her head, not wanting to explain. "The story is a complicated, one that I'm sure would only bore you."

"I can't imagine any stories you tell would be boring."

Ella's breath caught at the hint of admiration in his eyes as he held her gaze. For goodness' sake. What was wrong with her? Since when was her head turned by any man, even one who brought to mind a medieval knight from one of the stories their mother used to read to them?

It was just that she was off-balance, worried about what was to come as much as she was burdened by recent events. She gave herself a mental shake as they joined her sisters and Mrs. Whitsome.

"Ella. What happened to you?" Norah asked, her eyes wide with worry. "One moment you were behind us and the next you'd disappeared." But her expression softened as she took in Ella's escort.

"I'm here now thanks to the kindness of a stranger." She nodded at the gentleman as she released his arm. Something about the jostling crowd had her gripping her reticule even tighter. It couldn't be the loss of the handsome man's assistance that caused her to feel so uncertain.

"The pleasure has been mine." The man bowed, then turned to her sisters and bowed again. "Enjoy your time in London."

"Thank you," Ella managed as those hazel eyes fastened once more on her. Then in the blink of an eye, he was gone.

"Who was that?" Mrs. Whitsome asked.

"No introductions were made," Ella said.

"Very handsome," Lena whispered as she stared after him.

"And tall," Norah added. "He was dressed so finely. Do you think he was a lord?"

Guilt filled Ella. The thought hadn't crossed her mind. "I hope not, or I might've offended him by not properly addressing him."

"He didn't seem offended." Lena patted her arm. "Besides, it's not as if you'll ever see him again."

"True." Ella had more important things to worry over, such as whether the duke would even bother to meet them. "Let us call on our grandfather."

"There's a hackney cab stand just over there," Mrs. Whit-some advised. "Why don't we share one, and I'll see you to your grandfather's home before I'm on my way."

Ella nodded, then straightened her shoulders and told herself she was ready for whatever was to come. There was no argument the Duke of Rothwood could present that would dissuade her from insisting that he take them in.

Chapter Two

L EO COULDN'T DISMISS the blonde-haired beauty from his thoughts. Even after he'd found Viscount Worley, who was beside himself with excitement over the artifacts he'd brought, Leo caught himself searching the crowd for a glimpse of her.

"I didn't dare leave them in my bag. One never knows if someone told others about a find." Worley scowled as he drew to a halt and glared at Leo, his impressive mustache twitching. "Are you even listening?"

"Of course," Leo reassured his friend. "I look forward to seeing them for myself."

Leo's fixation on the lady was ridiculous. He'd met any number of beautiful women in his life, and none of them had distracted him like this. It was only that she'd looked lost, at least until they'd found her sisters. Her vulnerability had brought forth a protective streak he hadn't realized he was capable of.

What had led her to London? And why was she uncertain over her welcome? He couldn't imagine anyone turning aside her and her sisters.

"Are you sure?" Worley asked.

"About what?" Leo realized he had indeed lost track of their conversation.

"That you are paying attention. I'm not going to tell this story twice."

Leo knew that to be a lie. There was nothing his friend liked more than sharing his adventures from the field. Especially over a drink with an audience. The tale would be much embellished by the time he told it the third or fourth time. It was a good thing the viscount's father had deep pockets so that he could indulge his son's wanderlust.

Still, Leo appreciated Worley's enthusiasm for artifacts and new discoveries as it nearly matched his own.

"Rothwood is excited to see the items as well," Leo shared before his friend took him to task again.

"Oh?" Worley grinned. "All the better. Perhaps he'll be interested in funding my next adventure."

"How can you plan another when you've only just returned?" Travel could be exciting at times, but it was also uncomfortable, unpleasant, and frustrating. At least, that had been Leo's experience. He was too fond of his own bed and the finer comforts of life to want to venture to foreign shores more than once or twice a year.

"I can't help but wonder what's around the next corner. Or country," Worley added with a chuckle. "How is the duke?"

"I'm relieved that he's delighted to be included in reviewing your finds."

"That poorly, eh?" Worley shook his head, his mustache twitching once again. "It's odd to feel sorry for a duke, but when it comes to Rothwood, one does."

Leo gestured toward his carriage and adjusted course across the crowded dock. "Isn't it ridiculous how often people are hurt by love?"

As an only child, Leo had learned at an early age that love was a selfish emotion not to be trusted. He intended to avoid it at all costs after witnessing the misery it—or the lack thereof—caused his parents. His father never recovered from his broken heart, and his mother's unhappiness at being married to her lovesick husband had made Leo's childhood difficult at best, miserable at worst.

"True. Thank goodness I have not been subjected to its fearsome grip." Worley's dramatic tone nearly made Leo smile.

"I count myself lucky as well. Such a foul emotion that brings joy to so few." Leo nearly shuddered at the thought.

Worley clapped Leo's shoulder. "We should pledge to never succumb to it."

Leo knew his friend well enough to catch the flash of pain in his dark eyes. Society frowned upon who Worley tended to fall for. The fact caused him great pain and long bouts of depression. Was it any wonder he chose to seek adventure abroad? "And we must make certain to remember that lust is not love."

"True enough." Worley nodded. "But people are not meant to live in solitude with books as you seem to prefer."

"I like books. The knowledge they impart is a treasure hunt of its own." It was a familiar argument. One to which Leo did not take offense. "Would you prefer to stop by your home before we proceed to the Society offices?"

"No need. I will rest easier once the items I brought are in safekeeping." He patted the brown leather satchel he carried.

As Worley stepped into the carriage, Leo couldn't resist looking about one last time for the lady. He wished he would've gotten her name. Ridiculous, when he wouldn't ever see her again.

"THANK YOU SO much." Ella waved and forced a smile as Mrs. Whitsome departed in the hackney, leaving them before the Duke of Rothwood's home.

"Why didn't you allow her to wait?" Lena asked. "She wanted to see us safely inside."

"You mean she wanted to see the inside," Norah muttered as Ella followed her gaze toward the stern, imposing façade with its white pillars, red brick, and wrought-iron balconies. "Besides, we don't know if we're even going to be allowed entrance."

"Norah." Ella glared at her middle sister. No purpose would be served in upsetting Lena.

"She'll learn the truth soon enough." Norah lifted her chin in a rare hint of defiance.

"How do you mean?" Lena asked. "The duke is our grandfather."

"Who has yet to acknowledge us." Ella supposed Norah was right. Ella was surprised Lena hadn't sensed their concern but knew grief had smothered her ability to infer much of anything.

Lena pondered Ella's words for a moment, then met each of their gazes. "It's three against one. The odds are in our favor."

Norah nearly snorted with amusement as Ella chuckled.

"True enough." Ella squeezed Lena's arm, appreciating her attempt at levity, as well as her confidence. "That's an excellent reminder. Have I mentioned lately how much I love you both?" She only hoped they would return the sentiment no matter what happened once they raised the brass knocker in the shape of a lion's head that graced the front door.

Before they could do so, the door flew open to reveal an elderly man in a black suit. "What is the meaning of this?" His outrage as he glared at the three of them and the pile of bags behind them was intimidating. "Remove yourselves at once."

"Is that him?" Lena whispered as she stared with wide eyes at the angry man.

"I believe it's the butler," Norah countered.

Neither of her sisters moved from where they stood on the pavement. Ella resisted the urge to press a hand to her roiling stomach and, instead, strode along the walkway toward the butler as if she owned the place. Now was not the time for nerves to gain the better of her. "Good morning, sir."

Rather than answer, the servant lifted his nose in haughty disdain, his dark eyes chilled.

Holding tight to Lena's reminder about their odds, Ella smiled. "My name is Ella Wright, and I'm pleased to make your acquaintance."

The butler only glared at her.

Ella felt foolish for attempting to be friendly. "These are my sisters, Norah and Lena." She glanced at them, their worried expressions lending her courage. She refused to allow them to be left on the doorstep.

Or for their futures to be anything less than happy or to fail in her mission.

Her shoulders nearly sagged under the worry as she turned back to face the butler, holding his gaze. "We are—"

The man gasped, his eyes wide with shock as he stared at her, then each of her sisters, his entire body slowly softening. "Lady Bethany's daughters?"

Ella stiffened in surprise, his question more than she'd hoped for. "Yes. Yes, we are."

"I never thought...we've often wondered..." He shook his head. "The resemblance is uncanny. Allow me to express condolences on behalf of the staff for the loss of your dear mother. Many of us remember her fondly." He bowed elegantly, then glanced over his shoulder as if nervous. But that couldn't be, could it? "Now then. Let me think how we should proceed."

"Think?" What was there to think about? Either he allowed them entrance, or he didn't.

He waved at a footman who appeared in the doorway. The servant hurried forward, and the butler leaned close to whisper in his ear. The large man nodded, then bowed to Ella before stepping around her and walking to the baggage to heft one in each hand.

Norah and Lena came slowly up the walkway as if still uncertain about what was happening. That made three of them.

"We must approach this carefully." The butler tapped a finger on his top lip, his eyes darting about. "Mrs. Enfield will know what to do. Come inside while I fetch her." He said the last bit as a whisper as he cast his worried gaze about, confusing Ella all the more.

He bowed and then ushered them through the door where a black and white entrance hall with more white columns and marble floors awaited. He gestured toward a small reception room nearby, and Ella led the way inside followed by her sisters.

"If you would remain quiet until my return, that would be most helpful. Excuse me." Then he left, closing the door behind him.

"Where is he going?" Norah asked.

"To find Mrs. Enfield," Ella replied.

"Who is she?"

"I have no idea." Ella shook her head. "But he recognized us once he looked closely. That's good news." However, she was far from reassured.

"What an amazing house this is." Lena walked around the small space, studying the details, her blue eyes seeming to take in everything.

The elegant room was decorated in blue and white from the ceiling to the floor and everywhere in between except for a few touches of gold. The chairs boasted blue velvet cushions with elegantly carved legs as did the matching settee. But no fire burned in the hearth to take the chill from the room. Did that mean the duke didn't have many guests?

"Do you think Mother stood in here?" Norah asked, a smile gracing her lips as she tucked a strand of pale hair behind her ear.

The question brought a lump to Ella's throat. "I'm certain she did. If anyone came to call, they would've waited here to see if she was receiving."

"I like to think she stood in this very spot." Lena moved to stand just inside the doorway, facing the room. Her eyes filled with tears as she looked at Ella and Norah. "I miss her so much."

"So do I. I miss them both." Norah walked forward to take Lena's hand and then looked at Ella. "Do you think she'd approve of us coming here?"

Ella hesitated. She'd asked herself that question numerous times before they'd started the journey to London and had yet to determine the answer. "That is my hope."

Lena nodded. "But would Father?"

Ella couldn't answer. He'd never said much about his father-in-law's rejection. Whether that was because he understood it or simply out of respect for his wife, Ella didn't know. Perhaps his silence masked a deep dislike of the duke for the pain he'd caused them both.

Before Ella had thought of a response, the door opened to reveal a short, stout woman dressed in unrelenting black except for a snowy white apron and cap. Her grey hair was twisted into a tight bun at the base of her neck. The massive set of keys hanging from her waist marked her as the housekeeper.

Her lips pressed into a thin line as her assessing brown eyes in a round face swept over them.

Ella met her gaze openly. They had nothing to hide. Yet the tangled knot in her stomach tightened all the same. Based on the woman's grey hair and the lines on her face, she might've known their mother as well.

Ella felt her sisters' presence on either side of her and appreciated them standing nearby to present a united front. "Good afternoon," Ella said at last.

The woman's mouth slowly fell open as she turned to look at the butler, who remained in the doorway. "I never thought to see this day."

He grinned like a schoolboy released early from lessons. "Nor did I."

Mrs. Enfield looked back at them, then walked closer, her focus latched on Ella. "Your name?"

"Ella, ma'am. This is Norah and Lena." She gestured toward them in turn.

"It's remarkable how much you look like Lady Bethany." Her gaze shifted from one to the next to the next and back again. "As if each of you has a piece of her."

Ella smiled at the comforting thought.

"I'm Mrs. Enfield, the housekeeper. And you've already met

Davies." She gestured to the butler. "I was your mother's lady's maid before..." Her voice faltered as sorrow crossed her face. "Before she left."

"We're pleased to meet you," Lena said with a dip of her head, and Norah did the same.

"May we speak with the duke?" Ella couldn't forget for a moment that although these two servants were welcoming, it didn't mean their grandfather would be.

"His Grace is out riding but expected to return momentarily," Davies answered. "Needless to say, your arrival will come as a surprise." His puckered brow suggested it might not be a welcome one.

Given that the duke hadn't responded to their mother's or Ella's letters, that was expected.

"Perhaps we should mention that His Grace is often in poor spirits," Mrs. Enfield warned. "It may take time for him to realize how fortunate he is to have you here."

Ella bit back a sigh. Did she come right out and explain that they had nowhere else to go and little money to see them through the week, let alone longer?

"What is the meaning of this?" The angry, booming voice from the entrance hall had everyone in the room stiffening with alarm.

Davies winced. "I had hoped to move your baggage else-where before his return. Allow me to see if I can soothe his temper." The butler lifted his chin and strode out of the room.

"I will assist him," Mrs. Enfield said as she followed with a shake of her head. "It might be best if you wait here until all is calm. Or, at least, calmer."

Ella waited a moment after the housekeeper's departure, then shared a look with her sisters. "Shall we introduce ourselves to our grandfather?" By the sound of things, there was little hope of having it go well. She would much rather have this moment over and done.

"Yes." Norah gave a decisive nod as did Lena.

The three of them walked through the door.

Ella didn't know what she was expecting. But the tall, grey-haired man with bushy grey brows and long sideburns wasn't precisely it. Not when those brows were so low over his eyes that it was impossible to see their color. Not when his lips were pressed so tightly together as to be nearly invisible.

He tapped a riding crop against his thigh with impatience as he glared between the stacks of baggage and his servants.

"Some unexpected guests have arrived, Your Grace," Davies said.

"All will be sorted out soon," Mrs. Enfield added.

The duke pivoted and caught sight of Ella and her sisters. The loosely formed explanation Ella had prepared fell away at his glower. He was an imposing figure with an erect posture despite his years. His elegant attire fit perfectly. His boots were polished to a high shine. He looked every inch a duke. But he didn't look like a grandfather. Especially since his fierce expression didn't alter at the sight of them.

"Who are you?" he demanded.

Already, Ella's thoughts marched ahead as to where they could go from here. Perhaps Mrs. Whitsome's sister had room for them for a night or two until Ella could find a position of some sort.

Lena, bless her heart, dipped into a perfect curtsy, reminding Ella and Norah to do the same.

"Good afternoon, Your Grace," Ella managed, finding a bit of her own anger at his harshness. "We are your granddaughters." There seemed little purpose in giving their names when it was doubtful he would want to know them.

"I have no granddaughters." Yet his form stilled as he continued to stare at them as if perplexed by their presence. Was that a hint of uncertainty in his eyes?

"I am Ella," she began, not bothering to disagree with his statement. She turned to her sisters, whose expressions revealed the same worry she felt. "These are my sisters, Norah and Lena."

She faced him again. "Lady Bethany was our mother, and David Wright our father."

"Do not say his name in my presence. Do not say it in my house. Ever." He slapped the riding crop against his side as if to emphasize his point. No one moved.

Were all lords like this, Ella wondered? Angry and old, spitting out orders as if they owned the world and everyone should scurry to obey. She knew that wasn't true, but her mind rebelled at his demand.

Ella refused to apologize for speaking her father's name. Instead, she waited to see what the duke might say next. His anger was a waste as far as she was concerned. Besides, he had no right to be angry with them.

"We are pleased to make your acquaintance, Your Grace." Lena ignored his outburst and offered a smile, as did Norah.

Ella didn't, but she was proud of her sisters in this difficult moment. If the duke didn't want them, it was his loss. The realization lifted a weight from her shoulders. "As I believe you know, our mother passed away five years ago. Our father died more recently."

The duke's lips tightened at the mention of him, but Ella had followed his request to not speak his name.

"We've come to London to live. And to see you." Norah shared the last part casually as if coming to see him wasn't their sole purpose.

"I see." He took one step closer, his gaze shifting between them. Then he took another. His lips twisted as if he wasn't certain what to do with them. He came to stand directly before Ella.

She searched his face for something familiar, perhaps a sign of her mother. And for a sign as to whether there was any hope of them being welcome here. Sadly, she saw neither.

He moved to Norah, examining her with the same thoroughness. Then Lena.

If Ella hadn't been watching closely, she would've missed the suspicious moisture in his eyes as his anger seemed to slowly fade.

"Humph." He spun away to address his servants. "Did you find rooms for them?"

"Not yet, Your Grace," Davies advised.

"Do you have a preference for which ones?" Mrs. Enfield asked.

"The east wing. Keep them as far away from me as possible." Then he strode down the corridor toward the rear of the house without looking at them again. The click of his heels on the marble floor and the slam of a door were followed by silence.

"Well, that went more smoothly than I expected." Mrs. Enfield drew a breath as she shared a smile with Davies.

"Indeed." The butler looked relieved as well.

"It did?" Lena asked, giving voice to Ella's shock.

"Well, yes," Davies advised with a puzzled look. "He's invited you to stay."

"That didn't sound like an invitation." Ella sighed, only slightly less concerned than she had been before the meeting. "I suppose this means we've won the battle but not the war."

Based on the duke's response to their arrival, the outcome was far from certain.

Chapter Three

L EO STRODE INTO the Royal Geological Society on Savile Row just off Piccadilly. The one-hundred-year-old building was a rather cramped place and lacked any hint of panache. Many members complained that the Society, which had found its start as a dining club, needed a larger, more stately building to befit its purpose.

Since none had stepped forward with a suggestion of a different building or the funds to make a change, the present one would have to suffice. After all, they'd only been at this location for the past five years. Leo's only complaint was that their current location lacked a lecture hall. Given the growing interest in exploration and other similar matters, a large hall for experts in the various fields of geology to share new information would be helpful.

At least their current space had a decent map room, as well as rooms to hold smaller meetings, such as the one he was about to attend.

He and Viscount Worley had carefully examined and cataloged Worley's findings two days prior. Now they were to share the research each of them had completed with one another to see what additional conclusions could be drawn.

Leo's personal library held numerous tomes on the various areas in which he was interested. However, poring over texts took time and patience. It was always better to divide such tasks to speed up the process. He'd found several references to the location in which Worley had discovered the artifacts and looked forward to sharing the details with his friend.

"I thought you advised me that Rothwood was interested in the finds," Viscount Worley said as Leo entered the room.

"He is." Leo frowned. "At least he was. I received a brief message from him yesterday, advising he was unavailable for another day or two."

"Do you think he's under the weather?"

"He was fine when I had dinner with him the other night." In truth, the message had puzzled Leo. Its very briefness left more questions than it answered.

"I can't imagine that he's changed his mind." Worley stroked the end of his mustache as he contemplated the issue.

"Nor can I." Leo knew Worley was anxious to have the duke involved with the hope he'd help fund another expedition. Having the duke's support also improved the chances of gaining interest, and therefore funds, from other members as well. Worley tried not to always rely solely on his father. "If I don't hear from him soon, I'll call on him to make certain all is well."

As interested as Rothwood had been when Leo mentioned the artifacts, Leo was surprised he hadn't joined them. He normally enjoyed the research aspect of geological matters as much as Leo did.

It took nearly two hours for Worley and him to share and debate each of the details they'd learned. Leo made notes of the most relevant information both to document it, as well as to share with the duke once he became available.

Worley pushed away from the table where they'd set out a few maps to review. "I think that's enough for today, don't you? I'd like time to consider all we've learned before drawing any further conclusions."

"Agreed." Leo sat back in his chair. "It seems like we should celebrate your finds. Why don't we drop by Brooks's for a drink?"

"Perfect."

In short order, the two men were seated at a table in the gentlemen's club with whiskies in hand. They were careful not to discuss specifics of the artifacts outside of the Society. One never knew if any unscrupulous characters were listening to a conversation.

The treasure hunting business was filled with such people—those willing to do anything to put their hands on riches. These days, artifacts were considered treasure even if they weren't made of gold. Those items often brought significant sums of money from collectors. Precious metal or gems weren't a requirement to make it worthwhile to steal as information also held value.

However, Worley did share stories from his most recent trip. Within a quarter of an hour, several other gentlemen had gathered around their table to listen to Worley share an amusing encounter he'd had aboard the steamship.

"The woman insisted she didn't know how the turtle ended up in her luggage. That it must've crawled in there all by itself. The look on the captain's face was priceless."

The small group broke into laughter at the scene Worley painted so vividly. If he ever stopped traveling, Leo would suggest he write a book to share his adventures. Several other stories followed, along with another round of drinks. Life was always more interesting when Worley was in town, but Leo understood his need to travel. The demons that chased his friend rarely quieted.

Another entertaining hour passed before, at last, the group began to disband.

"Marbury, how is life treating you?"

Leo turned to see Charles Kimmer, Viscount Dyke, a friend and fellow Society member, approach. "Well, Dyke. And you?"

"Well enough." He pondered the drink he held. "Father is pestering me to marry before the end of the Season."

"I suppose it's something most of us will do eventually." Leo wasn't enthused at the idea. Luckily, his mother rarely raised the topic. He liked to think he could hold out several more years before marrying.

"You certainly don't sound as if you're in a hurry to do so."

"No, I can't say that I am," Leo replied with a smile.

"I heard Rothwood has taken in three beauties. I don't suppose you'd care to garner me an introduction, would you?"

"What are you talking about?" Leo asked.

"Haven't you heard? Rumors are circling that three young ladies claiming to be his granddaughters knocked on his door and demanded entrance."

Surprise held Leo rooted to the spot. Especially given the fact that he had recently been at Rothwood's for dinner, and there had been no mention of granddaughters, let alone any arriving soon. What on earth was going on? Worry for the duke took hold and wouldn't let go.

"Are you certain it's Rothwood to whom this has happened?" Leo asked.

"According to my mother. As you may remember, my parents live close to the duke's residence. She says the entire neighborhood is abuzz over the situation."

"Will you excuse me? I've just remembered something I must take care of." Leo left Dyke to quickly bid Worley goodbye and then departed for the duke's home. He didn't pretend to know what was going on, but he intended to get to the bottom of it as soon as possible.

The idea of someone taking advantage of a lonely, old man, especially a wealthy one, was something Leo wouldn't accept.

ELLA HELD BACK a growl of frustration as she took in Davies's presence once again outside the door of the duke's study.

"Why did he suggest we stay if he never intends to speak with us?" she asked the butler as she crossed her arms over her chest.

She'd come this afternoon with the intent of asking His Grace to help arrange for her and her sisters to be introduced into Society. The London Season for balls and other events was underway, and there was much to be done if they were going to find suitable matches for Norah and Lena.

Gowns would need to be ordered and a suitable lady would need to be found to provide the necessary introductions. Hopefully someone the duke knew would be willing to guide them in this new world.

None of that could be done without the duke's assistance.

"I would ask that you give him more time to adjust to the circumstances, Miss Ella." The butler's sympathy for their plight made her feel marginally better. But only just.

"How can he adjust if he doesn't see us? Pretending we're not here won't change the facts." Ella did her best not to let her feelings show. Given that those feelings ranged from anger to frustration to hurt, hiding them was for the best.

Ella had only caught one glimpse of the duke since their arrival. She'd been coming down the stairs, and he'd just returned home. After taking one look at her as he entered the house, he'd merely scowled and strode toward his study.

"Your Grace," she'd called out, determined to speak with him about the reason she'd brought her sisters to London. When he didn't respond, she hurried after him only to have his study door shut in her face.

She'd knocked, but Davies had quickly taken up the post as guard, which was where he was now.

"His Grace wasn't aware of having granddaughters, so you can imagine the shock of your arrival." Davies's loyalty to his employer took precedence over any sympathy he felt for her.

"I'm certain my mother wrote about us many times over the years."

"The duke chose not to read her letters. It was simply too painful for him. Give him more time, miss."

Ella sighed as she nodded reluctantly. What else could she do?

Yet part of her wondered if he'd ever come to accept them as family. If he'd had the will to cut off all contact with his only child, who he knew and loved, why would three granddaughters who were strangers be able to break through the wall he'd built around himself?

She slowly made her way back up the stairs to her bedroom, her hand trailing along the elegantly carved banister. The house was beautiful if rather formal in style. Though many of the rooms were closed off with dust covers over the furnishings, elegance was still visible everywhere. She wondered if her mother had assisted in choosing the décor, or perhaps it had been her grandmother, who'd died when Lady Bethany was young, who had done so.

Mrs. Enfield had been friendly and done her best to make them feel at home, but Ella felt the barrier that kept the woman from being truly welcoming. She knew her sisters felt it, as well. It was as if the housekeeper didn't want to be too friendly, since the duke had yet to speak to them. Ella was certain the other servants were of the same mind.

The past two days had allowed Ella and her sisters to rest and recover from the journey to London. Knowing they had a roof over their heads for the time being provided some relief and being here gave them an unexpected link to their mother, as well, something all three of them appreciated. To think she'd walked along the same corridor or enjoyed the music room the way they were was comforting.

This house wasn't home, but it was more than Ella had expected. Now if only she could find a way to get through to their grandfather. What might make him soften toward them?

Before she made it past the upper landing, a knock sounded at the front door. She paused, curious as to whom might be calling. No one had done so since their arrival that she'd seen.

The low rumble of voices as the footman greeted the visitor suggested it was a male guest. Her view of the entrance hall was limited from where she stood on the upper floor, but she didn't want to be caught gawking at the visitor.

She saw a glimpse of the back of a tall man with dark hair clipped short as he followed the footman down the corridor, no doubt toward the duke's study. She couldn't help but scowl at the idea of whomever it was gaining entrance when she could not.

With a flick of her skirts, she turned and went up to the next floor to check on her sisters. Both Norah and Lena were growing restless now that they'd recovered. Their current schedule allowed them too much time to think. They needed something to do. Norah definitely had something on her mind. A pensive look often came over her, suggesting she was troubled. Yet when Ella questioned her, she'd denied it.

Perhaps Ella would converse with Mrs. Enfield to see if she could help them order suitable fabric to sew a few gowns. Between the three of them, they were talented seamstresses. At least, talented enough to manage a few simple items. Trousseaus were expensive, and if they sewed a few gowns themselves, it would save money and give them something to keep them occupied.

※≫≪※

"Is it true?" Leo sank into the chair before Rothwood's massive mahogany desk.

"Is what true?" the duke asked, though Leo found it telling that he didn't meet his gaze.

"That you have visitors?" He wasn't going to call them granddaughters unless the duke was absolutely certain that was who they were.

"Yes." Still, the duke didn't look at him, his attention remaining on a letter before him.

"And?" Leo couldn't hold back the annoyance in his tone. Why he felt that way, he wasn't certain. Was it because the duke hadn't sent a message about his guests? Or was it their identity that caused this unsettled feeling?

"Marbury, if you have questions, simply ask them. I will not pretend to read your mind." At last, the duke's gaze shifted to meet Leo's.

The air left Leo's lungs in a silent whoosh. The worry in the depths of his blue eyes was enough to confirm the news.

"So, it's true then? They are your granddaughters?"

Rothwood's shoulders sagged. "I believe so."

"But you don't know for certain."

The duke's lips tightened, almost trembling, as he tapped the letter on his desk. "I opened a few of the letters Bethany sent. In one of them, she wrote of the birth of her child. A daughter named Ella."

"That matches one of the ladies who just arrived?"

He nodded slowly. "It does indeed."

Leo could hardly believe it. Yet the news didn't completely allay his suspicions. It seemed too coincidental that the anniversary of Lady Bethany's elopement had just passed and now, suddenly, her supposed daughters had arrived.

"Their father?" Leo asked.

"Dead."

"What other information have they shared?"

The duke turned away almost as if guilty. "I have yet to speak with them."

"Pardon me?" That made no sense. How could he allow them entrance but not hold a conversation with them?

"The eldest one has requested an audience several times."

"Ella?" It seemed like Rothwood should use their names if he had allowed them to stay.

"Yes, yes." The duke waved in a gesture of dismissal as if not appreciating Leo's reminder.

"What do you intend to do? How do you know for certain that they are who they say they are?" That was truly the question.

Rothwood's gaze held on Leo's, a well of emotion in his expression. The lines around his eyes and mouth looked deeper than usual. "They look so much like their mother. They each have a part of her in their face. It's uncanny."

Leo had never met Lady Bethany, of course. He wouldn't have the same emotional reaction that the duke had when he met her daughters.

"Why have they come?" Leo asked. Even if they truly were Rothwood's granddaughters, that didn't mean they could be trusted. Especially given who their father was.

"I...I don't know." The man's uncertainty tugged at Leo. He was normally decisive and confident, which made it clear how much the situation had upset him.

His gaze bounced around the room as if he sought an answer from the shelves of books that graced one wall or the artifacts displayed along the opposite wall.

Some lords liked to own and display fine art. But the duke preferred items from the past that had served a purpose. A Neolithic scraping stone chipped into a teardrop shape found near Stonehenge. An ancient German axe made of bone and sinew. A clay vessel unearthed near Silbury Hill chalk mound in Wiltshire. Each item had a story.

Leo would hazard a guess that the ladies upstairs did as well.

"Would you like me to speak with them?" Leo wasn't certain what caused him to offer. He supposed he didn't like the idea of anyone using the duke's emotions to gain the better of him. Tricksters came in all shapes and sizes.

The relief on Rothwood's face was clear. "Would you? I suppose I'm not feeling up to it as of yet. I would appreciate your opinion on their story, as well."

Since the duke hadn't yet heard it, Leo wasn't certain how much good that would do. Then again, he knew enough about the past to know if they told any falsehoods. The fact that the duke's heir was nowhere to be found wasn't a secret, and that fact might encourage three young ladies to pose as Rothwood's granddaughters.

"Of course. I would be happy to speak with them." Leo

stood. "No time like the present."

The duke's eyes went wide for a moment, then he nodded and slowly rose to ring the bell. "Excellent. I'll advise Davies."

The strains of a piano reached Leo's ears when Davies opened the door. It had been a long time since music had filled this house. The fact that one of Leo's favorite pieces echoed in the distance didn't soften the distrust that filled him.

Chapter Four

"THERE'S A GENTLEMAN to see you, miss," Davies advised from the doorway of the music room. "To see all of you." His gaze took in Ella and her sisters.

"Who?" Ella paused her hands over the piano keys. She didn't care for the idea of a strange gentleman calling on them. Not when their future was still so unsettled. "Isn't the duke at home?"

"Yes, he is. The Earl of Marbury is a friend of his."

"Will His Grace be joining us?" Norah asked.

"Not to my knowledge, miss."

"That seems odd," Lena said. "Why would we speak with him when we have yet to truly speak with our grandfather?"

Ella waited for Davies's response, as she had the same question.

"He is a *close* friend of the duke's." If the repetitive answer wasn't enough, the butler took a step back as if to suggest that was the only answer they'd receive. "If you'll follow me to the drawing room, the earl awaits you there."

Ella reluctantly stood as she shared a look with her sisters. While speaking with the earl seemed unusual, so were the circumstances. "He might be able to shed some light on the situation."

Based on the twist of Norah's lips, she thought that unlikely. As did Ella.

Lena waited for Davies to step out before drawing closer. "Perhaps we can convince him to help us with the duke." Her optimism was something Ella appreciated, since she had so little.

"It is certainly worth speaking to him," Ella agreed.

They followed the butler to the drawing room, where a tall gentleman stood with his back to them, staring out the window, his broad shoulders silhouetted against the afternoon light.

Ella led the way, only to halt when the man turned to face them. The very same man from the dock who she'd bumped into. Shock held her in place. Ella didn't know what to think. Apparently, neither did her sisters as they stared at him in surprise, as well.

The man's eyes narrowed as he studied them each in turn. Nothing in his expression shared whether he was as surprised as they were. "Good afternoon," he greeted them.

Ella dipped into a curtsy as did Norah and Lena.

"My apologies for not offering a proper introduction when we first met." His deep voice was as rich as Ella remembered, even if she wasn't sure she wanted to. Her admiration of him now seemed out of place when she didn't know if he was friend or foe.

"I am Ella Wright." She gestured to her sisters. "These are my sisters, Norah and Lena."

"Leo Stanton, the Earl of Marbury." He hesitated a moment as if expecting a reaction to his name, but Ella couldn't imagine why. "A friend of the Duke of Rothwood's."

Ella noted he didn't use the term "your grandfather'" to refer to the duke. Nor did his demeanor seem welcoming. Not compared to his smile and interest when they'd bumped into each other upon their arrival.

"How kind of you to call," Ella said. "Forgive me for mentioning it, but I find it too great of a coincidence that we met on the dock." She didn't bother to hide the suspicion she felt. How often had her father advised her to trust her instincts?

"Isn't it though?" He offered a somewhat insincere smile as he moved closer. "I assure you it was just that. After all, I don't think anyone here knew you were coming." The accusatory note in his voice had Ella stiffening in response.

"Actually, I wrote to the duke prior to our departure, though it seems he has a habit of not opening letters from family members."

Norah's gasp suggested Ella might have gone too far. But she wasn't about to allow this man to accuse them of anything. From his tight expression and lack of a warm greeting, she had to guess he didn't believe they were truly the duke's granddaughters.

"You mentioned on the dock that you traveled on the *Campania*?"

"That's right." Lena nodded, her chin lifted.

"And you journeyed here from…" He paused, a frown marring his handsome face.

Ella knew without a doubt that he remembered what she'd told him previously if only because he'd seemed interested. What game was he playing? But she said nothing while Lena shared a few more details.

"What brought you to London?" he asked.

Now Norah frowned. "We came to see our grandfather, of course."

"But why now after all these years? I don't believe you visited him before. Isn't that correct?"

"Our mother died five years ago, and our father more recently," Ella supplied, her anger building. "There was nothing left for us in Nova Scotia. We thought it best to come here to be with family."

"You don't intend to return home?" he asked.

"No." Of that much, Ella was certain. The chances of seeing her sisters happily married were far greater in London than they'd been back home. She wanted them to find happiness. Marrying a man whose only interest was eking out a living in a harsh environment didn't seem as if it would provide anything but hardship. They'd already endured their share of that. Though she'd loved her parents, the life they'd chosen had been difficult. She wouldn't trade that experience for anything. But the time had come to see what else the world had to offer.

"Your father didn't find the treasure he sought?" The knowing look in the earl's hazel eyes suggested he already knew the answer.

"Why are you asking all these questions?" Norah stepped forward, her body stiff. "Did the duke request you to do so?"

"I offered, as His Grace has been a friend of mine for many years. In fact, he was a friend of my father's." Again, he paused as if waiting for their reaction.

"Oh?" Ella prompted, puzzled as to why that mattered.

"You see, my father was the man your mother left standing at the altar the day she eloped."

Ella's breath caught, her thoughts reeling. She stared at him, thoroughly unsettled at the odd connection they had with this man. No wonder he seemed to resent their presence. The situation was complicated, one that left her feeling off-balance. The idea that fate had brought them together at the dock only to set them at odds with one another was staggering. She told herself the detail was the least of her worries, yet something deep inside her stirred in protest. Oh, my.

LEO CURSED HIMSELF as he walked down the steps of Rothwood's home toward his carriage. What had gotten into him that he'd allowed the truth about the past to escape? Never mind that he had told himself he wouldn't share those details given how personal they were. His mother would be appalled.

Yet, as Ella Wright had stood glaring at him with suspicion, his own anger had stirred.

He scowled at the thought. It hadn't been only anger that had been roused. Miss Wright was a beauty, as were her sisters. But

Ella was the one who caught his notice. Her intelligent blue eyes were the color of a bright summer sky. With blonde hair that held hints of honey and a heart-shaped face that balanced those wide blue eyes, she was very attractive. Beautiful, in fact. Her black gown lent a somberness to her character that was unusual for a woman her age. She moved with purpose as if she knew exactly what she wanted and intended to achieve it. That intrigued him as well.

Perhaps part of his anger came from the unwanted attraction he felt toward her. A chemical reaction sparked between them, something inevitable that had occurred both times they'd met.

He didn't want to admire her beauty or her courage. And it had certainly taken bravery to pack up their belongings from the only home they'd ever known to come to London to see a grandfather who had never acknowledged them. The three ladies each had a serious demeanor, emphasized by their mourning attire.

Obviously, the loss of their father still wore on them. How long ago had it been since he'd died, he wondered, only to shake his head. He didn't want to be curious about any part of their lives.

He rubbed a hand over the back of his neck as his carriage rolled away from the duke's residence. What a complicated snarl the situation was.

He'd cut short the meeting soon after he'd revealed his father's role in their past and returned to the duke's study. Unfortunately, he hadn't gained an answer to the one thing the duke wanted to know—what did the three women want? Why had they come? To be with family as Ella had suggested was difficult to believe. Rarely were people's motivations so simple in his experience. Leo supposed he could hazard a guess—money. At the very least, a dowry to ensure they made good matches.

What were the odds that the beauty he'd bumped into on the dock was the duke's granddaughter, the daughter of the woman Leo's father had loved so deeply that it had cast a shadow over his entire life?

Though he considered himself a proficient mathematician, the probability seemed unreasonable. But he had never put much faith in fate and refused to do so now, despite the unusual circumstances.

He'd been so annoyed with himself for speaking of his father to the ladies that he had only given Rothwood a perfunctory report as to what they'd said before taking his leave.

Some friend he was being.

The women looked so much alike that there was no question they were sisters. The duke was the one who had to decide if he believed their claim to be his granddaughters. If a portrait had ever been done of Lady Bethany, it must've been hidden away upon her departure, as Leo had never seen it. The letters the duke had should be able to confirm the facts if His Grace chose to read the rest of them.

Then again, based on the duke's upset, it seemed to Leo that Rothwood had already decided they were. Considering the three were of marriageable age, surely, they had come to London to find husbands.

None of that needed to involve Leo. He intended to stay as far away as possible from any events they attended. At least, he would until he managed to curtail the unusual reaction he had to Ella.

He wished he could blame it on the tangled connection of their pasts. But he'd felt this attraction on the dock before he'd known who she was. How strange. He'd simply ignore it until the sensation passed.

With a sigh, he braced himself as the carriage rounded a corner. The question was whether he told his mother of the granddaughters' arrival now, before the news spread.

There was only one answer.

"Where's the dowager countess?" he asked as he handed his hat and gloves to Niles, the butler.

"I believe she's in her sitting room, my lord," the stately man said with a bow.

"Thank you." Leo took the stairs two at a time to the upper level to his mother's suite of rooms.

She'd moved from her original bedroom nearly two years ago, a subtle hint that he should marry. Something else he ignored. The thought reassured him. Apparently, he was good at ignoring what he didn't want to acknowledge.

He knocked on the door before opening it to find his mother reading in a chair by the window. She'd decorated the room in shades of rose, something that suited her. Dark wood accents kept it from appearing overly feminine and made it a restful room. A fire burned in the hearth, and a beautifully woven cream blanket lay over her lap to keep away the chill.

"Good afternoon, Mother." He crossed the room to press a kiss on her cheek.

"Leo." Her smile was warm as her gaze swept over his face as if to gauge his mood.

Had she learned to do that because his father's moods so often varied? The thought made his heart heavy. She deserved more than his father had been able to give her.

"How was your day?" she asked, her eyes holding on his, suggesting some of his upset was visible.

"Interesting. And yours?" Though he knew he had to tell her, he was reluctant to raise the topic.

Her dark brown hair and brown eyes were the opposite of Ella and her sisters' appearance. Was that one of the reasons his father had chosen her? Because she looked nothing like Lady Bethany?

"Uneventful. Though I'm attending the Waterby musical this evening, which should prove entertaining."

A few social events were already being held now that it was spring. His mother's love of music had her going to concerts and musicals as often as possible. She also encouraged young ladies who had an interest in music. Lady Patricia, the Waterbys' eldest daughter, was talented on the piano, and his mother enjoyed her performances.

Leo's thoughts drifted to the music he'd heard at Rothwood's. Which granddaughter had been playing? Whoever it was, she had talent for the instrument, as well. Perhaps even better than Lady Patricia.

"Are you meeting friends there?" he asked as he settled in the chair next to her and stretched out his legs. He was lucky that his mother's circle of friends was a wide one. Otherwise, he might find himself escorting her to more than the handful of outings he already did.

"Yes. Lady Dyke and Lady Vermoth are joining me."

Then it was fortunate he had run into Viscount Dyke at the club. Otherwise, his mother would've heard the news from Lady Dyke. He hated to think she might've been blindsided by the news.

"You mentioned you had an interesting day." She placed a ribbon to mark the place in her book and set it aside. "Does that mean you had the chance to learn more about Worley's artifacts?"

"Yes. They are definitely intriguing." His mother had always appreciated his and his father's interest in exploration, though she didn't share it. "They show promise, but more research will be needed."

"Of course. At times like this, I am reminded of how much you are like your father." She shook her head as if the thought didn't necessarily please her.

It didn't please him either. He would never put his family through misery because he couldn't control his emotions. When it came time to marry, he'd select a suitable wife based on mutual interests and respect. Nothing else. Love was only a path to heartache.

He forced himself to return to the issue. "Something else unexpected has happened."

"What might that be?" The look of wariness that crossed her face pulled at Leo, making him resent the duke's visitors all the more.

"The Duke of Rothwood's granddaughters have arrived from Nova Scotia and are now staying with him." There was no point in suggesting he still questioned whether they were who they claimed to be. Not when the duke was already convinced. Rothwood might not have truly accepted them yet, but Leo thought he soon would.

"Oh?" His mother shifted her gaze to the flames of the cheerfully burning fire as if to give herself time to process the news. "Granddaughters? There's more than one?"

"Three."

"That is interesting." Her brow puckered, making him pleased he was the one to have delivered the news.

This way she didn't have to ponder the ramifications—if any—while enduring curious stares. And there would be curious stares. It never failed to amaze him how long the memories of some members of the *ton* were. This would stir old gossip.

"Their father?"

"Dead." Leo couldn't help the relief he felt that David Wright hadn't returned to London, even if guilt accompanied the feeling. It wasn't that he wished the man dead, only pleased he hadn't accompanied his daughters to London. That would've made a difficult situation worse.

"I see. How old are they?"

Leo considered the question. "Of marriageable age."

"How is Rothwood taking the news?" Her lips twisted with the question, something that often happened when she said his name. As if doing so left an unpleasant taste in her mouth.

"Not particularly well."

That caused his mother to offer a small smile. "I don't suppose. It must be something of a shock."

"Very much so. I don't think he knows what to do with them."

"Is he certain they're truly his granddaughters?" Now it was Leo's turn to smile at her skeptical tone.

"I had the same question." He folded his hands over his stomach. "However, he says they look so much like his daughter that I have to think it's impossible to doubt it." That was something else he wanted his mother to know. Otherwise, seeing them might have caused another shock.

His mother had known Lady Bethany, as they'd been introduced into Society the same year, one of the many details she'd shared with Leo. According to the stories he'd heard, often from his father during drunken tirades, Lady Bethany had been the pale-haired beauty that everyone noticed. Partly because she was the duke's only child. While Leo thought his mother beautiful, still, as she had aged well, she insisted she hadn't compared to Lady Bethany in looks or personality.

Her sympathy for Leo's father at being jilted had been what drew them together. Leo was certain she never expected her husband to remain lovesick his entire life for the woman who'd hurt him so.

Again, Leo reminded himself that regrets served no purpose. What had been done couldn't be undone. Not that such sayings made living with events any easier.

"I see." She breathed deeply, then straightened her already perfect posture. "I suppose we shall see them at some of the upcoming balls. The Season will soon be fully underway."

"I suppose." Not that Leo attended many, but his mother frequently did.

"Have you met them?"

"Yes." He hesitated, deciding against mentioning the brief few minutes when he'd literally bumped into Miss Wright on the dock. "I spoke with them."

"And?"

He pulled his gaze from the fire to his mother, wondering what she was asking. "How do you mean?"

"What did you think?"

Uncomfortable, he shifted in his chair. The question seemed like a potential pit from which he might not redeem himself. If he complimented them, his mother might think he was willing to put aside past events. Given that she wasn't, he didn't think she'd approve.

Yet if he discredited them, his mother could make their entrance into Society difficult. That didn't sit well with him either. He'd rather they both simply kept their distance.

"They seem nice enough, I suppose."

"Do they speak English?"

"Of course." He stared at her, surprised she'd asked such a thing.

She waved a hand in dismissal. "I don't believe I've ever met anyone raised in the wilds of Nova Scotia. I thought perhaps they spoke French."

"They might. They appear to be well educated, intelligent, and possessed of good manners." There. Surely that would be enough to assuage her curiosity.

"I see."

He stirred again under her continued regard, wondering what she thought she saw in his expression. He couldn't guess when he wasn't certain what he felt. "I suppose you'll meet them soon enough."

"Hmm. I suppose, though I confess, I'm not in any hurry to do so."

Leo nodded. He didn't intend to see them again either. The more distance he kept from them, the better. Hopefully, Rothwood would join the next discussion he and Worley were holding at the Society offices. Then he would certainly be able to avoid seeing the granddaughters.

Yet as he shifted the conversation to other topics, he couldn't dismiss the image of Miss Ella Wright from his thoughts. The lady intrigued him, and he had yet to understand why.

Chapter Five

E LLA SMOOTHED THE lavender silk fabric sample, awed by the way it shimmered beneath her hand. She'd never seen anything quite like it. Mrs. Enfield stood nearby, awaiting her decision. "But we're still in mourning." Her protest sounded weak even to her own ears.

"Forgive me, Miss Ella, but it's been six months since your father passed. Half-mourning is appropriate." The sympathy on the housekeeper's face was much appreciated, even if it didn't help Ella know the right thing to do.

She glanced down at her black gown and sighed, filled with equal measures of uncertainty and longing. Not wearing full mourning felt like letting go of her father—a choice she wasn't certain she was prepared to make.

Yet the idea of her and her sisters appearing in a ballroom for the first time dressed in black wouldn't do. They would be better off remaining home rather than attending events if they couldn't bring themselves to move out of full mourning.

She didn't want to wait another year for her sisters to be introduced to Society and therefore have the chance to find a suitable match. Especially since the duke had yet to speak with them. Ella couldn't imagine keeping her sisters in this awkward, uncomfortable existence for an entire year. Better that they have new experiences with the hope they found someone they could care for who would make a suitable husband.

In truth, she was beginning to think the duke would never soften in his attitude toward them. Given that he'd sent the Earl of Marbury to speak with them rather than visiting with them himself, she was right to be concerned. The shared past they had with the earl had been a shock, one she was still sorting through. That wasn't the only point about him that bothered her. Her reaction to him was even more concerning.

She quickly brushed away the thought. Far more important matters required her attention. Uppermost was the worry that perhaps the duke wouldn't support her goal of her sisters entering Society. The concern had her lifting her chin. She refused to allow that to happen, especially when she had no idea what to do if it did.

"Yes, you're right," Ella said at last. "However, allow me to speak with my sisters before any purchases are made. I want to make certain they're comfortable with this."

She had the feeling they wouldn't be as reluctant as she was to put mourning attire behind them. They missed their father terribly, but they also held an appreciation for fashion and finer things because they'd had so little of them.

"Of course, miss." Mrs. Enfield smiled approvingly. "Let me know when you'd like to proceed with ordering additional fabric." The housekeeper departed, leaving Ella alone in her bedroom with her thoughts.

Ella appreciated new items as well but couldn't release the guilt her longing brought. As if she were somehow betraying their father by desiring them. She knew he'd want them to be happy, though she wasn't certain they shared the same definition of happiness. What had brought him joy hadn't always given the rest of his family the same pleasure.

Was that selfish of him? Yes, it was. A sliver of resentment—something that was always inside her—reared its head. Their lives would've been much different if Father hadn't pursued his dream of finding buried treasure. Life in their simple cottage on Oak

Island hadn't been easy. Winters were long and harsh and part of it had been spent on the mainland. Survival in the area was not a given, but something for which one had to strive.

However, the biggest resentment she carried was that her father—and possibly her mother—would still be alive if he hadn't insisted on following his dream.

The guilt the thought brought had her breath catching. Along with it came a terrible wave of grief, bringing tears to her eyes. She loved her father more than anything but had yet to reconcile her mixed feelings about him pursuing his goal. Or her mother for giving up everything, including her own father, to support him when she chose to marry a commoner. Pursuing dreams meant releasing something precious in order to reach for something else. That seemed a terrible bargain.

Thinking so made her a horrible daughter, of that she had no doubt.

She'd sifted through her circling thoughts many times without finding resolution. Doing so again now would solve nothing.

She walked to the wardrobe and opened the doors to view her few possessions. She only had a handful of gowns to her name, most of which were now black. She and her sisters had dyed the ones they could soon after their father's death.

Perhaps it was time to move into half-mourning as Mrs. Enfield had suggested. Shades of grey and lavender were certainly more appealing than black, yet still gave respect to their father. Mrs. Enfield had said there were funds in the household budget that could be spent on fabric for a few gowns. Doing so might get them by until the duke approved of having a modiste call to assist with new attire suitable for the Season and give them something to do.

Ella had wanted to correct the housekeeper—*if* the duke approved of such a thing. Davies still wouldn't allow Ella entrance to his study, so Ella had resorted to writing another letter to him. This time, it was from within his own house. She'd done her best to explain their presence and that she realized their arrival was unexpected and caused him a shock. Though tempted, she'd resisted the urge to state that if he'd opened her previous letter, it wouldn't have been so.

Such remarks wouldn't gain them anything.

She had also shared her hope for her and her sisters to begin a new life in London and that they wanted him to be part of it. Whether her words would change anything, she didn't know. But she would write another letter along with anything else she could think of until he agreed to speak with them. The least he could do was hear them out. Surely if he came to know them, he could find it in his heart to accept them as family.

As she sorted through the gowns hanging inside the wardrobe, considering whether any of the trim could be reused on a new gown, her reticule in the bottom caught her notice.

She couldn't resist pulling it out to carry it to the bed. There were four items sewn into the lining that had been found on Oak Island. Three were ones her father had found during his digs. The fourth was one Norah had found while walking along the shoreline.

The journal was what Ella appreciated the most, which had been too large to hide in the lining. To see her father's handwriting on the pages along with the small drawings he'd made of the various locations he'd searched as he tried to puzzle out the location of the treasure was like a peek into his mind. He'd written many journals during his time on the island, but Ella had only kept the most recent one. The others remained with his partner, Edward Peterson, on Oak Island.

She opened the reticule and pulled out the brown leatherbound notebook only to have her heart stop. The cover was all wrong. She ran her hands over it, certain she had to be mistaken. But no. It looked too new. The leather too dark. She opened the journal.

The pages were empty. Untouched. Pristine.

Panicked, her heart thumping painfully and unable to believe her eyes, she thumbed through it, certain she had to be wrong.

Yet only blank page after blank page greeted her. She closed it again to study the cover which contained none of the familiar stains or nicks that marked it as David Wright's.

How could this be, she wondered as she pressed a trembling hand to her mouth. Where was her father's journal? She gripped the new one tight, took her reticule, and hurried to share the terrible news with her sisters.

→»»«««

LEO PAUSED IN the doorway of the duke's drawing room the following morning to find Rothwood standing at the window with his back to the room. His three granddaughters were seated on the low couch with their hands linked as they stared blankly across the room.

The atmosphere was positively chilly. Silent. Heavy.

The message he'd received from Rothwood earlier hadn't shared any details but stated there was an urgent matter that required his assistance. Leo had no idea what that could be.

"Good morning," he said as he stepped into the room, curiosity drawing him forward.

Ella and her sisters jerked to their feet, their faces pale as they curtsied.

"Good morning." Ella seemed to be the speaker for her sisters on most occasions which made sense as she was the eldest. Worry and anger lingered in the depths of her blue eyes as she met his gaze, making him more curious as to what had happened.

The duke turned to face Leo, lines bracketing his mouth. He looked anything but pleased. The fact that he was in the same room as his granddaughters came as a surprise. Leo would've taken that as a good sign except for the fact that they all appeared distraught.

"Your Grace," Leo greeted him with a bow.

Rothwood nodded. "Thank you for coming, Marbury."

"Of course." His gaze caught on Ella again, noting her obvious upset. He was surprised how it tugged at him. Much like their brief meeting on the dock, he felt compelled to offer help. Yet nothing could erase the thought of how much pain her father and mother had caused his own parents, and therefore him.

He turned to face the duke, a reminder that if he could help, it would be for Rothwood's sake. "How can I be of assistance?"

The older man was several inches shorter than Leo. His bearing was erect as always as if his title alone provided a frame in which he resided that didn't allow for anything else. While a serious man in general, his demeanor today was especially somber.

The duke's lips tightened, then he gestured toward the ladies. "Perhaps you should explain."

Leo reluctantly turned to face them, his attention once again landing on Ella.

"My father's journal has been stolen." Heated anger snapped in her eyes as she glared at him.

"Don't you mean it's missing?" Leo countered. Surely, she didn't suspect him, yet he could think of no other reason for her anger.

"No. I used the correct word. Someone took it without our knowledge or permission."

"Perhaps it's simply been misplaced." He didn't appreciate her accusatory expression.

"Someone took it and replaced it with another." Norah, the middle granddaughter, shared this information. She was an inch or two shorter than Ella and more petite. Her eyes were a blue-grey shade whereas Ella's were brighter and bluer. And angrier at the moment.

The news sent Leo's thoughts in several directions. "What did the journal contain? Why would anyone want it?"

Ella's chin lifted. "It was our father's and contained detailed notes of his efforts over the years."

"Efforts?"

"His pursuit for treasure on Oak Island," Lena added. She was slightly taller than Ella with a hint of green in her eyes, her hair so pale as to appear nearly silver.

"You mean the supposed treasure." Leo couldn't have held back the correction if his life had depended on it.

"No, she means the treasure," Norah countered with a frown, though her expression lacked the heat of Ella's. "Why is it that you continually question our word choice?"

Leo nearly scowled in response, deciding it best if he didn't answer. "When did you last see the journal?"

"On the ship." Ella pressed her index finger to her upper lip, which caused Leo to stare in surprise. Rothwood often did the exact same thing. "I placed it in my reticule the morning we disembarked."

"You're certain it wasn't the replacement you mentioned?"

"I know what my father's journal looks like," she said with no small amount of exasperation.

"We would appreciate your assistance in helping discover who might have taken it," Rothwood said as he took a step closer, his gaze on Leo rather than on his granddaughters.

Leo surmised that the duke supported their claim that the journal truly had been stolen. However, his request didn't mean Leo had to do the same.

"Why would anyone want it?" Leo asked. "I don't mean to be offensive, but reading through years of unsuccessful efforts hardly seems worth stealing." He knew he should've been more diplomatic in how he stated his point, but his loyalty was with his own father.

"I don't think you appreciate the complications he encountered while digging." Ella clasped her hands before her as if doing so might help her keep her patience. "There is not just a single location but numerous ones. It was often a matter of trial and error to attempt to discover the exact place to search."

But mostly errors, Leo thought, pleased he managed to keep the words to himself. Insulting their father wouldn't serve any purpose.

"Given that Wright's notes could be of interest to another treasure hunter, I thought it best to request that you become involved," Rothwood explained.

"Why?" Norah asked the duke.

"The Earl of Marbury is a well-respected expert on pirate artifacts," Rothwood answered with a brief glance at her. "Now if you'll excuse me, I'll leave you to discuss it further, as I have other matters requiring my attention." He turned to Leo. "I trust you'll keep me apprised of the situation?"

"Of course, Your Grace." Leo nearly cursed at his agreement to this impossible task. However, he was apparently unable to refuse Rothwood's request.

The duke nodded, then quit the room without a word to his granddaughters. Leo appreciated the difficulty of the situation for the older man but didn't care to be placed in the middle of it.

He'd do enough to convince them he tried to find the missing journal and then let the matter go. He might have expertise in pirate lore and artifacts, but that didn't mean he had a knowledge of thieves.

"Is there anyone you suspect?" Leo asked.

"Yes." Ella nodded with certainty. "You."

Leo stared at her in shock, wondering how his life had suddenly become so complicated.

ELLA WAS PLEASED the duke had left so she didn't have to accuse the earl in front of him. Given that the two were friends, she feared the duke would be insulted by her accusation.

The fact that she'd failed to protect her father's journal rested heavily on her shoulders. She would do everything—anything— in her power to gain it back.

How could she not suspect the earl when he'd been at the

dock not long after she'd last seen the journal? Had the moment she'd been bumped and her reticule landed on the ground been the opportunity he'd needed to take the journal? While she didn't know how the earl could've managed it without her noticing, perhaps he was working with someone else. It seemed too great of a coincidence that Marbury was an expert in pirate treasure and had been at the dock and was a friend of her grandfather's. Never mind that he was also the son of the man her mother had jilted.

"Me?" The earl appeared amused by her accusation rather than offended.

"Yes, that's right." Ella had already mentioned her suspicion to her sisters. As far as she was concerned, it was up to the earl to prove his innocence. This was one time when she wished Lena might have one of her feelings to point them in the right direction.

Her father had been vigilant about secrecy and always leery of anyone who came to visit, something that had bothered her mother. It had been difficult enough to have friends in the remote area of Nova Scotia. Having her husband suspect everyone they encountered made it doubly so.

"I would have no use for the journal." The earl shook his head, not seeming to be bothered by her accusation. "I wouldn't read it if you handed it to me, so it makes no sense for me to steal it. I have never believed there's any pirate treasure on Oak Island." The casualness with which he spoke annoyed Ella. He acted as if he wasn't taking her claim seriously.

"Perhaps not. But other treasure hunters do," Ella advised.

"How do you know?" Leo asked, his expression curious.

"Our father mentioned it on numerous occasions." Norah took a step closer as she spoke. "There were several attempts to steal his maps and plans over the years."

"Hmm." His expression suggested he doubted her statement, which only served to irritate Ella further.

"For all we know, you might have taken it so you could sell it for your own personal gain." Lena folded her arms over her chest as she studied him with narrowed eyes.

His mouth quirked at one end, although he tried to hide it. "As I said, I wouldn't have any use for it. Nor do I know of anyone interested in Oak Island."

Ella watched him closely as he spoke, noting how his brow puckered as he stated the last part. She'd bet her last coin that someone came to his mind despite what he'd said.

His gaze lifted to meet hers, the earnestness there taking her aback. "You have my word that I have nothing to do with the missing—"

"You mean stolen," she interrupted him.

He dipped his head to acknowledge her correction. "Yes. Stolen journal. Let us not waste time on the concern that I'm involved." He waved a hand in the air as if to dismiss the thought. "Who else do you suspect?"

Ella wasn't about to trust him, despite the fact that he met her eyes so easily. Why was it that, even though circumstances demanded she suspect him because of their supposedly chance meeting on the dock and his parents' relationship to hers, she still found him incredibly appealing?

His dark hair was brushed to the side, leaving a lock on his forehead her fingers itched to smooth back. Who knew that a man could have such long eyelashes? It simply wasn't fair, as his attractiveness made her more inclined to believe anything he said.

She glanced away before her fanciful thoughts got the better of her.

"We've discussed possible suspects, but considering we've only just arrived in London and know few people, the list is far from complete," Norah advised.

"Do you think it was taken before you left the ship?" the earl asked.

"No," Ella said. "I checked to make certain it was in my possession immediately after—" She halted midsentence to look at her sisters as remorse filled her. She hadn't wanted to tell them about the search.

"After what?" Lena asked, her eyes filled with concern.

Ella sighed. "Our room was searched the night before we arrived in London."

"What?" Norah stared at her as if she couldn't believe her ears.

"I'm sorry I didn't tell you." Ella looked at each of them in turn. "You were already so worried, and nothing seemed to be missing. I didn't want to concern you more than you already were. Mrs. Whitsome helped me put the room to rights before you returned from dinner."

"Mrs. Whitsome." Lena's eyes went wide. "Could she have something to do with it?"

"That seems unlikely." Norah frowned. "The few times we mentioned our father's work she didn't seem interested and always changed the subject."

Lena slumped. "I forgot that."

"Who is Mrs. Whitsome?" the earl asked.

"She is a widow who served as our chaperone during our journey," Ella supplied. "I approached her on the recommendation of an acquaintance."

"That makes her less likely of a suspect," Marbury agreed. "Was there anyone else on the ship?"

"Mr. Conway. Julius Conway," Norah said. "But he couldn't have anything to do with it, given how kind he was to us."

Ella nearly smiled. Norah was always determined to believe the best of everyone.

"Though he did act fascinated by our stories of living on the island and digging for treasure." Lena unfolded her arms and sighed. "I hate to think he could be involved."

"Do you make a habit of telling everyone you encounter about your father's search?" Marbury frowned as if surprised by the idea.

"No, of course not." Ella quickly denied his suggestion. She normally went out of her way to avoid the topic. Her father had always advised them to be cautious and would've been appalled to learn how many people they'd told on board the ship.

"It's just that it was a long trip," Lena said. "There was little to do except visit with the other passengers."

"Are you suggesting that most of those onboard knew?"

"Not at all." Norah scowled at the earl as if he'd insulted them. "Less than a handful."

"Who may have told a few others and soon most of the passengers would be aware," Marbury said. "As you may know, treasure hunting is best kept secret."

Ella glared at Marbury. "We have lived with it our entire lives and are well aware of the need for secrecy."

"Except for during your trip." He shook his head again. "Let us focus on what happened after you disembarked."

Ella allowed her sisters to share the details, her spirits sinking even lower. Discovering who took the journal seemed more impossible than ever. Speaking with the earl made her feel as if she were even more to blame.

Despair swept over her. She shouldn't have suggested they come to London. The duke had no interest in getting to know them. They would've been better off remaining in Nova Scotia and seeking some way to claim a future there. Now they'd lost the most important tie they had with their father, and she was to blame.

Chapter Six

L EO NOTED HOW the light in Ella's bright blue eyes dimmed, and her head lowered along with her shoulders. Blast it all. She was obviously upset about the missing journal, especially since it had been in her possession nearly the entire journey to London.

The urge to reassure her swept over him, taking him by surprise once again. He much preferred when she displayed the spirit she'd shown earlier, even if it held a hint of temper.

"I shall make a few inquiries to see if any rumors in the treasure hunting community have surfaced," he found himself offering. What else could he do when the duke had asked him to help, not to mention the three pairs of blue eyes that stared at him? Anyone in his position would be compelled to do the same.

"Thank you, my lord." Norah's tight smile suggested she didn't believe he meant what he said.

"We certainly appreciate any help you can lend," Lena added, equally politely.

The three sisters shared a look, and Leo had the distinct impression they thought his efforts would be mediocre—if he bothered to follow through with his offer at all.

The feeling annoyed him. Never mind that he hadn't intended to put forth significant energy on the search. Guilt had him reevaluating his intent. He'd given his word to Rothwood, and he needed to try his best.

Though it was on the tip of his tongue to caution them from hoping the journal would be returned, he held back. Ella already appeared distraught. No doubt the entire situation was wearing on her, beginning with her father's death to their arrival at Rothwood's with a less than warm welcome to this moment.

Norah and Lena moved together toward the window, whispering to each other, leaving him and Ella together.

"I am sorry for the circumstances in which you find yourself," he began, uncertain what he hoped to gain by offering his sympathies.

Her lovely eyes met his. The pain and worry in their depths tempted him to place a comforting hand on her arm or better yet, hold her. She continued to have a curious effect on him, and he didn't care for it.

"Thank you." She seemed to gather herself, regaining a hint of her spirit. "I'm surprised the duke requested your aid with this matter. How have you and His Grace come to be such good friends?"

"I know most of those involved in geological exploration, so I often hear rumblings of discoveries. As to our friendship, my father became close to His Grace after proposing to your mother. That continued after she left and even after my father married my mother. I've known Rothwood my entire life. The three of us also shared an interest in exploration. The duke has been much like a grandfather to me all these years."

"Your father passed away?" Her expression softened with her question.

"Nearly five years ago. Interestingly, it wasn't long after your mother died." He didn't know why he'd mentioned that.

Ella seemed to consider the news for a moment. "And your mother?"

"She is alive and well. You'll most likely meet her at some point if you attend a ball or another function, as she goes to many events."

"Does she think your relationship with the duke strange?"

Leo smiled at the familiar topic. He could imagine his mother's answer all too well. "Yes, but she has become resigned to it after all these years."

"I see." Ella glanced at her sisters who continued to converse several feet away.

From what little he'd witnessed, the three were very close. "Have you made progress with the duke?"

Ella shook her head, her discouragement obvious. "No. Davies advised him of our unfortunate news. He asked a few questions and then said he knew someone who might be able to help. I didn't realize that person would be you."

"I don't know how much I can assist, but I will see what I can do. I appreciate that the journal was important to you." He certainly wouldn't be pleased if something of his father's had been stolen.

"I have been so careful since Father passed to keep it close to me. I'm horrified to think someone would go to the effort of switching another one for my father's."

That detail concerned Leo as well. Obviously, someone thought the journal was of enough value to go to great lengths to take it. Whoever it was had seen the journal or knew of it. Then again, if David Wright had been using it for a year or two to document his search, chances were it wasn't as much of a secret as the man would've liked.

Though Leo had told the ladies he didn't know of anyone interested in Oak Island, that wasn't quite true. He knew of three men who were highly interested in the supposed treasure there. Or perhaps it was the series of flood tunnels purported to have been used to keep the treasure out of the wrong hands that caught their notice. Many adventurers enjoyed the chase and the puzzle as much as finding riches. He'd start with them and see where it led.

"Did your father believe he was searching for Captain Kidd's treasure?" Leo asked. Most of those who believed riches were buried on the island thought the pirate was the one who had put his plunder there.

Leo had studied Kidd's movements, but his research suggested Madagascar was the more likely location of his treasure—if there was any. However, he didn't think Ella or her sisters would want to hear his opinion at the moment, if ever.

"Captain Kidd was one of the possibilities." Ella didn't seem inclined to share additional information, so he decided against asking further questions.

"Interesting." Leo would've enjoyed debating the topic but now wasn't the time. "As I said, I will make some discreet inquiries and see what arises."

"Why is it that I feel as if you have little interest in helping us?" Ella's eyes narrowed as she looked at him.

Her question was a bold one. Did he dare answer in the same vein?

"I have said I will help, and I will. As a favor to Rothwood. But I won't make any promises. Unless whoever took the journal chooses to sell it or starts digging on the island, we might not locate it."

Ella closed her eyes briefly as if his words pained her. Yet he didn't see any point in giving her false hope. "Thank you."

"You're welcome," he replied, unsure whether she was being sarcastic. Though tempted to ask if her father had ever found anything in his searches that hinted at treasure, Leo held back. Asking seemed as if it would suggest he thought such a thing possible when he didn't.

Even if Wright had found a gold coin or two in such a remote location, it didn't mean there was buried treasure nearby. It only meant someone who'd been there had dropped something. Small finds were rarely a reason to mount an expedition or dig for gold.

"I hope you'll let us know if you discover any information," Ella said, her tone resigned.

"Of course, though it might take time."

"I'm sure." The long fringe of her lashes lowered, hiding her thoughts. Her expression was pinched with worry, and that didn't settle well with him.

"Perhaps something good will come of this," Leo offered, wanting to lift her mood for reasons he didn't begin to understand.

"How?" Ella's frown suggested she believed that unlikely.

"It might encourage an understanding between you and your grandfather. Or at least provide a reason for a conversation or two."

"As you may have noticed, he left the room as quickly as possible." Ella sighed as she glanced at the doorway as if the duke might reappear. "I don't think he is ready for a true conversation. I'm not even certain if he read my letter."

"Your letter?"

"I wrote one the day before yesterday with the hope of explaining our point of view. If he won't see us, it seemed like the only way to reach him."

Leo's sympathies tugged again. Though he understood the duke's pain, none of the situation was the fault of these three ladies. In all honesty, they appeared to be pleasant in both looks and manner, just as he'd told his mother. With their beauty and connection to the duke, assuming he provided a dowry, they would make fine marriages.

Would Rothwood be willing to eventually open his heart to his granddaughters? That was something Leo didn't know. He supposed Rothwood didn't either. Knowing the stubbornness of the older man, Leo would hazard a guess that His Grace planned to allow them to stay, find someone to introduce them to Society, and arrange suitable marriages for them, all without involving his own emotions.

The thought nearly made Leo smile. He had the feeling that Rothwood didn't stand a chance against these three.

ELLA WAS WAGING war.

That was how she was beginning to think of her effort to convince the duke to speak with them. She still avoided thinking of him as their grandfather. How could she when he had yet to hold a true conversation with them?

She'd finished another letter to him, though she didn't know if he'd opened the first one. Davies advised her that he'd placed it in the center of his desk. But the butler hadn't mentioned whether he'd seen the duke reading it.

Mrs. Enfield had shared that the duke used to enjoy listening to their mother play music, so each day when they thought the duke was at home, the three made their way to the music room, left the door open wide, and played for a time. Their mother had taught them music, among other things. During the long winters, they had often stayed with friends on the mainland who had music rooms where they'd increased their skills.

Her sisters agreed they couldn't remain in mourning attire and attend events, so Mrs. Enfield had ordered fabric in various shades of lavender for half-mourning.

Lena had already taken apart one of Norah's gowns, which they'd decided was the most up-to-date style they owned, to use as a pattern. The pair were cutting the fabric for a gown for Norah first, then one for Lena. Ella had advised them to do theirs first. She wouldn't worry about her own future until she had seen them both happily settled.

"Miss Ella?"

She looked up to find Davies in the doorway of the drawing room where she was embroidering as she considered what else she could do to win over the duke.

"The Dowager Marchioness of Havenby is calling."

"For me?"

"Yes, miss. Should I tell her you're receiving?"

"Please show her in." Ella rose, curious as to who the woman was and why she'd asked to see her.

Within a few short minutes, Davies reappeared. "The Dowager Marchioness of Havenby."

About the same age as her mother would've been, the lady's good taste and elegance was immediately apparent. Her crimson gown with a modest bustle and striped underskirt and black trim might've been something in one of the fashion magazines of which Lena was fond.

Her brown hair was wound into an intricate chignon at the back of her head just visible beneath a small, feathered black hat perched to the side. Her skin was flawless alabaster with only a few lines around her eyes that revealed her age. Brown eyes wide with curiosity beneath arched brows held on Ella.

Ella dropped into a curtsy, surprised when the lady came forward to take her hand as if entranced by her appearance.

"Look at you," she whispered, her eyes shining with unshed tears. "Ella. So much like your mother."

Ella smiled. She liked to think part of their mother lived on in her and her sisters, and meeting someone who'd known Lady Bethany was special. "It's a pleasure to meet you, my lady."

"Not nearly as much of a pleasure as it is for me to meet you." The older woman continued to study Ella so closely that she wondered what she looked for—or what she saw. "I was a friend of your mother's, you see."

"How lovely."

At last, Lady Havenby released her hands, and Ella gestured toward the couch. "Would you care to sit down?"

"I would indeed." The lady sank gracefully onto the cushion, the folds of her full gown falling perfectly into place, her gloved hands resting on her lap as Ella joined her. "Are your sisters here?"

"They're upstairs." Ella looked at Davies who hovered in the doorway. "Perhaps you could advise them we have a caller?"

"Of course, miss." He bowed and left the room.

"When I received Rothwood's message telling me of your arrival and asking me to call, I could hardly believe it. I didn't know your mother had children, let alone three daughters."

The realization that the lady and her mother hadn't kept in touch was disappointing. Had that been the preference of Lady Havenby or her mother? Ella imagined it would have been difficult for her mother to stay in touch with those she left behind. Perhaps it had been too painful to do so.

"Please accept my condolences for the passing of both your mother and your father." She reached out to place a gloved hand on Ella's arm. "How terrible to be so far away and all alone."

"It has been difficult. We miss them both dearly."

"Rothwood asked if I would introduce you to Society. I'm honored he thought of me." She waved a hand in the air. "Of course, you know all of that."

Ella knew she didn't hide her surprise very well. "Actually, he didn't mention it." She decided against sharing the lack of the duke's welcome. Not until she knew what type of person Lady Havenby was and how close she'd truly been to her mother.

"Did Lady Bethany mention me?" Her dark brows arched with hope.

"Not that I can recall." Ella didn't like to think her answer hurt the lady's feelings.

"Oh, sweet Bethany." She sighed and shook her head. "I missed her terribly when she left. To think she had the courage to leave all this behind with the choice she made." She glanced around the room with its formal touches and rich décor as if she couldn't imagine doing so.

"The two of you were close?"

"Quite. We had our presentation to the queen at the same time. Both of our fathers were adamant we make good marriages. Back then, we felt so much pressure to never make a mistake lest we risk our futures."

"I'm sure." Unease had Ella drawing a deep breath, wondering if she and her sisters would feel the same way. Yet how could they disappoint the duke when he didn't speak to them?

"Your mother always enjoyed meeting new people and having new experiences. It shouldn't have come as a surprise that she eloped with David Wright."

"But you were surprised?"

"Very. She liked Marbury." Lady Havenby caught Ella's gaze. "I don't know if you were aware that she was betrothed to someone else."

"She mentioned that."

"Marbury would've been an excellent match for her. Their temperaments were much the same. He also had an interest in new experiences, though his were through studying exploration and geology rather than actually doing it. I suppose that part of your father appealed to her. He was quite the adventurer."

"You knew my father as well?" Ella's curiosity stirred even more.

"We were introduced, but I wouldn't say I knew him well. He was quite the charmer and so handsome. Rothwood met him through a friend who'd funded one of his expeditions. In fact, Rothwood introduced him to Lady Bethany, something I'm sure he came to regret. When your father shared his adventures, as he'd already been on several before coming to London, your mother's face lit with interest. I didn't realize their feelings ran so deep until they left."

"They were devoted to one another." How ironic that the quality her mother found appealing about David Wright was the same quality that frustrated her the most. His single-minded pursuit of treasure to the exclusion of all else had caused disagreements between her parents on more than one occasion.

"A marriage based on love is unique. It's unfortunate that what they felt for each other hurt so many." Lady Havenby shook her head. "That is life, I suppose. Though I don't think making enemies was new to your father. He already had several, even as a young man."

"Truly?" Ella had difficulty believing that.

"Treasure hunting is a dangerous business, my dear." She paused to study Ella. "I'm surprised you aren't aware of more of his past."

"My parents always said they preferred to look forward rather than back." How she wished she knew more to better prepare herself and her sisters for the coming months.

"I think it best if you hear the more significant details from me rather than the old gossip that is certain to stir when you are introduced."

"I appreciate that," Ella said, even as unease settled over her. She wasn't certain she wanted to know everything.

"It's the least I can do given my friendship with your mother." She stared into the distance as if gathering her memories once more. "Your father was desperate to become a member of the Royal Geological Society before the elopement. If Rothwood would've given the nod, he might've been admitted. Obviously, that was impossible after they'd married. Especially with Marbury looking on."

Ella hadn't known any of that. How much more had she been unaware of?

"Marbury eventually married, of course," Lady Havenby continued. "But it was no love match. It was obvious that Bethany leaving broke his heart."

Ella nearly cringed to hear this again. "So we've been told."

"Oh? Did Rothwood mention it?" She appeared astounded by the possibility of the duke sharing such a detail.

As she should. The idea nearly made Ella laugh. If he did speak with them eventually, she was certain it wouldn't be about that situation. "No. The present Earl of Marbury did."

Lady Havenby's eyes went even wider. "You've met him?"

"Yes. He's called twice."

"Oh my. What did he say exactly?"

Heat filled Ella's cheeks as the memory of his doubtful expression filled her. "I believe he was concerned as to whether we are who we claim to be."

"Of course. Marbury is quite close to Rothwood, as was his father. He's the protective sort. Isn't this just a delightful tangle?" Lady Havenby's smile suggested she found it fascinating.

"How so?" Delightful wasn't the word Ella would use.

"Marbury is the grandson Rothwood never had." The lady leaned close to impart that detail as if sharing a dark secret. "Now that you're here, where does that leave him?"

"I can't believe our arrival will have any effect on their friendship." A sliver of envy took hold at what Ella had already suspected about the earl's place in the duke's life. Apparently, it didn't matter that Ella and her sisters were his true grandchildren, as Marbury had already filled the role of family. Would they eventually convince the duke to allow them a place as well?

"Perhaps, but it will certainly complicate it." The lady chuckled. "I do wish my own son, Arthur, wasn't already married. I would welcome you as a daughter-in-law with open arms."

"How kind of you." Ella couldn't take the compliment seriously given that Lady Havenby didn't know her. This woman was so different than her mother had been. Ella had difficulty imagining the two as friends. Yet she appreciated all the lady had shared. Forewarned was forearmed, and it appeared as if there was much she didn't know about the past.

Norah and Lena arrived, and Ella made the introductions. Lady Havenby had the same delighted reaction to their appearance, studying them in turn.

"You all look so much like your mother. What a sensation you'll make at your first ball. Those who knew her won't be able to take their eyes from you. Those who haven't will be eager to hear the story and meet you." She clasped her gloved hands before her chest and beamed. "You'll be the talk of the Season."

Ella noted the worried look Norah shared with Lena. The lady's prediction made Ella nervous as well. They were out of their element here. None of them were used to being at the center of attention. Surely the woman exaggerated.

"I am sorry to hear about your father's death," Lady Havenby continued as she eyed their black gowns with a furrowed brow. "How long ago was it?"

"Just past six months, my lady," Norah answered.

Again, Ella noted worry tighten her sister's features. Could whatever was bothering her have to do with their father's passing?

Relief swept over Lady Havenby's face. "Then half-mourning will be acceptable. Excellent." She seemed to realize how poorly that sounded. "Not that you shouldn't honor your father's memory. But I'm sure he'd want you to be happy and move on with your lives."

That much Ella knew for certain. Whether he would've agreed with her decision to move to London to live with the duke was something she'd never know. It didn't seem to matter how many times she told herself they had no other choice. She still felt guilty. The duke had been an ongoing source of contention between her parents. The fact that he'd never accepted David Wright as a son-in-law had not set well with her father.

"Now then, I've taken the liberty of making an appointment with my favorite modiste. Madame Drury has a fabulous eye for design. We shall venture there tomorrow. However, I would love a good visit with you now so I might come to know you better. Your mother was a dear friend, and I'm honored to be asked to assist you to take your rightful place in Society. This is where you belong."

Did they belong here? Ella was not yet convinced. The coming weeks now seemed as if they'd be incredibly difficult to navigate. Perhaps even more so than what they'd already endured. Ella shared a look with her sisters and saw the same concerns reflected in their expressions.

Lady Havenby cleared her throat, finally seeming to realize how overwhelming this all was. "Shall we ring for tea?" she asked with a purposefully bright tone. "I want to hear all about your lives."

Ella appreciated the lady's enthusiasm and hoped it would be enough for all of them. Though she feared the water ahead would be anything but smooth sailing, she couldn't change course now. They had to make the best of it. And it was a relief to feel as if at least one person appreciated their arrival in London.

Chapter Seven

E LLA'S STOMACH TINGLED with a combination of nerves and excitement the following afternoon as the carriage rumbled along the street. Lena scooted forward to the edge of the tufted bench seat to peer out the window, suggesting she felt much the same. Norah showed a bit more restraint, though her eyes sparkled with anticipation.

This was their first outing since arriving in London. Whether that was the cause of their uplifted spirits or the promise of new gowns they wouldn't have to sew themselves, Ella didn't know.

Lady Havenby had asked them to meet her at Madame Drury's establishment on Bond Street. However, Ella had reservations. Had the duke approved of this trip along with the money that would be required to order suitable gowns for them? She could easily see Lady Havenby overstepping her bounds when it came to spending Rothwood's wealth.

At the earliest opportunity, she intended to pull aside the lady to ask if the duke had been specific about that detail.

"Do you think it is much farther?" Lena asked.

"I have no idea, though we seem to be nearing the shops now," Ella advised as she shared a smile with Sally, the maid who accompanied them. "Are we close, Sally?"

"Yes, miss," the maid confirmed as she glanced out the window. "Not much farther now."

"Would it be possible for us to do a little window shopping before we return home?" Norah asked.

"I don't see why not." Ella only wished she had more funds so they could make a few purchases. However, the majority of what their father left had been spent on purchasing tickets for the steamship. She had also compensated Mrs. Whitsome for chaperoning them on the journey.

The little money remaining she wanted to save in case the duke asked them to leave. Their meager savings wouldn't last long, but it would tide them over until Ella could find work. Would their arrival in London come to that? Her stomach tightened at the thought. She had been so certain that, by now, their future would be clear, but it was far from being so.

The carriage rolled to a halt, and Norah and Lena exchanged an excited smile. Ella was grateful they weren't privy to her worries. She wanted them to enjoy the outing.

A moment later, the footman put down the step, then opened the door, and assisted them to alight. The modiste's shop stood directly before them, but Ella slowed to look up and down the street with curiosity as did her sisters.

"Shopping in London," Norah whispered. "How exciting."

"Isn't it though?" Lena agreed.

The street bustled with people, carriages, horses, and riders. A jeweler, an antique shop, and a store specializing in musical instruments were all nearby, their goods displayed in their windows to lure in customers. A few finely dressed gentlemen and many more ladies in elegant gowns, some with parasols, several with maids trailing behind, paused at storefronts to admire the displays.

Ella's excitement grew, if only because she welcomed the chance to see more of London. She and her sisters were ready to do something other than sew, play music, or walk in the garden. They were eager to explore the city they now called home. Hopefully, this would be the first of many outings.

Despite her excitement, she need only look at their mourning gowns to remember what had propelled them to come to London. It seemed as if every moment of happiness was tainted by the grief that still gripped them. Waves of sadness washed over them at the smallest reminder of their father, leaving them hollow.

"Would you prefer we wait for you or return with the carriage?" William, the footman, asked.

Ella hesitated, uncertain what the appropriate thing to do would be. There were so many things she didn't know, both big and small. "Why don't you return in an hour's time?"

"Do you think that will be long enough?" Norah asked.

"No worries, miss," William said with a nod and a smile. "If you're not yet done, we'll wait nearby."

"Thank you, William." All the servants had been so helpful and supportive, which helped to ease the chilliness they felt because of the duke's lack of welcome.

"Let us see if Lady Havenby is waiting for us," Ella advised her sisters before the clever displays in the nearby shop windows drew them.

They followed her, though they continued to look about as Sally held open the door. The shop didn't look like much from the outside, but the interior was warm and inviting. Full-length mirrors stood around the room, and white lace curtains allowed the light in but offered some privacy from the street.

Silk screens created areas for customers to work with a dressmaker. A half-dozen ladies were inside, some studying their reflection as they tried on a gown, others being measured by seamstresses. Most paused to glance at them, then take a second look, perhaps because of their mourning attire. Partially sewn gowns were draped over mannequins, and lengths of fabric were strewn across tables in the center of the shop.

"There you are." Lady Havenby beamed as she walked forward to greet them. She wore a vivid green gown with a square neckline and a matching hat that flattered her. There was no denying she had impeccable taste. "Won't this be fun?"

"May I have a word with you before we get started?" Ella asked.

"Of course. What is on your mind?" the lady asked as she accompanied Ella to one of the areas partitioned by a screen.

"Does the duke know we are here?"

"Why yes, my dear." Her furrowed brow suggested she was puzzled by Ella's question. "Why do you ask?"

"Did His Grace specify a budget by which we should abide?" She did her best to set aside her embarrassment at having to ask the question.

"Darling, you are the granddaughters of the Duke of Rothwood. A budget is nothing with which you need to concern yourself."

Despite her reassurance and the confidence with which she spoke, Ella was still uncertain. Perhaps the time had come to explain that they hadn't exactly been welcomed upon their arrival. It only made sense that the duke would not want to open his pocketbook to them either.

A seamstress with a strong French accent approached her sisters, tut-tutting over their simple black gowns.

Relieved they were occupied and wouldn't hear her, Ella continued, "I'm not certain the duke is happy to have us under his roof. Given the circumstances, it seems doubtful that he would want to pay for our gowns."

"Oh, you poor dear." The lady looked at her with pity which left Ella uncomfortable. "Do not worry so. Rothwood is an honorable and responsible man. He would never turn away his own family."

Ella stared at her, waiting to see if she realized what she had said.

Immediately the woman's eyes grew wide, and she pressed a gloved hand to her mouth. "Perhaps he did turn his back on Lady Bethany, but her actions were part of his decision. None of that is the fault of you or your sisters."

"Still, I'm sure you can understand my concern. I do not have the funds to see both of my sisters with new wardrobes."

"You are worrying over nothing. I will speak with your grandfather, though I don't think it necessary. He asked me to help introduce you to Society and that cannot be done without the proper attire. His Grace is well aware of that."

Even as Ella opened her mouth to further protest, Lady Havenby shook her head. "You must trust me in this. We will see you all in new gowns. But if it makes you feel better, we will keep our purchases modest until I speak with Rothwood again. You wouldn't want to be an embarrassment to him, would you?"

Ella was taken aback by her words, as that was a possibility she hadn't considered. The last thing she wanted to do was embarrass the duke in any way. Bringing shame to him would not aid her in trying to win him over. However, neither would she spend significant sums of his money without his prior approval. Her best hope was somewhere in between.

"You have a point," Ella relented. "But let us proceed conservatively."

Lady Havenby's eyes brightened as she gave two enthusiastic claps of her gloved hands. "Excellent. Now let us begin. We have much to do."

She took Ella's hand in hers and guided her toward the seamstress who was already draping a length of fabric over Norah's shoulder.

Ella smiled at Norah's excited grin. Nothing made Ella happier than seeing her sisters happy. With a determined lift of her chin, she made a concerted effort to set aside her worries and enjoy the afternoon.

In short order, under the direction of Lady Havenby, who would have rivaled any military officer in the way she orchestrated the Wright sisters and the seamstresses, a variety of fabric and styles were presented. Madame Drury made suggestions as well. The seamstresses busily scribbled notes as to the specifics.

"It is important that you each have your own style," Lady Havenby advised as she studied them in turn. Madame Drury nodded in agreement. "You already look so much alike that we can't have your gowns similar as well. Though all your coloring favors bolder colors, Miss Lena is the youngest, so she will wear paler shades, and her gowns will be simpler."

Lena's slight frown suggested she wasn't certain if she liked the suggestion.

Lady Havenby reached to give her arm a reassuring squeeze. "Your beauty is such that you need little embellishment to bring it out."

Lena brightened at the compliment.

"Miss Norah, your style will be slightly more sophisticated with deeper jewel tones." The seamstress nodded her approval as the lady continued, "Miss Ella, you shall be the queen of the trio."

"Oh no." Alarm filled her and caused her heart to pound. She felt like a fish out of water, gasping for breath. "One or two simple gowns in lavender or grey is all I require."

Lady Havenby smiled politely, even as she shook her head. She leaned close to whisper, "You must lead by example. Your sisters will follow what you do."

"But I don't want to be the center of attention," Ella replied, hoping that wasn't a whine evident in her own tone. She didn't mean to sound ungrateful, but the thought of being stared at during a ball caused her stomach to knot. "My wish is to see my sisters introduced properly."

"You cannot possibly do that if you are not at the ball with them, now can you? If you don't dress equally well, potential suitors will receive the wrong impression."

Ella could see her logic but that didn't mean she cared for it. How had ordering a few gowns become quite so complicated?

At the end of two hours, Ella was exhausted, as were her sisters. They'd been poked, prodded, measured, studied, and measured again. They'd tried on numerous gowns in more styles than Ella had realized existed. Small bustles and larger ones. Ruffled necklines and square ones. Layers of silk, wool, and muslin had been draped and pinned on each of them.

Lady Havenby was relentless in her determination to see them properly attired. Not just properly but perfectly, Ella amended.

Ella couldn't have managed any of this on her own, which made her even more grateful. The fashion plates in the magazines her sisters were so fond of poring over had been months old. Who knew styles could change so quickly? Bows sewn on the top of bustles were no longer in fashion. Necklines had changed, as well as the tightness of sleeves. They'd also ordered corsets and crinolines, chemises and nightgowns.

"Next, we shall go to the haberdashery."

Out of view of Lady Havenby, Norah caught Ella's gaze and shook her head with a pleading look. She looked as exhausted by what they'd already accomplished as Ella felt.

"Would it be possible for us to do that another day?" Ella asked. "I think we're all beyond making another decision."

Lena hid a smile at that lie—out of Lady Havenby's view, of course. She was right. They hadn't made any decisions. The lady had made them all.

"Certainly," Lady Havenby readily agreed. "I'm sure this is all a bit much when you aren't accustomed to it."

Before they could respond, another lady entered the shop.

"Lady Havenby, how lovely to see you," she said as she approached. Her greeting seemed at odds with her displeased expression. "Ordering some new gowns?" The newcomer studied Lady Havenby from head to toe with a wrinkled brow as if to suggest something different was needed.

"Heavens, no." Lady Havenby chuckled even as she smoothed her skirts, her smile tight. The tension in the air was palpable. "I am assisting my new friends."

The lady's attention moved to Ella and her sisters along with their mourning gowns. "Who do we have here?"

Lady Havenby hesitated. "I suppose you'll hear of their arrival soon enough. These are the granddaughters of the Duke of Rothwood."

The shock on the newcomer's face was clear. "Truly? Lady Bethany's daughters?"

Ella had enough of being talked about as if she wasn't there. "Yes, Lady Bethany was our mother," she said. Had so few known their father? Or was it just that they refused to mention his name out of deference to the duke?

"How...lovely." Whoever the woman was, she was an expert at saying the opposite of what she meant. She didn't look pleased at the news.

"We're just on our way out," Lady Havenby said as she reached to guide Lena and Norah toward the door. "Enjoy your visit with the modiste. I'm sure she can help you." Her gaze swept over the woman's fussy gown with multiple ruffles, the curl of her lip making it clear she found it less than desirable. "Good day."

They took a moment to thank the seamstresses who'd helped them, then stepped out the door. It hadn't escaped Ella's notice that Lady Havenby hadn't bothered to formally introduce them. Should they feel slighted or had the slight been meant for the other woman?

Lady Havenby led the way down the pavement several steps to take them out of the view of the modiste's windows then paused to heave a huge sigh. "How I detest that woman."

"Who was she?" Lena asked.

"The Countess of Davenport. One of your mother's former rivals. If she suddenly decides to befriend you, be certain not to take her seriously. And whatever you do, do not tell her anything in confidence. She's a notorious gossip."

The subtle jabs and looks the ladies had exchanged only made Ella worry more about their introduction to Society. How did one attempt to make friends, let alone find potential husbands, when people rarely said what they meant?

At least with the Earl of Marbury, she knew what he thought as he made it clear. She just hoped he was taking his promise to help find her father's journal to heart. He was their best—their only—hope to get it back.

Chapter Eight

L EO LISTENED WITH half an ear to the report at the Royal Geological Society council meeting the following afternoon. His thoughts were on two of the men in attendance. Well, three actually, if he counted Rothwood.

He was surprised the duke had come to the meeting as he'd half-expected His Grace to avoid social outings of any sort for a time. Leo knew the older man wouldn't relish answering questions about his three guests.

News of the granddaughters had spread like wildfire. Even the members of the Society were intrigued by the story from a few remarks Leo had overheard. He could only imagine how taken the *ton* would be by the three young ladies once they attended their first ball, assuming they did so eventually. Would the duke want them to? Would he guide them as they entered Society or leave them to fend for themselves? Leo hoped he'd do the right thing by them, as the *ton* could be a difficult and less-than-welcoming world for the uninitiated.

Rothwood scowled even though his gaze was firmly fixed on Lord Fremont, who served as treasurer and read the financial report for the first quarter of the year. Leo would hazard a guess that it wasn't only the limited funds in the Society's account that caused his foul mood. The duke had garnered more curious stares since his arrival than a flock of birds hovering over a dead rabbit.

No doubt he'd been subjected to similar stares after Lady Bethany had left decades ago.

Leo forced his attention away from his friend to study Lord Mortenson, one of the men Leo considered a potential suspect for the missing journal.

The man had more than a passing interest in pirate treasure, particularly Captain Kidd's. He'd even taken a trip to Oak Island five or six years ago. At the time, he'd insisted his interest was not solely on the treasure but the area in general.

Leo had difficulty believing that. While Nova Scotia was said to be beautiful, it wasn't a common destination for most people. The forested area had little to offer in the way of entertainment for men like Mortenson, who made no secret of his preference for fine dining and elegant accommodations.

The lord didn't always act as a gentleman should, pushing the boundaries of right and wrong where it suited him. Nothing illegal that Leo knew of, but not exactly ethical either. Leo was certain he wouldn't bat an eye at buying a stolen object if it was one he desired.

Leo had spoken with Mortenson the previous day, bringing up both Oak Island and Captain Kidd's treasure in an effort to gain a reaction but hadn't noted anything unusual. One could often see a hum of excitement in a fellow member when they discovered something new. He had experienced that feeling himself, and it was difficult to hide, especially when among other members of the Society who shared the same passion. Speaking of newfound treasure lit a fire that was often impossible to smother.

Mortenson had spent a good portion of his fortune pursuing riches in various parts of the world. Perhaps that made him desperate for funds. His potential involvement was certainly worth further inquiry.

Leo wondered whether spreading the news about the theft of David Wright's journal would shake loose any information. If it was commonly known the journal had been taken, selling it would become more difficult.

Most members of the Society abhorred thievery. At least, that was what they claimed. Whether they chose to dabble in stolen artifacts was another thing altogether. The rules they held themselves to often changed when the item was something in which they were greatly interested.

Ruthless was one way to describe the single-minded focus that some explorers had. In fact, Leo had heard that term used for David Wright on more than one occasion.

Leo's gaze shifted to the other person present who had come to mind—Stephen Rayburn, Viscount Ludham. His charming smile hid an iron resolve to take what he wanted. He had also chased pirate treasure on numerous occasions, though he seemed to prefer to acquire what others had discovered rather than find his own. Leo intended to speak with him soon.

Leo wasn't interested in only who might buy the journal if it were offered for sale but also in who had taken it. Logic insisted it wasn't a random theft. He should've pressed Ella further on exactly when she had last seen the journal to narrow the time as to when it could have been taken. That might be beneficial in determining who had done so. He needed to call on her again to discuss that, as well as learn more about the man from the steamship she mentioned.

"What do you think, Marbury?" Lord Fremont asked.

Leo looked up to realize everyone had their gaze on him, waiting for a response, but he had lost track of the conversation. His focus shifted to Rothwood with the hope of finding a clue as to what the question was.

"Money must be found for a new location." The duke's lips tightened with determination as he glared at Leo, making it clear he wanted him to agree.

Leo smothered a sigh. The discussion was an ongoing one that showed no sign of resolution. While most members agreed that a larger building would be preferable, no one had discovered a way to raise the funds to do so.

"Until we have more money at our disposal, arguing about it won't help." Leo knew that wasn't the response the duke wanted, but the topic was the last thing on his mind at the moment. The same should be true for the duke as well.

The council members all begin speaking at once, which only made Leo shake his head. He held tight to his patience as he waited for Fremont to call the meeting back to order and finally adjourn.

Rothwood caught Leo's gaze as the other men stood, many renewing their arguments as they slowly made their way out the door. The duke rose and approached Leo. "I expected you to list the reasons a larger building is vital."

"I would think that would be the least of your worries given the arrival of your granddaughters and the missing journal. Or are you still pretending they aren't staying with you?" Leo asked in a quiet tone.

Rothwood glanced about as if to make certain no one could hear them. "I don't know what you mean."

"I mean that you need to come to grips with their presence. And we should be working together to try to find the journal. You know as well as I do that there were two men in this meeting who would love to get their hands on it."

Rothwood's face tightened with displeasure. "I thought I made it clear that you are better suited to deal with the matter of the missing item than I."

"You asked for my help. You didn't mention handing the search over to me completely." Leo was well aware his tone held a bite, but he didn't appreciate being thrust into the situation only to have the duke step away.

Besides, he had as much of a reason to keep his distance from David and Bethany Wright's daughters as Rothwood, if only for his mother's sake. He wished he could remember that when he looked into Ella's wide blue eyes.

He gave a mental shake at the thought. At the very least, he could use some assistance in his inquiries. Perhaps he should involve Worley in the investigation since the duke apparently had no intention of helping.

While Leo appreciated how difficult the situation was, he didn't see the purpose of Rothwood attempting to ignore his granddaughters. In truth, he had hoped that during the past few days, the duke would've become reconciled to having them in his home.

The situation was nothing he could control. He could only offer his opinion, something he intended to do, despite the fact that he knew the duke wouldn't welcome it. Rothwood was nothing if not stubborn.

"You are more than capable of dealing with it yourself," the duke insisted. "I have little to offer."

"Have you spoken further with them?"

"Who?"

"Your granddaughters." Leo realized his voice had risen, but he was beyond caring.

"I can't." The sudden wash of sorrow in the older man's eyes took Leo aback. "They are so like Bethany. It hurts to look at them. I can't possibly go through all that pain again."

Sympathy filled Leo at the stark confession. He could only imagine how much the memories pained him. "What if they help to heal the past?"

Rothwood's eyes closed briefly. "No. Impossible. You must deal with the journal on your own. Know that you have my thanks."

Before Leo could argue, the duke strode from the room without looking back.

"What was all that about?" Worley asked as he joined Leo.

"A tangle that refuses to unwind."

"Do tell." His friend raised a brow. "It sounds as if it's an interesting story."

"It's an old one, though apparently, it hasn't lost the power to hurt."

"Now you have to tell me as I'm beyond curious." Worley

tipped his head toward the door. "Buy me a drink and share the details."

Leo nodded. If the duke wasn't going to aid him, he was certain Worley would. Perhaps between the two of them, they could find a way to uncover the thief.

⫸⫷

"THE EARL OF Marbury to see you, Miss Ella," Davies announced from the doorway of the music room where Ella had been playing the piano by herself later that afternoon.

"Oh?" Hope filled her at his unexpected visit. Had he found the journal or at least brought some news of it?

She'd been restless since the outing to the modiste the previous day, and she placed the blame for it on the duke. If he would converse with her so she knew where they stood and what to expect, her worries would ease.

Living in limbo was nothing she enjoyed. Lady Havenby hadn't provided any clarification yet either. Had she remembered her promise to speak with the duke? The situation was unsettling enough without her regret over her father's missing journal.

Ella attempted to cast aside her worries as she asked the butler to show in the earl, hoping beyond hope he had information to share.

The moment he appeared in the doorway, she knew he didn't. His expression said it all.

"My lord." She curtsied, wondering if he at least had something to tell her. "Does the day find you well?"

"Well enough. And you?"

"Fine. Thank you." She waited for him to say something more but when he only watched her, she raised a brow. "Do you have news?" Surely this wasn't a social call.

His lips twisted. "Not yet. I still have doubts as to the possibility of recovering the journal. As you may have noticed, London is a big city. It could be anywhere."

"Surely your expertise in pirate treasure is of some assistance." The idea of never getting it back was impossible to consider. While they still had the artifacts her father had found, they didn't have the personal touch his journal had. At least not for Ella. Reading his handwritten notes was like hearing him speak. She cherished that connection. She'd left her father's previous journals with his partner on Oak Island, who intended to review them to help decide where he should dig next.

"My expertise is regarding the possible locations of artifacts. Not finding lost journals."

"You mean stolen." Irritation flooded her at his statement. Did he think she had simply misplaced such a precious item?

"Yes, of course. Stolen." Yet the casual way he said it suggested there was little difference in the terms to him.

There was a world of difference to her.

"Then what brings you by this afternoon?" She held tight to her manners. Her mother had always insisted on civility to keep tempers reined in. Little could be accomplished when emotions ruled rather than logic.

"I wanted to review the details of when you last saw it."

"Do you truly intend to conduct a search?" She didn't want to waste her time sharing them if he didn't.

His lips tightened, suggesting she'd either offended him or struck upon the truth. "I have begun inquiries, though nothing of importance has arisen thus far." He gestured toward the bench where she'd been sitting. "Please sit." He turned to draw a nearby chair closer. "I heard you playing. You're quite talented."

"Thank you. I enjoy it."

"Do you play other instruments as well?"

His question was confusing. Why did he pretend to want to know her better when he was so clearly displeased by their arrival?

"I do." She chose not to expand on her answer. Now was not the time for pleasantries. Besides, nothing she said could erase the pain her parents had caused his family.

After a moment of silence, he apparently grasped her intent to stay focused on the journal.

He cleared his throat. "Now then, you are certain you had it the last night on the steamship despite the search of your room."

"Yes. In fact, I slept with it under my pillow that night, as I was so upset over the search. The following morning, I placed it in my reticule."

"So, to your knowledge, you left the ship with it. Then what happened?"

"We made our way down the gangway and onto the dock. The crowd was significant, as you saw for yourself."

He nodded. "You mentioned that you spoke with someone else. Another passenger."

"Julius Conway."

"What do you know of him?"

"Very little. He befriended us on the journey and helped to brighten our spirits."

"Does he live in Nova Scotia?"

"No. He shared that he had visited family there and was returning to his home in London."

"Did he act especially interested in your father's search?"

Ella tried to think back to when Lena had first mentioned their father to the man. "He said he had never met a treasure hunter before and seemed curious about what Father was digging for and how he knew where to look. Then again, nearly everyone who finds out about our father shows interest."

"Hmm." The earl turned his head to look out the nearby window as if processing what she'd shared.

Ella studied his handsome profile. With high cheekbones and a strong jaw, he had an arresting face. His sun-kissed skin suggested he spent a significant amount of time outdoors. His effortless grace, part confidence, part arrogance, was surprisingly attractive. Did he look like his father had?

Despite her mixed feelings about this man, she couldn't deny the tingle of awareness that crept over her each time she was with him. It was as if her body reacted to his presence, regardless of her thoughts.

His attention returned to her, and that small tingle changed to a full shiver as her stomach did a slow somersault. What was this odd feeling? She lowered her gaze to her hands in an attempt to regain her composure.

"Did he see the journal?"

Ella shifted on the bench, wishing she had a different answer. "Yes. Lena wanted to show it to him one evening on the ship. He had already noted our mourning attire and expressed his sympathies. We shared a few things about our father with him. One story led to another, and we probably said more than we should have."

Rather than the reprimand she expected, she saw only empathy in his expression.

"Grief makes us want to share things about our loved ones, doesn't it? As if doing so will help make certain we don't forget them."

"Yes. Exactly that." Ella's heart pinched at his quiet words. He'd obviously felt that way at one time. Perhaps when his own father had died.

"I'm sure it's difficult not to discuss your father's occupation," he added. "Especially when so many in London heard the story of him and your mother."

"And your father." She had no doubt the late earl had been part of the gossip at the time as well.

He slowly nodded. "My mother and father are certainly part of the story."

"Does…does your mother know of us?" Ella was curious about her, both because she was part of the past and because she was Leo's mother.

Again, he nodded. "I thought it important to tell her myself."

"I hope it didn't upset her."

"Your arrival certainly surprised her. But she has become adept at dealing with difficult situations over her lifetime." His

85

expression softened, giving Ella the impression that he loved his mother. The idea melted her heart a bit.

"You haven't seen Mr. Conway since the dock?" When she shook her head, he asked, "Do you know where he lives?"

"I don't believe he said. I can ask Norah and Lena if they heard him mention it if you'd like."

"That would be helpful. Then what happened?"

"I was pushed into you." She no longer suspected he'd taken the journal. There was something trustworthy about the earl. Something that spoke of honesty and integrity when one looked at him. Though she knew she shouldn't believe in anyone given the situation, she couldn't deny she was beginning to trust this man.

"And after I left you with your sisters on the dock?"

"We hired a hackney and traveled directly here. Mrs. Whitsome accompanied us, then took the hackney on to her sister's."

"Where were your things while you..." His hesitation nearly made her smile.

"While we waited to see if we would be allowed entrance?" She took pity on him and finished the question.

He smiled. "That is a blunt way to state it."

"My mother often said sometimes blunt is best." Ella missed her wisdom. "The baggage sat on the pavement outside the house for a few minutes, though Davies was quick to have it hauled inside. That must've set the neighbors' tongues wagging if they saw the stack."

His chuckle sent warmth through her chest. While he was handsome all the time, when he smiled, he was even more so. Perhaps it would be best if she avoided making him smile. It was having an unfortunate effect on her focus.

"And the journal?" he asked.

"Still with me in my reticule." She frowned. "Although I only felt the weight of it inside. I suppose there's a chance that by then, the fake one had been switched for the real one." With a shake of her head, she searched his face. "I can't believe that any of the staff here would've taken it. But how could I not have noticed if someone had taken it out and replaced it with another while we were on the dock?"

"Those with nimble fingers are talented. Considering how distracted you must've been with all you had on your mind, it might've been possible."

She closed her eyes briefly as guilt swept over her once again, bringing a lump to her throat. A touch on her hand had her eyes flying open, only to see Leo beside her, his expression one of sympathy.

"Try not to worry. We will do all we can to find it. I'm sure that no matter what it contained, it was precious to you and your sisters."

"It truly was. Is," she quickly corrected. "I have to find it. I don't want to lose the memories of our Father."

"It's difficult, isn't it? My own father fades in my mind a little more each year no matter how I wish that wasn't the case." He clasped her hand, his gaze holding on her.

The connection she'd felt with him earlier expanded. Deepened. How odd to think she had something in common with this man whose past was so tangled with her own.

Then he rose and returned to his seat. "I am going to share the theft of the journal with a few acquaintances, mainly members of the Royal Geological Society, to see if anyone shows an unusual reaction to it."

"You think that will help?"

"It might. The more who know of the theft, the more difficult it will be for whoever took it to sell it."

"If that's their intent," she countered.

"It's the most likely outcome, don't you think?"

"Unless they want to use the information it contains to search for the Oak Island treasure themselves."

He scoffed. "It's possible, I suppose." He held up a hand, palm out, as if realizing she was about to argue. "If your father searched for all these years without success, it seems unlikely anyone else would be eager to take up where he left off."

"I don't think you understand the complexity of searching

there." She held tight to her mother's reminder about using logic over emotions to hold back her frustration. "There are only a few months of each year that allow for searching, let alone digging. And there's more than one theory as to where the treasure might be and how it was put there."

"The infamous flood tunnels."

"Yes." She was pleased he knew about the box drains in the cove that her father believed were connected to the money pit where the treasure was said to be. If someone attempted to dig without knowing how to properly access the treasure, the drains would cause seawater to fill the tunnels, making it impossible to reach the money pit. "Along with the damage previous searchers caused."

"How do you mean?"

"Father felt important clues had been lost by others, as some dug in various locations with the hope of circumventing the flood tunnels."

"But without success," he suggested.

"Yes, though that won't be known for certain until someone finds the treasure."

He tilted his head to the side as he considered her. "So, you're a believer?"

"Of course," she replied with a smile. "You couldn't live with my father and not be. If you had heard him speak of it, I think he might've convinced you as well."

Leo chuckled again. The sound of it along with the light in his eyes lifted her heart.

"Perhaps listening to you will eventually change my mind. You make a compelling argument," he added. His remark suggested he welcomed the chance to learn more about the treasure.

"Perhaps so." Her breath caught at the realization that she looked forward to sharing what she knew with Leo, if only because doing so gave her an excuse to be with him. He was charming when he bothered. It was difficult to believe that her opinion of him was improving, but she couldn't deny it.

Chapter Nine

"Y OU KNOW, THIS is a bit like a treasure hunt," Worley whispered to Leo as they entered the club the next evening.

"Hmm." Leo hadn't considered the similarities before. "I suppose there's some truth to that. Unfortunately, we have very few clues to follow."

"Which is how all good treasure hunts start." Worley clapped Leo's shoulder. "At first, there's only a spark. Then it slowly builds."

"In that case, I'm ready for the fire," Leo replied wryly.

"It's like falling in love," his friend continued. "A spark of interest. A second look. A breathless moment." He grinned at Leo. "Then passion arises and refuses to let go."

Leo paused mid-stride as a shocking realization took hold. He'd experienced the first three only yesterday. With Ella Wright of all people.

The spark of interest he'd felt on the dock had struck again while he'd spoken to her in the music room where the sunlight from the windows had cast her features in a warm glow.

A second look, and a third if he were honest, the first day he'd officially met her and again.

A breathless moment when he'd held her hand as they'd commiserated over losing a loved one. He'd felt...linked in an inexplicable way with her.

Leo scoffed and dismissed the revelation. Those moments were nothing. Meant nothing.

"What is it?" Worley asked as he paused beside Leo.

"Nothing." He suppressed the urge to shiver as something unsettling crept along his spine. Developing a tendre for David Wright's daughter was inconceivable. It would be a betrayal of his parents, especially to his mother, since she still lived.

A brief moment of connection with Ella didn't mean anything. Reassured, he moved forward again, forcing his thoughts to the evening ahead.

"You remember our plan?" he asked Worley.

"Of course. Stir up trouble."

"That isn't exactly what we discussed."

"It amounts to the same thing." Worley smiled. "We shall see if anyone looks guilty when we raise the topic of the stolen journal. Nothing like a few drinks to loosen one's tongue and make it more difficult to hide secrets."

"Chances are this won't amount to anything, but we have to start somewhere." Leo was pleased he'd involved Worley. Having another person to discuss the proper steps to take was helpful, and they'd be able to cover twice as much ground as Leo would've done by himself. Given Worley's storytelling ability, he'd soon spread the news far and wide, and hopefully, a clue would arise.

"Shall we start with Ludham?" Leo asked when he spotted the viscount across the room.

"Mortenson is also here. It's our lucky night to find them both. Who would you prefer to speak with first?"

"Mortenson, I think." Leo eyed the lord who sat at a table by himself. "Since I've already spoken with him, it shouldn't take long to see if he acts suspiciously in any way."

"Excellent. I'm pleased you're buying the drinks tonight," Worley said with a grin.

"I'll insist the duke reimburse me if we find the blasted journal."

With that, Leo walked to Mortenson's table. "Good evening, Mortenson. Can we join you?"

"Of course." The lord nodded, only to scowl at Leo. "You're not going to go on about the new location for the Society, are you? I've grown weary of that particular topic."

"You're not alone," Leo reassured him. "What purpose is there in discussing it at every meeting when we lack the funds to consider a move?"

"Exactly." Mortenson appeared relieved at his remark.

"Until someone finds a clever way to raise money or one of our wealthier members offers the funds, there's no point in looking at options." Worley signaled for a waiter.

"Care for another drink?" Leo asked as he settled into a chair.

"Don't mind if I do."

After they received their drinks, Worley raised the topic of his own recent success. There was nothing treasure hunters liked better than discussing their finds or hearing how others had located theirs.

Mortenson was eager to hear the story, and Worley enjoyed telling it.

"Marbury, did you mention the journal to Lord Mortenson?" Worley asked when he'd finished his tale.

"I've only shared the news with a few." Leo did his best to act uncomfortable at the topic as if reluctant to speak of it, although the conversation was proceeding exactly as he and Worley had planned.

"Mortenson might have some insight." Worley tipped his head toward the lord.

Leo pretended to hesitate, then sat forward in his chair. "You remember David Wright, don't you? The one who was so interested in Oak Island."

"Of course." Mortenson nodded. "You mentioned the place the other day when we spoke. Many believed Wright crazy for pursuing treasure on the island. Harsh conditions, you know. I spoke with him briefly when I traveled there a few years ago."

"He kept journals documenting his progress." Leo paused for what he hoped was a dramatic effect. "The last one he used before his death has gone missing." Leo watched the man closely to see his reaction.

"As in stolen?" Mortenson appeared surprised.

Leo nodded.

"Didn't he die last year?" the lord asked.

"I believe he did," Worley said. "I wonder who could've known about the journal."

Mortenson scoffed. "You know how the treasure hunting community is. One whiff of a rumor and the hounds are on the chase."

"True," Leo agreed. "But I, for one, would have no interest in it." He frowned, realizing he could no longer say that with certainty. After listening to Ella, a part of him wanted to know what Wright had found in his many years of exploring the island. "I have never believed pirate treasure was buried there."

"But it's been proven Captain Kidd ventured to Oak Island, hasn't it?" Mortenson asked.

Leo studied the lord as Worley took up the conversation, and the pair discussed what little was known.

"I still think Kidd's treasure is in Madagascar," Leo said as the discussion dwindled.

"You're probably right," Mortenson admitted. "But you know what they say—where there's smoke, there's fire."

Leo shared a look with Worley and could see the same conclusion in his friend's expression. It seemed unlikely that Mortenson was their man. With luck, maybe he'd share news of the missing journal with a few friends, and rumors would begin to swirl. That would hopefully make whoever took it nervous and more likely to take a misstep.

Leo would prefer to distance himself from spreading the news, if possible. Otherwise, someone would eventually think of his friendship with Rothwood, and given that the duke's granddaughters had arrived in London, might guess that Leo was helping to search for the missing item. Those involved might then take extra care to guard what they said around him.

After a few more minutes, Worley gestured toward the far side of the room. "I see a friend I must speak with. Care to join me, Marbury?"

"Of course." Leo stood, and they both bid Mortenson goodbye, then strolled toward where Viscount Ludham stood at the bar.

"Didn't seem like Mortenson was our man," Worley whispered as they approached the viscount.

"Agreed. Let us see how Ludham reacts to our news." Leo looked around the club to see if any other possibilities came to mind but didn't see anyone else who might be interested.

Though he'd been certain he would regret telling Ella he would try to locate the stolen journal, he was more determined than ever to do all he could after visiting with her. He dearly wanted to be able to give her some good news and lift the guilt she felt, along with some of the grief present in her eyes.

Yet something more nagged at him. Something that suggested there was more to his wish to see her spirits lift and a smile curve those lush lips.

He shoved away the concern before it took hold, reminding himself that an attraction between them was unthinkable.

Wasn't it?

ELLA WATCHED AS her sisters moved from one hat to another in the milliner shop on Bond Street. Their excitement over the various styles had Ella sharing a pleased smile with Lady Havenby.

"I simply cannot wait until the three of you attend your first ball." Lady Havenby clapped her hands twice, a gesture Ella had noted she did often. "You will all look stunning."

"You're so kind to help us with everything that goes along with attending the various events." Ella was still nervous about going. Especially when Lady Havenby was convinced they would garner so much attention.

"The pleasure is mine." She took a step closer to Ella. "I spoke with Rothwood and advised him of my intention of ordering trousseaus for each of you. He didn't bat an eye."

"I'm pleased to hear that." The news was somewhat reassuring to Ella. But she would rather he had agreed with enthusiasm.

Ella's continued attempts to connect with him had gone unanswered. He'd become adept at avoiding them. Davies and the other servants guarded him while he was in his study, and he rarely ate at home. It was beginning to feel hopeless to write him notes if he wasn't going to read them. Was that how her mother had felt when she realized he wasn't going to answer any of her letters?

A tug of sympathy filled her at the thought. Carrying on a one-sided conversation was never pleasant or easy, no matter the method of communication.

How isolated her mother must've felt in Nova Scotia, despite having her husband at her side. Being so far from home would be challenging. Being a new mother couldn't have been easy either. But experiencing both without additional support must've been incredibly difficult.

Then again, Lady Bethany had made that choice. Ella liked to think that her mother had believed she'd made the best one for herself and her family. Ella supposed she needed to start believing she'd done the same for herself and her sisters as well.

With that firmly in mind, she reached for a red hat with a narrow brim and a black plume that was terribly clever. "Norah, you must try on this one."

Norah grinned as she reached for it and moved to stand before a mirror as she put it on. "I love the style, though not the color, of course."

"We could order it in black to complement one of your gowns," Lady Havenby suggested. "That would be perfect."

Next, they found an even smaller hat for Lena with small violet roses made of ribbon.

She tried it on, turning this way and that in the mirror. "I'm not sure why they call these hats when so little of the head is covered."

Norah chuckled. "True. They're more like decorations."

Lena turned to face them, still wearing the hat. "Do you like my décor?" she asked as she tipped her head from side to side with her nose in the air.

The three sisters laughed, gaining curious stares from the other ladies in the shop.

After selecting a few plain hats, they moved on to the haberdashery to pick out various feathers, ribbons, and netting to decorate the hats themselves. Ella was pleased they'd have something else to do at the duke's and said as much to Lady Havenby.

"Do not worry. Soon you will be longing for a quiet day at home," the lady warned with a smile. "The numerous events you'll be attending will be exhausting."

Ella wasn't certain they were ready for that, but the evening of the first ball they were to attend would arrive before they knew it.

Next, they strolled along the shops and enjoyed watching people, as well as looking in the various windows that displayed goods. A few people stared at them, but Lady Havenby only smiled and whispered for them to keep walking.

"As I said, the three of you will be the talk of the *ton* once you've been introduced to the right people."

Ella wondered who the "right" people were. Would they have known their mother? Coming to London made her realize she'd only known a small part of her parents' existence. It was unsettling to think she didn't know them as well as she thought. They had lived a much different life here than their quiet one in

Nova Scotia.

She shook off the concern. Her own memories of them were more important than anything she was told by others. None of that could change her love for them.

⟫⟫✕⟪⟪

LENA RUSHED INTO the drawing room where Ella and Norah were reading that evening before dinner. "I have the best idea," she declared.

Ella smiled at her sister's enthusiasm. "What might that be?"

Lena drew closer, her eyes sparkling in a way that made Ella nervous. She'd seen that look before, and it didn't always bode well.

"Davies is preparing the table for dinner."

Ella frowned. That information was nothing new. The three of them had eaten alone at every meal since their arrival. Where or when the duke ate remained a mystery. Ella guessed he frequently ate at his club. Whether it was a new habit of his, she didn't know. No doubt, he did it to avoid them.

"He is also preparing the table in the small dining room," Lena said.

"The one we use for breakfast?" Norah asked.

"Yes." Lena nodded with enthusiasm.

"Why would he do that?" Norah asked, clearly puzzled. "We always eat dinner in the large dining room."

But Lena's words were beginning to make sense to Ella. She set aside her book and rose, her thoughts swirling as her gaze held on Lena. "You think the duke will be dining at home this evening but separately."

"That is nothing new," Norah said in a frustrated tone. "He has never eaten with us."

"Don't you see?" Lena asked. "This is our chance."

"Davies will never allow it," Ella warned. Although the butler

96

was sympathetic to their plight, he guarded the duke fiercely. Then again, keeping his position probably depended on doing so. Ella couldn't blame him for that.

"What if we simply go to the dining room, pick up our plates, and carry them into the small dining room ourselves?" Lena's blue eyes rounded with hope as she looked at them.

Ella was tempted. A bold move was certainly needed to gain the duke's attention. "He might simply leave if we join him. He is quite good at doing that."

"But what if he doesn't?" Lena asked. "What if we are able to spend even just five minutes in his company? That would be more than what we've been able to do since the day we arrived."

"Except for when the journal went missing." Norah tapped a finger on her chin, suggesting she, too, was tempted. "He spent several minutes with us then. Of course, most of them were in silence as we waited for the Earl of Marbury to arrive."

"If the letters aren't working, it seems like we should try something else," Ella said, her mind made up.

"Do you think he just needs more time to adjust to us?" Norah asked. She didn't care for conflict.

Neither did Ella. But what they'd been doing hadn't gotten them anywhere.

"If we do this, we must take care to remain respectful," Ella said as she thought it through. "We don't want to give him a reason not to like us." Or to demand that they leave the house and find somewhere else to stay. But she didn't say that.

Just because Lady Havenby had convinced him to pay for a few gowns didn't mean he was close to accepting them. But Ella was determined for the duke to come to know them. That wouldn't happen if they never spent any time with him.

"I think we should try," Lena said. "Dealing with the duke is rather like dealing with a colt. One must warm up to it, then coax it forward."

Norah looked at her as if she had lost her mind. "I don't think comparing His Grace to a horse is helpful in the least. It would only offend him."

Lena gave her sister an exasperated look. "I'm not going to tell him that. I'm just saying we need to try and convince him to like us. Even if we only have a few minutes with him."

Norah worried her lower lip, and Ella knew how concerned she was about the proposed plan. "This might make him like us even less."

"I'm not sure that's possible, but the idea does hold risk." Ella sighed. "I, for one, think we need to try a new way to reach him. This could work. What do you think?"

Norah slowly nodded. "Very well. I can already see it is two against one. But we must all be on our best behavior with our best manners."

"Agreed." Ella nodded and looked at Lena.

"Agreed." Lena nodded as well.

The clock chimed the hour, which meant it was time for dinner. Ella hoped the duke was eating at the same time as they were.

"Shall we?" With a lift of her brow, she led the way down the stairs to the dining room where the table had been set for three as usual.

"Do we take them now?" Lena asked in a whisper as she moved to stand behind her chair.

"I think we wait until the meal has started," Ella said. "That would make it less likely for him to get up and leave."

Just then William, the footman, entered the room—an unusual occurrence, as Davies normally served them. "Good evening." He greeted them with a bow.

"Good evening," they replied.

He rounded the table to help them take their seats.

"Where is Davies?" Lena asked.

William hesitated as if uncertain how to answer. "He is otherwise occupied, so I will be serving you this evening."

The three sisters shared a look. Surely that meant Davies was serving the duke at this exact moment as well.

The footman stepped out and then returned with a large tray holding the first course of cream of celery soup.

The cook was talented, and the food was always delicious. Mrs. Enfield assisted in deciding the meals, though the house-keeper had asked if there was anything in particular they wanted. The lady of the house normally helped plan meals for the week, but Ella hadn't been asked to take on that responsibility. That was one of the many reasons Ella felt as if they were only guests here. This wasn't home.

They ate the creamy soup, but Ella noted her sisters were as nervous as she was and weren't enjoying the food.

The footman cleared their bowls and left the room again.

"Once the main course is served and William steps out, we will take our plates to join the duke," Ella whispered, her stomach knotting. She could already picture the cold look of disdain he would give them as he stood and left the room.

Lena nodded, her enthusiasm for her idea noticeably reduced now that the time had come to implement it.

Ella hoped that wasn't a sign of what was to come.

Chapter Ten

"**Y**OU LEAD THE way," Lena whispered once the footman had left the dining room after serving the main course.

Ella rose, well aware the footman would be back at any moment to see if they needed anything. She hoped they wouldn't regret this. She picked up her napkin, silverware, and the plate filled with roasted mutton and vegetables, then rose to wait for her sisters to do the same.

She walked down the hall the short distance to the smaller dining room that easily sat eight, where they normally ate breakfast, and paused at the door to look at Lena and Norah. "Smiles."

They both attempted one, though it was far from their best. Ella did the same, determined to do everything in her power to make this go well, and pushed open the door.

To her surprise, the duke truly was sitting at the table alone. He looked up in surprise at their entrance, his fork halting in midair.

"Good evening, Your Grace," Ella said as she set down her plate and other items on the table, then curtsied, hoping her sisters were doing the same.

"We were feeling lonely in the other dining room," Lena began as she pulled out a chair. "We wondered if we might join you briefly?"

The duke only blinked as he slowly lowered his fork to his plate, clearly at a loss how to reply. His grey hair was smoothed to the side. His evening dress was impeccable even though he dined alone. His plate held the same mutton and vegetables as theirs.

Sympathy tugged at Ella. Was this how he spent most meals, dining alone? She didn't care for the idea, which made her even more determined to convince him to let them into his life. Since he hadn't refused their request, she took a seat.

"We hope you don't mind," Norah added as she sank into a chair. "Perhaps just for this course?"

Ella was pleased none of them sat too close to the duke, so as not to crowd him. Maybe Lena's analogy of him being like a colt wasn't so wrong after all. If they moved with care, perhaps he wouldn't bolt like he had before.

"Just for this course," Ella repeated as she scooted in her chair.

Davies entered the room from the door that led down to the kitchen with a bottle of wine in hand only to halt abruptly, his expression alarmed as he took in their presence.

"We're joining His Grace for this one course," Ella advised the butler, who shifted his gaze to the duke.

"Your Grace?" Davies asked quietly. Perhaps he, too, understood that quick movements or loud noises would cause the duke to quit the room.

The lord's lips twisted, then he gave a single nod. "One course."

Ella's relief caused her to take a deep breath. "Thank you, Your Grace." She picked up her fork, uncertain what topic they might discuss. In truth, she hadn't thought they'd make it this far.

"The weather was particularly fine today, don't you think?" Norah asked no one in particular.

"It was," Lena responded with enthusiasm. "The sunlight feels so fragile this time of year. As if it wants to be bold and bright but hasn't quite worked up the energy to do so."

Ella couldn't have been prouder of her sisters. They spoke quietly, with a genuineness that should keep any awkward moments at bay.

"I believe we are to venture out with Lady Havenby again tomorrow afternoon," Ella added, wanting to do her part.

"She is very kind." Norah smiled at the duke. "I'm so pleased you suggested she help guide us."

He didn't respond, though his gaze caught on each of them as they spoke before once again dropping to his plate. He ate at a steady pace but didn't seem to rush through as Ella had expected.

They continued conversing, leaving pauses for the duke to comment, though he didn't. Ella avoided asking him any direct questions, as did her sisters.

Once they'd finished, Ella set down her fork and rose, determined to keep their word about only staying for one course. "Thank you, Your Grace. We very much appreciate your company."

Her sisters rose as well and added their thanks, curtsied, then the three of them departed. Her grandfather had only uttered two words. But more importantly, he hadn't asked them to leave.

As far as Ella was concerned, that was one battle they'd won. Perhaps there was a chance of winning the war after all. She couldn't help but smile at the thought.

⟫⟫⟫✖⟪⟪⟪

LEO ENTERED THE bookshop in Finsbury Square that he frequented and glanced around to see if any fellow Society members were there.

This shop specialized in research books. Mr. Filpin, the owner, had sent a note stating he'd found an interesting book on Madagascar, in which Leo might be interested. Leo had already purchased several items from the shop to add to his collection and was eager to see what the owner had found. Leo also wanted to ask Mr. Filpin to be on the watch for any treasure hunter journals and notify him if he heard anything.

Three days had passed since he and Worley started their efforts to find David Wright's journal. Unfortunately, no clues had yet arisen, nor had they found anyone who'd heard of Julius Conway. A new method of approaching the situation was needed, but none had come to mind as of yet.

To his surprise, Ella perused a shelf near the front of the shop. He drew slowly closer, appreciating the chance to watch her unobserved for a moment.

A shaft of afternoon sunlight shone through the front window, casting her in a golden light. The sun drew out the honey tones of her hair, making him realize how many different shades the strands held.

She looked different than when he'd last seen her, and he stared, trying to determine why. It took a moment for him to realize this was the first time he'd seen her in something other than black.

Her new gown was a deep lavender that gave her skin a creamy glow. A small matching hat trimmed in black perched on one side of her head, giving her a jaunty appearance. The hint of color in her cheeks spoke of her good health.

She truly was a beautiful woman. That beauty—said to be so much like her mother's—made him wonder what Lady Bethany had looked like. He had gained a certain appreciation for his father's adoration of the lady, given his own attraction to Ella.

"Miss Wright," he said.

She turned from her study of a book to look at him, smiling as recognition came. "My lord." She dipped into a curtsy. "How lovely to see you this afternoon."

"And you." He glanced at the book she held, curious as to what had caught her interest. "Are you in search of something in particular?"

"My sisters are in the shop next door, but I couldn't resist seeing what books this establishment has to offer." Her gaze caught on a maid who waited near the door.

"And have you found it to your liking?"

"I thought to find one on the history of London but came across this book on Captain Kidd."

He was so surprised he didn't immediately respond. "Surely your father had a book or two on the subject."

"Yes, but isn't it interesting how each account shares a different version of the same story?" The way she watched him suggested she truly wanted to hear his opinion.

"True, though some go to great lengths to dramatize events."

"Which makes it difficult to sift through the information to find the facts."

He nodded, pleased she understood that just because something was printed in a book didn't mean it was true. "Cross-referencing details with other sources is vital when doing a thorough study."

"Have you written any articles about the pirate?" Her blue eyes sparkled with interest.

"Marbury has written numerous articles on every topic."

Leo turned to see Viscount Ludham approach.

"Ludham." Leo gave a polite nod, wishing the man would go on his way and find someone else to bother.

Ludham's brow rose as he looked at Ella. "Aren't you going to introduce me to the lady?"

Leo watched as Ella's gaze shifted from the viscount back to Leo, caution in her expression.

"Miss Ella Wright, may I introduce you to Stephen Rayburn, Viscount Ludham."

"What a pleasure, Miss Wright." Ludham reached for her hand just as she started to curtsy, which seemed to take Ella aback. "I can't believe we haven't met before now."

Ella glanced at Leo as if seeking his guidance. "I'm new to London."

Leo had the sudden urge to take Ella by the arm and march her out of the bookshop and as far from Ludham as possible. The man looked at her as if she were a tasty morsel to devour rather than a woman with thoughts and feelings. Leo didn't like it.

"Will you be staying in London long?" Ludham asked.

"For a time," Ella replied noncommittally.

"Then you'll be enjoying the Season. Perhaps attending a few balls and the like?"

"I believe so." Ella glanced toward the door, and Leo imagined she was wondering how soon she could escape.

That made two of them.

"Forgive me, but I can't help but wonder what a beautiful lady like you is doing in a dusty old place like this." Ludham glanced about as if to prove his point.

"I rather like shops like this," Ella countered. "One never knows what might be discovered in the pages of a book. Wouldn't you agree?"

"If you like books that much, Marbury would make an excellent companion." Ludham leaned close to Ella. So close that she drew back slightly. "But if you prefer true adventure that thrills you to the marrow of your bones, then you and I should become better acquainted." The viscount offered a smile that Leo imagined he thought was irresistible.

It was all Leo could do not to roll his eyes at Ludham's blatant attempt at charm.

"How...interesting," Ella replied with a polite tone that held a distinct chill. "I believe I've had enough adventures in my life. At least for now, I'd prefer to merely read about them."

Based on the way the viscount stared at her as if fascinated, her answer had only further piqued his interest.

"Then I look forward to exchanging stories with you soon." He glanced at Leo, then returned his attention to Ella. "It's been a pleasure to meet you." He dipped his head and then strode toward the exit.

"How do you know the viscount?" she asked after the door shut behind him.

"A fellow member of the Royal Geological Society. One I

don't especially care for." He knew Ella could form her own opinion, but he hoped she could see beyond the man's attempt to charm.

Ludham remained on Leo's shortlist of suspects. His reaction to news of Wright's missing journal had been difficult to read when Leo and Worley had spoken with him at Brooks's a few nights ago. There was something untrustworthy about the viscount, though Leo had yet to put his finger on the reason.

However, it was interesting that Ludham hadn't latched onto Ella's last name when Leo had introduced her. That was actually a point in the viscount's favor. Surely if he had David Wright's journal, he would've had more of a reaction to meeting someone with the same last name.

"Is what he said true?" Ella asked. "Have you written many articles?"

"I have written several. Mainly on pirate treasure, of course, as that is where my focus is."

"Why? What makes you so interested in that? It seems unusual for someone like yourself to study the subject rather than exploring it firsthand."

"I traveled extensively when I first left university and made occasional trips in the years that followed. But I have found I prefer to attempt to solve the puzzles of buried treasure from home. Being distant from the sites allows for greater objectivity, in my opinion. Also, my research books are here. I don't care to pursue clues until I can investigate the possibility of them bearing fruit."

"Objectivity." Ella nodded slowly. "That is not a word I would use to describe most treasure hunters."

"Including your father?"

"Most definitely." She smiled, though grief dimmed it. "Obsessed, perhaps. But not objective."

"I think passion is a requirement to dig for treasure. Along with a great deal of stubbornness. Otherwise, many would give up long before they found anything."

"He had those qualities as well. Of course, he questioned information before he invested the time and energy to pursue it."

"Did he believe in the curse?" Only too late, Leo realized how terrible the question was, especially when Ella shivered slightly. "My apologies. That was a thoughtless question."

Legend said that seven men must die before the Oak Island treasure could be found. If Leo was correct, her father was the second.

"No, it's all right. The supposed curse is a big part of the lure of Oak Island. Father believed it was invented by whoever first searched for the treasure to ward off other hunters."

"Logical." Leo nodded, keeping his focus on Ella and hoping he hadn't upset her. "I truly am sorry for mentioning it."

"You won't be the last one to do so. Besides, my father didn't believe in it. He insisted all treasure hunting was dangerous. That it was a risk one had to be willing to take. If the actual search didn't threaten one's safety, fellow treasure hunters eager to share in the riches might."

"I confess to having written an article that said much the same thing."

Ella's smile was genuine. "Did you offer a solution to the problem?"

"I suggested that working together would bring results more quickly. It wasn't one of my more popular articles," he added with a wry smile.

"A delicate subject, I'm sure."

"Indeed."

"Why Captain Kidd in particular? What about him captures your interest?"

"Imagine being hired by European royalty to attack and steal from other ships. He was hired by England to protect ships in the Caribbean from France. A pirate hunter who became a pirate. I find the line between protecting and attacking in these situations fascinating."

"A hero to one side and an enemy to the other."

"Exactly," Leo said, warming to the subject. "Kidd and others like him were allowed to keep whatever loot they found on enemy ships. It was like being handed the keys to a gold mine."

"It's no wonder he's said to have accumulated masses of treasure."

"Indeed. However, not much of it has been found. It's out there somewhere."

"Which is why you enjoy studying various accounts of his life in an attempt to uncover where it might be."

"Yes!" Leo chuckled at his overly enthusiastic reply which gained him stares from several others in the shop. "Forgive me. It's always a pleasure when someone actually understands the reason behind my interest."

"Not at all. It's enjoyable to hear a different perspective from my father's. But his passion was similar."

Passion.

Somehow, the word uttered by Ella tripped a trigger inside Leo. His world narrowed, and all he could see was her, her eyes full of light. The curve of her rosy lips drew him like a siren. The urge to kiss her shoved aside thoughts of his favorite topic.

Leo forced himself to look away before he did something he would regret. Now was not the time or place for such thoughts. If only his body would listen.

"I should be getting back to my sisters," Ella said with a glance at her maid, who still waited patiently by the door. She returned the book to the shelf. "They'll be wondering what's become of me."

"It was a pleasure speaking with you," Leo managed, hoping his attraction wasn't as evident as it felt.

"Oh." She paused to meet his gaze. "I wondered if it would be worth having a conversation with the shop owner to advise him to watch for anyone attempting to sell my father's journal."

"That's one of the reasons I'm here today." Leo nodded. "I will speak with him."

Ella smiled. "Thank you." She curtsied and moved to the door, leaving him standing there, wondering what was happening to him and to his heart.

Chapter Eleven

"WHAT HAVE YOU discovered?"

Leo looked up from the article he was reading at a table at the Society offices to find the Duke of Rothwood standing before him, his brow furrowed.

"Good day, Your Grace." Leo stood and dipped his head. "I hope the day finds you well." Since when had they dispensed with pleasantries? The duke was normally a stickler about such things.

Rothwood's lips tightened with impatience. "Yes, yes. I'm well. You're well. All is well." He glanced about as if to make certain no one else could overhear them. "Except for the theft of my granddaughters' journal."

Leo blinked at that statement, trying to digest what it meant. For the duke to say the word "granddaughters" was one thing. For him to mention the stolen journal was another. Last time they'd spoken, the duke hadn't wanted anything to do with the search. Or his granddaughters for that matter.

Now he was suddenly demanding answers?

Three days had passed since Leo had seen Ella at the bookshop. He had visited several others that specialized in unique items with the purpose of warning them about the stolen journal. Neither he nor Worley had found anyone who knew Conway, nor had any new rumors arisen about David Wright or his notes.

In truth, Leo wasn't certain what other action to take. However, he didn't appreciate the duke questioning him in this manner when he'd refused to help from the start.

"What's happened?" Leo asked as he sat down again. There had to be a reason for his questions.

"Apparently nothing, as the journal has not been returned."

"I meant what has happened to cause your sudden interest in the topic?"

"It's been several days since you started looking for it. I thought by now you'd have news."

"If I did, I would've called on you to advise you."

The duke shook his head, clearly dissatisfied with Leo's answer. He pulled out a chair to join Leo at the table, his expression grim. "It simply must be found."

"Do you have any helpful suggestions, or do you simply intend to make impossible demands?" Leo surprised himself with the question yet couldn't have kept it back even if he'd tried. Did the duke think he hadn't been trying? That it wasn't constantly on his mind? Granted, he hadn't been overly enthusiastic to begin with, something he thought the duke had understood. But he certainly had been attempting to find the journal.

Rothwood had the good sense to look sheepish. "My apologies. But I would like this matter resolved expediently."

"As would I." Perhaps then Leo could stop thinking of Ella. "Has something happened with your granddaughters to cause your concern?"

Rothwood's mouth opened and then closed as if he thought better of what he was about to say. Then he repeated the gesture.

"Out with it," Leo suggested, hiding his amusement at the duke's apparent befuddlement. "You know you can tell me in confidence."

"They insist on dining with me." Rothwood glanced around again as if to make certain no one had heard his odd confession. He shook his head, suggesting he found the situation impossible and had no idea what to do about it.

"Dining with you," Leo repeated, struggling to understand

why this was an issue. Of course, he was shocked Rothwood was doing anything with the ladies. The last he'd heard, the duke had been going out of his way to avoid them.

"Not the entire dinner. Just one course. Not necessarily the same one, mind you. I don't know at which they'll appear. Last night, it was the first course. The night before, it was dessert."

"I see." Leo did his best to smother his amusement.

"It's maddening."

"I'm sure." It sounded as if Ella and her sisters were doing their best to get under the duke's skin. How interesting that their efforts seemed to be working.

"Why don't they join me for the entire meal? It's ridiculous."

"Perhaps they're waiting for an invitation." Leo thought the idea brilliant. He would've been the first to acknowledge how lonely the duke had been all these years. Now he had not one but three granddaughters. Lovely women who seemed intelligent and pleasant, despite the difficulties life had dealt them.

"The situation is outrageous." The duke frowned again, clearly perplexed.

If Leo had to guess, he'd say Rothwood longed to have a connection with his granddaughters. But it wasn't easy to overcome the past. To forgive and let go, although Ella and her sisters hadn't caused the harm. Nor was it easy to risk being hurt. A long time had passed since the duke had someone in his life to care about.

"Did you enjoy it?" Leo asked. At Rothwood's blank look, he added, "The dinner. Or rather, their company."

"That's not the point."

"It should be. If you enjoyed dining with them, then why not ask them to join you for an entire meal?"

"Humph." The duke tapped his finger on his lip as he considered it, the gesture bringing Ella to Leo's mind. "I don't know if that's wise."

"Do you truly believe they are your granddaughters?"

"Of course. I said as much."

"Do you intend to ask them to leave?"

"Where else would they go?" Rothwood glared at him as if he'd suggested he kick a puppy.

Leo nodded. Now they were getting somewhere. Only too late did Leo realize that he was taking Ella and her sisters' side in this matter. Perhaps he and Rothwood had more in common than he'd realized. His own opinion of them had changed as much or more than the duke's.

"If they're here to stay, then why not come to know them?"

"Because eventually, they'll leave. I'll be alone again." The sorrow etched in the older man's expression caused a wave of sympathy to roll through Leo.

"Perhaps," Leo admitted. "But perhaps not." He leaned forward to hold the duke's gaze. "No doubt they'll marry eventually. That doesn't mean they'll be out of your life. Who knows? Within a few years, you might be entertaining great-grandchildren."

Rothwood's eyes softened before a hint of a smile curved his lips.

"If you don't take this chance now, why would they remain in your life in the coming years? Give them a reason to do so."

It wasn't long ago that Leo had wished for the duke to have both a family and a purpose. Now he could have both if he'd just allow his granddaughters a place in his heart.

"You've given me much to consider. I shall think upon it." Rothwood sat back in the chair for the first time, seeming to relax. "How unfortunate that the journal has not appeared."

"Indeed. However, I am far from giving up." Leo had no intention of admitting it to anyone, but each time he spent a few minutes with Ella, he came away more determined than ever to find it.

He still didn't think the journal held any great revelations about treasure on Oak Island. But its value was in other forms. That much he would admit. No treasure of any sort should be stolen. Especially not when they were as personal as Wright's notes.

At the very least, David Wright had tenacity. And Leo had no doubt his daughters, especially Ella, did as well.

ELLA PRESSED A handkerchief against her mouth, desperate not to breathe in any more dust. The particles were everywhere in the shaft, lingering in the air, coating her eyes and lungs. A torch hung nearby on one of the evenly spaced, rough-hewn timbers that held back the earth and cast a narrow circle of light around them.

Her father stood just ahead of her, using a pickaxe to dig deeper. Sweat beaded his brow and dust covered his stained shirt. A lock of dark hair fell onto his forehead as he toiled, and he grunted with his efforts.

How did he stand it day after day? The darkness. The dust. The loneliness and hard work. And at times, hopelessness. All those were part of his daily life. Yet still, he dug.

Ella admired his perseverance but being in the shaft was uncomfortable and caused a sense of dread in the pit of her stomach. She desperately wanted to leave.

The dirt walls rumbled as if in protest at his efforts even as the ground beneath her feet shifted. Fear pulsed through her, and she tugged on his shirt. "Father, we must go."

But it was as if he couldn't hear her or feel her touch. His focus remained on the earthen wall before him. He leaned forward to examine it, then reached for the torch to have a closer look. She followed his gaze to see a shiny object glittering in the light, barely visible in the dirt.

He hefted the pickaxe and tapped around that gleam as the walls continued to shake. More dust filled the air and chunks of rock began to fall.

"Father," she yelled above the terrifying roar, pulling on his shirt again as panic gripped her.

Still, he ignored her.

As he plucked the shiny metal object from the wall, the rumble intensified. Dirt and broken timbers rained down on them as the shaft started to collapse.

Ella jerked awake with a gasp, chest heaving in an effort to draw a breath. Her heart thundered and her palms were damp. She sat up and blinked at the sight of the elegant bedroom and the soft, clean bedclothes beneath her hands, confused as to where she was.

Slowly, her panic subsided as she realized it had been a nightmare. Unable to remain in bed, she threw back the covers and stood, hoping to dispel the terrible images that lingered in her mind. Chills ran along her skin, and she rubbed her arms to ward them off.

She stalked to the window to look out at the dark garden below. But the shadows there did nothing to chase away the nightmare. She pressed a hand to her chest and drew a deep breath, yet still felt as if she were sucking in dust.

Was this merely her imagination running wild, or was her father somehow showing her what had happened? Had his final moments been anything like what she'd witnessed in the dream? She shuddered at the thought.

She hadn't ventured into the shafts with him since her youth. Not after they'd been dug so deep. Her mother had forbidden it, certain it was too dangerous. The deeper the shaft, the greater the danger.

Her father's partner, Edward Peterson, had been as devastated at his death as they were. He had gathered men from the nearby town to help recover her father's body. It had taken several days for them to clear the debris and pull him out.

In the bleak days following his death, Ella had finally worked up the courage to open the journal and look at what he'd written the day before he'd lost his life.

He'd been hopeful that he was close to a discovery. That the area he was searching consisted of disturbed soil, possibly dug and then refilled by whoever had buried the treasure. Only a small amount of water had been trickling into the shaft where he was working, which had been another positive sign. Digging on an island meant one was always in danger of being flooded.

Mr. Peterson had been working in another location that week. Having two grown men in the same shaft was uncomfortable but sometimes required. When that had been the case, they'd taken turns, working in shifts, with one watching over the other during the more dangerous digging. But the shaft that had claimed her father's life wasn't supposed to be dangerous as it descended at an angle rather than straight down. However, many things could go wrong.

Had gone wrong, she silently corrected herself.

Perhaps her worry over the missing journal had caused the nightmare. She needed to do everything in her power to get it back. Her sisters might not blame her, but she blamed herself.

When morning came, she would send a message to Marbury and request an update. Surely by now, he knew something, given all his connections.

Then again, maybe she was relying too heavily on him. Perhaps the time had come for her to make a few inquiries of her own. Somebody had to know something. She would search the whole city if she had to, but she was determined to find the journal.

With a sigh, Ella returned to bed. But her thoughts continued to circle and refused to let her rest.

LEO ENTERED ROTHWOOD House late the following morning in response to a message he'd received from Ella. It had been abrupt and not particularly friendly, making him wonder if something had upset her.

He greeted Davies and was shown directly to the drawing room where Ella sat, writing at a desk tucked in the corner. Her sisters were nowhere in sight, but the faint strains of a harp echoed through the house, suggesting they were in the music room.

He studied her for a moment, wishing he didn't feel this tug of awareness each time they were together. The freshness of her beauty caught at him. With her pale hair and the strength of her chin, the sweep of her lashes and the arch of her brow, all combined to create a symmetry that also reflected the strength of her spirit.

She had endured much in her life, and he couldn't imagine any other ladies he knew managing it as well as she had. Before he could offer a greeting, she looked up.

He nearly grimaced as he didn't care to be caught staring like a schoolboy.

"Good morning." He tipped his head toward her. "I didn't want to interrupt what looked to be an important task."

She raised one brow as if she didn't completely believe his excuse. "While I expected to hear from you this morning, I didn't expect to see you." She set aside the pen and stood. "Does this mean you have news?"

"Unfortunately, no." He drew closer, trying to gain a sense of her mood. Shadows beneath her eyes spoke of a less than restful night. "As I mentioned, these things take time."

Her lips tightened with disapproval. "It seems to me as if the more time the thief is given, the easier it is to lose his trail."

"Given that there was no trail, I'm not sure that applies in this case." Leo couldn't help but defend himself, uncertain why he felt the need. Though he'd given her reason to question his efforts, it still rankled that she didn't seem to believe he was doing the best he could under the circumstances. "Of course, if you have any suggestions on where to look or who to question, I would be pleased to hear them."

"Actually, I do." She reached for one of the sheets of paper on the desk. "I've compiled a list of places that might be worth visiting from adverts in the news sheet along with the help of the servants. Though these businesses might not have the journal, warning them of someone trying to sell it might be worthwhile."

Leo took the paper she offered, astounded at the number of places she'd noted in her neat, feminine script. "Antiquity dealers, import and export shops, and museums. This is a rather lengthy list."

She gave a single nod. "Some are less likely than others, but I still thought them worth mentioning."

"The lending library?" He raised a brow, unable to understand why she'd included it.

Her cheeks heated under his stare. "I don't know how they work, as I've never been to one. We didn't have any in our area."

"I suppose not. But I think it's an unlikely source."

"Those who work there surely have an interest in books. Therefore, they might hear of the journal."

"Hmm. I suppose that is possible." The list provided an interesting insight into how her mind worked. Damn if it didn't make him admire her all the more. "How do you propose I approach this many places?"

Her blue eyes narrowed. "One at a time?"

"Doing so will take months. It's not as if I can spend each and every day working on this."

"Perhaps not. But I can." She made to take back the list, clearly displeased with his response.

He held it out of her reach, rather liking the fact that she drew closer to try to take it. She smelled wonderful—a mix of fresh flowers and sunshine, with a hint of citrus.

Her skin was clear and smooth, her eyes sparkling with her efforts—or maybe that was temper. Her lips were a deep pink, the bottom one fuller. The sudden urge to kiss her swept over him, shocking him to his core.

Leo gave himself a mental shake. Kissing Ella wasn't part of his plan. Yet the fringe of her lashes, the delicate shell of her ear, and the curve of her cheek all added to her beauty and pulled at him.

"Marbury, return it if you can't help," she insisted, even as she continued to reach for it.

"I didn't say I couldn't help." He moved the paper higher, hoping she'd come closer still.

"Then what exactly are you saying?" Those bright blue eyes met his, and he caught his breath.

She truly was stunning. The numerous reasons he should keep his distance fell away.

"Ella? Might I call you Ella?" he asked.

She blinked several times, and he could almost see a rush of awareness come over her, revealed by the deepening color in her cheeks and the widening of her eyes.

"Yes. Yes, of course." Her voice dropped to barely a whisper.

"I would be honored if you called me Leo." He slowly lowered his arm, hoping not to break the spell that bound them.

"Leo," she said.

How was it that his given name on her lips could bring forth such a fierce desire? So much so that he leaned closer, unable to resist the lure of her. He paused to see if she'd move away. Instead, her gaze dropped to his mouth and held.

Yes, he wanted to whisper. Me, too. Rather than say anything, he closed the distance between them until their breath mingled. Until awareness gripped them both. Then he shut his eyes and took her mouth with his, everything within him shouting yes.

She tasted even sweeter than he'd imagined. Her lips were soft and warm, firm beneath his. She leaned into him, making the moment all the more enjoyable.

The gentle touch of her fingers along his cheek nearly made him shudder. The level of need swirling inside him shocked him. He'd had more than his fair share of women. They'd been experienced widows or the like. Never an innocent like Ella. He made it a point not to dally with innocents. How could he experience this reaction to her of all people?

The thought had him jerking back to stare into her eyes. She looked back at him, seemingly as surprised by their kiss as he was.

Then she dropped her gaze and stepped away, clasping her hands tightly before her. "That was...unexpected."

"Wasn't it though?" And terribly inconvenient. He didn't want to feel this passion for her. What would his mother say? The thought had him scowling. Involving himself with Ella would hurt her, and that was something he couldn't permit.

"I will prioritize your list and do what I can to visit these places," he said. "I'll continue my other inquiries as well. But don't be surprised if nothing comes from either avenue."

"Very well." Ella lifted her chin. Damn if that simple gesture didn't make him want to kiss her again. "I would appreciate it if you would keep me apprised of your efforts."

"Of course. Now, I must be going." He bowed, then turned on his heel and departed before he did something foolish. Like kiss her again.

Chapter Twelve

"**D**O YOU THINK this wise?" Norah asked as she walked down the street beside Ella while Lena trailed behind with the maid. The carriage waited at the corner.

"Not particularly." Ella was certain of it, in fact. But what choice did she have when it was clear that Leo—or rather, Marbury—wasn't going to make a concerted effort to find the journal?

She nearly groaned at her use of his given name. It had been better when she had thought of him as Marbury. At least that allowed for some distance between them.

Still, if he wasn't going to truly try to find her father's notebook, it was up to her to do so.

She'd wasted nearly an entire day reliving and analyzing his kiss. Good heavens. Did all earls kiss like he did? In a way that caused her toes to curl? Even now, the memory of it made her shiver.

"What is it?" Lena asked as she quickened her pace to better hear the conversation.

"Whatever do you mean?" Ella asked. At times, Lena's sensitivity and intuitiveness were a nuisance, though Ella would never tell her so.

Ella didn't want to share anything about the lovely, heated kiss with her sisters. They would read far too much into it.

Besides, it hadn't meant anything, had it?

"I think it best if we start an investigation of our own. Relying on...Marbury would be a mistake. I'm sure he has other matters with which to concern himself." Ella realized if she weren't careful, she'd be calling him Leo all the time. What else might she do if she allowed their association to progress further?

"Why do you think that?" Lena walked even quicker, making Ella realize she'd increased her own pace.

With a sigh, she slowed. It was impossible to outpace her thoughts. She should've learned that yesterday when she had practically forged a path across the drawing room floor with her pacing after the kiss. "As you know, he doesn't believe Father's work has much merit. Therefore, it's logical to assume he doesn't think the journal does either." Their conversation about Captain Kidd and the challenges of digging on Oak Island might've given him a better understanding of her father's efforts, but she didn't think he'd truly changed his mind.

"Humph." Norah lifted her chin. "I had hoped he realized his opinion was incorrect. But if he hasn't, we certainly should take matters into our own hands."

"Exactly. Hence our visit to Henley's Antiquities. The shop should be just ahead." This one had been in the middle of the list she'd given Leo. If he investigated any of the places she'd noted, he'd most likely start at the beginning. Thank goodness she'd made a copy for herself. There were several other similar shops in the area that she also intended to visit after this one.

As Ella glanced about, she realized this neighborhood was far different than Bond Street or Piccadilly, where they had shopped several times.

The buildings here had a worn appearance, with soot-covered, crumbling brick faces and dirty windows that held displays that looked as if they'd been placed there a decade ago. The people walking past weren't finely dressed but rather working class.

A closer look at a man they passed made her wonder if he had a place to call home. The layers of filth on his clothes made it look as though they'd stand on their own if he stepped out of them.

Ella said a silent prayer for him and made a mental note to bring a few coins to give to those who truly seemed in need in case they came upon another person like him. The city's disparity shocked her. The well-to-do with money to spare shopped a block or two away from streets lined with the less fortunate.

"I think the earl still intends to help us," Lena said as her gaze fell on a stooped old man who leaned on a cane, walking ever so slowly. "His opinion about the journal doesn't matter. He gave his word he would assist us."

"Hmm." Lena's opinion made Ella feel slightly better as her sister was often right. "Still, we shall do what we can to help in the search. Agreed?"

"Agreed," Lena and Norah replied together.

"Here we are." Ella eyed the exterior of the shop, already feeling her spirits drop, not that she'd expected immediate results.

Mr. Henley, if there was such a person, must've fallen on hard times as the exterior of his shop was one of the worst on the street. It had bricks missing in several places and little paint on the door. The filthy windows suggested few customers were lured inside by the items visible.

"Oh dear." Norah hesitated before reaching for the door, obviously sharing the same worry as Ella.

"We must keep our wits about us during these excursions," Ella whispered. "Be on guard at all times."

"Excellent idea." Norah gestured for Ella to precede her, then followed along with Lena and Sally.

Entering the dark shop with its numerous pieces of furniture stacked haphazardly on top of one another on the right and shelves overflowing with smaller items on the left, didn't allay Ella's concern. It seemed as if something might fall on them at any moment.

"Definitely not a good idea," she muttered under her breath.

Norah glared at her with no small measure of exasperation.

"Too late now. We must make the best of it."

"What is that smell?" Lena held a gloved hand to her nose as she paused to look at a large wooden desk.

"Most unpleasant." Norah scrunched her nose in response.

The musty odor of the interior suggested the place needed a thorough cleaning. And perhaps a few cats to chase away the faint rustle that could be heard from a nearby desk drawer.

"May I help you?" The slightly nasal voice belonged to a thin man who stood behind a counter halfway into the shop. His bald head, bushy sideburns, and reddened nose reminded Ella of a clown they'd seen perform in Quebec years ago.

"We are in search of a journal with notes of a treasure hunter. Have you come across anything like that of late?"

"Hmm. I'm not certain, though we do have several books on the topic over there." He pointed toward a small stack on a nearby shelf.

While Sally waited by the door, Ella led her sisters to the area but could see immediately that their father's journal wasn't among them. "Let us see what they contain for curiosity's sake." She didn't want their visit to be completely wasted.

"Yes," Norah agreed. "After all, we are not only looking for the journal but gathering information."

Ella appreciated her supportive remark. They each took a book and paged through them. The one Ella picked up shared details about a legend in South America. The next covered a story about a chest of gold found in Spain. None were of any use to them.

"Has anyone been by trying to sell a journal of that sort?" Ella asked.

"No, miss."

Ella left her card with the request that he contact them if someone did, then joined her sisters who waited by the door, trying not to be disappointed. "I knew this wouldn't be easy, but I hoped to feel as if we were getting somewhere."

"We are." Lena looped her arm through Ella's. "We can cross

this shop from your list. We have only fifty or so more to visit."

Norah chuckled. "That certainly makes me feel better. What of you, Ella?"

"Indeed. Much better." She shook her head wryly. "Am I a fool for even trying?" The task before them seemed insurmountable. It wasn't as if the list she'd made was complete. The chance of finding success was small. Nearly nonexistent, in fact.

"We must try." Lena tightened her grip on Ella's arm. "Therefore, we are doing the right thing. Besides, I was only trying to make you smile."

"You succeeded. Thank you for that."

Norah slowed her pace, her focus on something in the distance. "Does that person look familiar?"

Ella followed her gaze to see a man striding briskly across the street. Her heartbeat sped. "Isn't that Julius Conway?" She could hardly believe her eyes. Yet the bright pumpkin-colored suit coat suggested it was him.

"It is." Norah looked at Ella. "Should we try to catch him?"

Yet even as Ella watched, Mr. Conway hopped into a hansom cab and was quickly gone. "Oh dear. To think we might've run into him if we'd been just a few minutes quicker."

"I think he must've been in that shop." Lena pointed to one nearby.

"Far East Imports and Exports," Ella murmured as she read the sign. "That will be the next one we visit."

"Do you truly think he took the journal?" Norah asked.

"It seems impossible, doesn't it?" Lena shook her head. "He was so kind to us."

"I have difficulty believing it as well," Ella admitted. "But I would certainly like to question him. Surely, he wouldn't be able to hide any guilt if we confronted him."

"True." Norah scowled. "Especially if the three of us did so."

Unfortunately, that shop didn't have the journal, and the shopkeeper insisted he didn't know anything about it. He also claimed not to know Mr. Conway. They visited three other shops on the street without success.

"I believe I've had enough of dusty places for one day." Norah brushed off her gloves as they exited another one. "It must be time for tea."

"I would have to agree." Ella forced a smile, pushing aside her discouragement. She'd known this wouldn't be easy. As she and Sally followed her sisters to where the carriage waited, she couldn't help glancing over her shoulder to the Far East Imports and Exports shop.

To think they'd been so close to bumping into Julius Conway was maddening. At the very least, she would share the details the next time she saw Leo. Never mind the flutter she felt at the idea of seeing him again.

⫸⫷

Leo paced the drawing room, waiting for Ella to make an appearance. He held a tight leash on his frustration. Over the past two days, he had searched high and low for the journal only to be told by two different shops that Ella had been there before him.

The worst part was that the shops had questionable reputations and resided in questionable neighborhoods. Did she not realize the danger? Who knew what unsavory sort of characters roamed about those streets? If anything happened to her, the duke would never forgive him. And he would never forgive himself either.

He should have communicated what his plan was. She must've decided to do some searching of her own, as she believed he wasn't going to. But he'd needed some time and distance after that kiss.

It shouldn't have mattered. After all, it was only one kiss. Yet he found himself constantly thinking about it. Thinking about her. She unsettled him in a way he couldn't process.

He'd spent the evening after the kiss having dinner with his mother. It had taken only one look at her across the table for him to be awash in guilt. She'd already endured more than any person should have to because of David Wright and Lady Bethany. Associating himself in any way with their daughter more than he already had would be a mistake. Not just for his own well-being but for his mother's. His loyalty lay with her, not Ella Wright.

The fact that part of the blame remained on his father for not letting go of the past and embracing his life rather than lamenting over what could've been didn't change the situation.

Yet when Leo looked at Ella, he no longer saw David Wright. He only saw her. She was beautiful, charming, and intelligent. No matter how many times he told himself none of that mattered, it did. She caught his interest in a way he couldn't explain. Each time he attempted to analyze his physical reaction to her, his mind shied away. As if pondering it only gave more merit to his concern.

If only he could dismiss his attraction. Perhaps he could if not for the damned journal. Searching for it kept her in the forefront of his thoughts. Sadly, he'd had little to no success in finding even a mention of the thing.

He paced the length of the room again, wondering how long Ella intended to keep him waiting. He pivoted to pace in the other direction, only to come to an abrupt halt at the sight of her standing in the doorway.

"Good afternoon." She dipped into a curtsy. Only then did he realize she was out of breath. Where had she been? And why did the thought of her rushing to see him cause his chest to tighten?

"Good afternoon." He briefly bowed, then raised a brow. "I hope my visit isn't inconvenient."

"I was walking in the garden."

The image of her strolling among the blooming flowers brought a lovely vision to his mind.

"Do you bring news?"

At the abruptness of her tone, the image fell away much like the fog dissipating under the spring sun, there one minute, gone the next.

"No. But perhaps you can explain why the owner of Sanderson's Antiquities mentioned you had already been there when I paid a visit."

Ella walked slowly forward, her gaze holding on him. "Surely you didn't expect me to simply wait to see whether you decided to take action."

"I thought I made my intentions clear."

A flash of temper crossed her face, lending more color to her cheeks, even as her shoulders straightened. "Perhaps if you could communicate with me so I know what your plans are, we could work together."

Together?

His mind latched on to the image. But it had nothing to do with working. Instead, he could only think of holding her. Of the two of them entwined. He never should have kissed her. It was as if he had crossed a line, a point of no return. He gave himself a mental shake. He was an intelligent man of free will. This woman had no hold on him.

Why couldn't he remember that?

"I don't think you realize how dangerous this search might be." Leo rubbed the back of his neck, hoping to ease the tension there. "Did you notice that the shop you visited was not in the best area?"

"Of course. I am not so foolish as to venture there alone. Both of my sisters were with me, along with our maid."

He paused to stare at her in disbelief. "How would they protect you if something went awry?"

"You cannot be implying that a group of four women would be accosted in broad daylight. The city is not that unsafe." Yet her frown suggested he might be reaching her.

"You'd be surprised. Not only is the area you were in dangerous, but those interested in treasure hunting aren't always honest. If someone believes riches could be gained by taking you or one of your sisters by force..." He shook his head, unable to finish the thought. "If you can't think of your own safety, think of your sisters. Think of the duke."

Her brow furrowed. "What about the duke?"

Once again, Leo stared at her in disbelief. "He would be beside himself with worry if anything were to happen to you."

Ella scoffed. "I don't think he would notice if one of us went missing. In fact, I rather think he would be pleased."

"What happened to the dinners, or rather the courses, you were having with him?"

"We continue to join him when he's home, though I wonder whether it is worth the effort. He only answers our questions with a yes or a no or a grunt. I wouldn't call that progress." She waved a hand in the air that spoke of her frustration.

Leo smiled. "I think you are making more of an impact than you realize."

"You do?" The hopeful tone in her voice made him understand how much the situation bothered her. The thought caused his frustration to lessen.

"I thought it was very clever of you," Leo continued. "He seemed quite flustered when he spoke of it."

"I suppose the fact that he mentioned our efforts is a good sign. But at this rate, it will take years before we can have an entire dinner together, let alone a true conversation."

Leo started to disagree only to hold back. What was it about Ella that made him forget his loyalties? He should let her and the duke work through their relationship rather than interfere.

"But I digress." Ella drew closer. "Have you found any traces of the journal?"

"None." He frowned, wishing he had better news. How strange that no one seemed to know anything about the notebook. It was as if the journal had disappeared. Perhaps whoever had taken it didn't intend to sell it. Maybe they wanted to use it for their own research. But who?

Then again, it wasn't as if he knew all treasure hunters and explorers. Only a small portion were members of the Royal

Geological Society. However, he'd hoped to bring some information to light by now.

"That is all the more reason my sisters and I should help with inquiries."

Leo opened his mouth to forbid her from doing so but promptly closed it. Such an order, especially coming from him, would only make her more determined. There was no purpose in wasting his breath.

Instead, he asked the other question that had crossed his mind as he'd searched. "Why didn't your father's partner keep his last journal?"

"He read through it while we were settling Father's affairs." She glanced away as if upset.

He remembered all too well how he'd felt when his father passed. A wave of grief would catch him at an unexpected moment. The smallest thing could cause his sorrow to feel as fresh as the day his father had died.

Ella cleared her throat as she met his gaze again. "He returned it to us before our journey. He didn't seem to think it contained anything that he didn't already know. He and Father had taken turns digging in that particular shaft, and they'd had numerous conversations about it previously."

"I see. He intends to continue the search?"

"Yes. At least, that was his plan when we last spoke. As I mentioned, the weather plays a large part in when he can dig."

"I'm sure." Leo couldn't imagine living in the harsh winters of the area, let alone conducting a search in those conditions.

A part of him—a very small part—envied David Wright. What might it be like to give oneself fully over to such a passion? Leo had experienced a burning need for answers several times. Only once had it compelled him to leave home in pursuit. But not for long. Did that show a lack in him? Or logic that he'd realized the unlikelihood of discovering what he sought after all?

"Did you read the journal?" He was trying to understand what it held—or what someone might think it held—that would cause them to steal it.

"Some but not all." Again, her grief seemed to gain the better of her. Pain pinched her features. "It was too painful."

Leo's heart tugged at her obvious distress, and he stepped close to take her hand. Though tempted to hold her, that would be a mistake, especially with so much emotion swirling through him. "I'm sure reading his thoughts was difficult."

She blinked back tears. "It was. I could hear his voice as I read. And while that was somewhat comforting..."

"It also hurt." He released her hand and gathered her close, unable to bear seeing her upset when he was the one who'd caused it by asking so many questions. "I'm sorry."

At his apology, her body relaxed as if she were allowing herself to take the comfort he offered. "It's impossible to think the journal could be gone forever. If only I had been more careful."

"It sounds as if you were very careful. The blame lies on the thief who took it. Not you."

She drew a shuddering breath. "I've had so much on my mind these recent months that I'm not always thinking clearly."

"You wouldn't be normal if that weren't the case."

She rested her head on his shoulder, her sweet scent slowly filling his senses. She fit against him perfectly, and for a moment, he couldn't help but think that she belonged there.

Leo shut his eyes tight, hoping to block out the thought. He was merely being gentlemanly by holding her, something anyone in his position would do. Yet the idea rang false. He shared a connection with Ella he couldn't explain. One that defied logic. Did it have something to do with their parents' relationship, as disastrous as it had proven?

The concern had him easing back. He had no wish to repeat the past. A glance at her face suggested she had reservations as well, for her gaze flickered briefly to his before falling again.

To his relief and dismay—in equal measure, she stepped back and out of his arms.

"Thank you for your kindness," she whispered. "I think I am

managing well and then suddenly I'm not."

"As I said, understandable." He studied her, wishing he had the right words to comfort her. Unable to think of any, he could only share his hope. "With luck, we will find your father's journal which will help to ease your grief."

"That would mean so much." She nodded. "It would also comfort my sisters and me if we could help."

He stilled, not liking her statement. "I don't believe that's wise."

"While I appreciate your concern for our safety, I must insist. We can visit some of the businesses and make inquiries as easily as you. That will speed up the process. And with luck, bring results sooner."

"I want results as well, but not when it places you or your sisters in danger."

"We will take your warning to heart and be careful. But I can't rest until the journal is returned to us."

He wanted to correct her to say "if," but it seemed as if that would only make her more determined. She left him little choice. She and her sisters would proceed with their efforts regardless of what he said. The only option that remained was for him to communicate with Ella and guide her efforts. That way, he could keep an eye on her and her sisters.

"Very well. Why don't we meet tomorrow afternoon at one o'clock at the Museum of Treasures on Trenary Street? It is next on my list of possibilities. From there, we will form a plan to divide up the other places of interest in the area."

"Perfect." Her beaming smile kicked up his pulse.

Why did he feel as if he were going to regret this?

Chapter Thirteen

ELLA FOLLOWED LENA and Norah into the Museum of Treasures the following afternoon, curious as to what a smaller establishment such as this would have to offer. And more specifically, why Leo thought it was a good place for them to meet.

From the exterior, the three-story structure looked much like a residence. In fact, she was certain several of the other houses on the street were. Only a small sign near the front gate declared its current purpose.

"You would think we'd have grown used to that smell after venturing into so many of these places," Lena whispered as she wrinkled her nose.

The same musty smell that permeated the air at most of the other establishments they'd visited was evident here.

"I prefer the scent of lemon and beeswax." Norah frowned as she cautiously sniffed the air.

"You mean you prefer cleanliness over dustiness and mildew," Lena corrected, bringing a smile to them all.

The small entrance hall with its wood trim and floral wallpaper in shades of red was at least tidy. What the rest of the museum offered remained to be seen. A podium of sorts stood to the side and the sign attached to its front stated the cost for a tour.

"Greetings!" A small man with a large mustache waxed to

curl upward at the tips strode into the entrance hall with a broad smile. His black hair was carefully parted in the middle and smoothed down. Spectacles lent him a scholarly appearance. "Welcome to you. Are you here for a tour?"

Norah and Lena glanced at Ella, who considered their options. They were early, and Leo had yet to arrive. He hadn't mentioned whether he intended to simply speak with the proprietor or wanted to view the exhibits.

"We would like a tour, please," she said. From what little she could see of the nearby room, it appeared as if the museum had many items and could prove interesting.

"Excellent." The man's enthusiasm as he rubbed his hands together made her smile. "You won't be disappointed. Treasures abound." His eyebrows moved up and down with his words.

Ella hid her amusement. She wondered if he'd been an actor before taking up the role of tour guide.

"Now then," he said as he moved behind the podium. "Let us take care of the pesky little fee before we begin."

The modest price for admission made Ella wonder how many actual treasures they'd see. Still, she was pleased to have something entertaining to do even if the treasures were questionable.

"I'll wait here for you, miss," Sally said as she looked about with a hint of distaste. The poor maid had probably grown weary of their frequent outings.

"Thank you, Sally." Ella was pleased there was a chair for her. "I appreciate your patience."

"Of course, miss." She smiled as if grateful for Ella's remark.

"I'm Mr. Cartland, and I'll be your tour guide. What you'll see today will astound and amaze you," the man promised in a theatrical tone. "What sort of treasure do you seek?"

Ella hesitated, wondering if it was a rhetorical question. Perhaps she should leave speaking about the journal to Leo. She glanced at her pin watch, realizing it would be another quarter of an hour or better before he arrived.

"If it's Inca gold, come this way." Mr. Cartland turned to the stairs and gestured for them to follow.

With a bemused look at each other, Ella and her sisters followed him up. He continued to the second floor while he shared the story of a treasure hunter lost in the wild jungles of South America with only a trusty guide to aid him.

"It was by pure accident that they cut through the vines of undergrowth to discover this." With a flourish, Mr. Cartland drew back a curtain to reveal a clever exhibit made to look like an ancient stone wall. Bits of moss and vines clung to the fake stones.

"These bricks were hand-chiseled with rudimentary tools. Look with amazement at what they built." He gestured toward a drawing of a large temple-like structure that was at least two stories tall.

After giving them a moment to view the drawing, he directed their attention to additional stones decorated with swirls, objects, and people with elaborate headdresses. "These carvings were all done by craftsmen the likes of which we are only beginning to appreciate."

The tour continued, embellished by Mr. Cartland, and included various artifacts that truly looked as if they might have been discovered in the jungle. Clay vessels, stone carvings, and small beads were among the treasures.

While Ella thought their tour guide was a bit theatrical, she appreciated hearing the stories of discovery while viewing the items. From the rapt look on her sisters' faces, she could see they felt the same.

He escorted them around the large room, sharing additional details, some of which she was certain had to be invented or, at least, embellished by either Mr. Cartland or whoever had provided the artifacts.

"Next, we will help search for pirate treasure." Again, Mr. Cartland's brows wiggled up and down, causing Lena to giggle.

Luckily, their tour guide didn't take offense to her amusement. He led them up another level where more displays were visible. An old wooden chest that looked as if it had been lifted from the sea was filled with crudely shaped gold coins.

"Are those truly gold?" Norah asked as she leaned close to study them.

"Unfortunately, they're reproductions," Mr. Cartland admitted with a wry smile. "We couldn't risk someone stealing them if we displayed real ones. Treasure hunters aren't so different from pirates, you know. Willing to take anything within reach."

Ella bristled at his statement and shared a disgruntled look with her sisters. Not all treasure hunters were thieves. Even Leo would agree with that.

"However, we do have several actual coins over here." Mr. Cartland pointed to a locked glass display case. "These are fine examples of the ones actually found."

He continued sharing stories as he led them to yet another room. This one had artifacts from Egypt and again seemed to be a mix of real and reproduced items.

Ella left her sisters' side to explore the room on her own, passing by a window that overlooked the front. A movement below caught her eye, and she paused to look closer. At first, she thought the male figure walking below might be Leo, so she watched another moment.

To her shock, the man resembled Julius Conway, especially his bright gold suit coat. She stiffened as her thoughts spun, wondering what she should do. What were the chances of seeing him twice? And why was he in this area? Was there another import and export shop nearby? She had to try to speak with him. Surely, she could tell by his reaction to her presence whether he had anything to do with the theft of her father's journal.

Ella approached Norah, doing her best to act calm. "I'm going to see if the earl has arrived." Ella couldn't explain why she didn't tell her the truth. But what point was there in worrying her when chances were she wouldn't be able to catch him?

After a nod from a distracted Norah, Ella rushed down the stairs. "I'll return directly, Sally," she advised once she reached the entrance.

"Very well, miss."

As quickly as possible, Ella hurried out of the museum, her focus on where she'd last seen Mr. Conway. The building near where he'd disappeared proved to be an antiquity dealer. At least, that was what she thought it was. Little could be seen through the filthy window, and she couldn't determine for certain whether the place was open for business. After a glance up at the museum window where she'd caught sight of the man, she was even more convinced he was inside.

She tried the door, somewhat surprised to find it unlocked. The interior was dim, dark even, as so many shops were. A lone lamp sat on a counter halfway through the store, and she moved slowly toward it as she looked about.

The shop appeared to be deserted. No customers were visible, nor any shopkeeper to watch over things. However, the multitude of items stacked nearly to the ceiling made it difficult to see. Rows of shelves and furniture blocked her view with only narrow aisles between them.

"Hello?" she called.

When no one answered, she turned her attention to the items on display, still listening carefully. She hesitated to call it a display, as there seemed to be little thought given to the arrangement of the goods.

A large ornate brass vase sat on a shelf next to a carved wooden figure of a nude woman, which was next to a stack of colorfully woven rugs. Several books briefly caught her notice and lured her closer. But the texts were written in a foreign language.

Unable to see between the rows, as the merchandise was packed so tightly, she continued toward the back until another item had her pausing briefly. The farther she wandered with no one in sight, the more she thought she was mistaken. It either hadn't been this shop or it hadn't been Mr. Conway she'd seen. Apparently, in her desperation, she was imagining him.

"Hello?" She tried one more time, about to give up.

The faint murmur of whispers reached her from the rear of the business, bringing with it a shiver that crawled along her spine as if to remind her that she was alone and without protection. Leo's warning echoed in her mind, adding to her unease. Her sisters weren't far, but they might as well be on another street since they didn't know where she was.

Yet she couldn't allow this opportunity to pass. If Mr. Conway was here, she needed to speak with him. With that thought in mind, she continued toward the back. "Hello?"

The whispers hushed and a heavy silence fell over the air.

"Excuse me," she called as she neared a curtain that served as a barrier to the rear of the shop. "I'm looking for Mr. Julius Conway."

The curtain parted to reveal a rather stout man, a few inches taller than her. "Can I help you?"

"Yes, please." Ella did her best to sound confident. "I believe I saw someone I know enter the shop." She glanced past him. "A Mr. Conway. Do you know him?"

"No one else is here." He drew closer, but the dim light kept his features hidden.

"I thought I heard voices." In fact, she knew she had.

"I must've been talking to myself," he offered with a smile. The sound of something sliding along the floor behind the curtain made a liar of him.

"Are you certain?" Ella moved closer, trying to peek through the slit in the curtain. Why would he lie unless he had something to hide?

"I'm sorry, miss, but we're closing early today. I'll have to ask you to leave." He took hold of her arm and pushed her backward between the towering shelves.

Ella wrenched free, a mix of fear and outrage swirling through her. "Do not touch me. If you'd tell Mr. Conway that I'm a friend, I'm certain he'll want to see me."

"There's no one here by that name."

Doubt flooded her. Could she be wrong? "Very well." She turned and took several steps toward the entrance as she searched her memory. The more she thought on it, the more convinced she was that it had been Mr. Conway she'd seen from the museum window.

"No, I'm certain he entered the shop." She turned back only to see one of the nearby shelves toppling toward her. With a gasp, she reached up a moment too late as a large brass chest fell from the shelf. Then all went dark.

❯❯❯❮❮❮

LEO ENTERED THE museum and found chaos. Ella's two sisters were there along with their maid, and all of the ladies were speaking at once. A man he assumed was with the museum tried to reassure them with little effect. But Ella was noticeably absent.

"Good afternoon," Leo offered, hoping one of them would explain the problem and allay the chilling worry creeping over him. "Where is Ella?"

"We don't know, but I'm telling you something is wrong," Lena insisted. She turned to Leo. "She was looking upstairs with us, then told Norah she was coming down here to see if you'd arrived."

"Sally, did she say where she went?" Norah asked.

"She told me she'd return directly, then stepped outside." The maid seemed as confused and worried as the sisters.

Leo didn't know what had happened, but he didn't like the sound of it. Rather than asking questions to which no one had the answer, he returned outside to the street and glanced about. He hadn't seen Ella before he entered, but she couldn't have gone far.

Yet there was no sign of her anywhere. He glanced at the buildings nearby, a mixture of homes and shops. It took only a moment longer to realize which one had the power to lure her inside.

He rushed to the entrance of what appeared to be an antique shop, only to see the shopkeeper reaching to lock the door. The tall, thin man froze, his eyes widening in alarm at the sight of Leo through the window. The questionable behavior had Leo jerking open the door. "Where is she?"

"Who?" the man sputtered as he held up both hands, palms out as if to protest his innocence. He glanced over his shoulder to where a shelf had tipped forward and leaned against another, too close to each other to have fallen to the floor. However, numerous objects and debris were scattered everywhere. "We were just closing to clean up an accident."

Leo didn't bother to argue but strode toward the fallen items in the middle of the shop, the hair on the back of his neck standing on end. A bit of plum-colored fabric was just visible beneath the pile.

Not just fabric—a gown.

"Ella?" Heart hammering, he quickly began tossing aside the items on top of her. The sight of her laying on her side, eyes closed amidst the debris, chilled his blood. With a tentative touch, he reached to brush a finger along her pale cheek. "Ella."

Her faint moan was the sweetest sound he'd ever heard.

"Where are you hurt?" He studied her form in search of an injury, glancing warily at a brass chest nearby. If that had struck her...

She turned her head only to wince. "My...head." She lifted a hand to her forehead and touched just below the small hat she still wore. "Something...fell on me." Her gloved fingers showed blood when she pulled them away. "Ouch."

Leo studied the area, confused as to how this could have happened.

"I-I was just preparing to aid her when you arrived." The shopkeeper stood nearby, wringing his hands. "Thank goodness the lady is all right."

"That remains to be seen." Leo glared at the man in disbelief.

Why had he attempted to lock the door before helping Ella? Added to that was his nervous demeanor. The situation made no sense.

But that didn't matter at the moment. Only Ella's well-being did.

"Can you sit up?" Leo placed a hand behind her shoulders as she shifted onto her elbows. "Go slowly." Given that she was bleeding, her head had to be throbbing.

She managed to do what he asked, hissing as she eased upright. He kept his arm around her to help brace her and make certain she didn't rise too quickly.

He studied her injury but could see little in the dim light.

"We'll have a closer look once you can manage to step outside," he murmured as he studied her pale face. "Do you know what happened?"

"I was speaking with someone." She grimaced, then turned to look at the shopkeeper with narrowed eyes. "It wasn't you. Then the shelf fell."

"What made you come in here?" Alone. But Leo didn't add that. A lecture on her safety would have to wait until she was feeling better.

"I-I saw someone I knew." She blinked several times as she studied the blood on her gloved fingers. "We were upstairs in the museum, and I saw Julius Conway step in here. At least I thought I did."

Leo stilled. He had the feeling it was no coincidence that she thought she'd seen the only real suspect they had and suddenly a shelf fell on her.

"I wanted—" she began.

He placed a finger over her lips to prevent her from saying anything more. If this man, Conway, was involved, Leo didn't want him or any of his acquaintances to know what she'd been about to say.

Her gaze held on him, her eyes dark with worry and slightly glazed with pain.

As he continued to hold her, her sisters entered the shop along with the maid, their expressions frantic.

"Ella!" Norah wound her way toward them with the other two directly behind her. "What happened?"

"The shelf tipped over and something hit me on the head." Ella shifted to gain her feet, and Leo stood to aid her, careful to move slowly, so as not to cause her additional pain.

Once she seemed steady, he released her to allow her sisters closer. Now that she was in good hands, he turned to face the shopkeeper.

The man had moved to stand behind the counter, his attention riveted on them, both hands flattened on the dull surface as if to brace himself. At Leo's approach, his mouth gaped open, though no explanation came forth.

"Would you care to explain what happened?" Leo asked, pleased that only an edge of steel was apparent in his tone rather than a sharp blade.

"I-I can't say that I know. I d-didn't see anything. I was in the back and didn't realize someone was in the shop."

"In the back with whom?"

"No one."

Leo scowled at what he had to think was a lie. While it seemed unlikely that this timid man had done something to hurt Ella, Leo was doubtful the shelf had suddenly toppled over on its own.

"I-I mean, the owner, Mr. Abbott was there. He was speaking with a business associate. But I wasn't with anyone."

"What is the name of this associate?"

"I don't know. I've never seen him before."

"Where's Mr. Abbott?"

"He left through the back with the other gentleman."

"Before or after the accident?" Leo was certain he already knew the answer.

"After." His shoulders lowered as he looked at Ella again. "He told me a shelf had fallen and to clean it up. Then the two left. I didn't realize a customer was involved, let alone hurt." He swallowed hard. "Not until I heard a moan."

Leo stiffened at that. "Why lock the door before you helped her?"

The man shook his head. "I-I shouldn't have. I wasn't thinking. I just didn't want any customers to come in and see what happened. Bad for business, you know."

Leo didn't want to believe the man, yet his story held a ring of truth.

The store clerk lifted a shaking hand to touch his forehead as if his head ached in sympathy with Ella's. "Is the lady going to be all right?"

Leo didn't bother to answer. Not when he was left with more questions than answers from the man. "Where can I find Mr. Abbott?"

The shopkeeper visibly paled. "I'm not allowed to share that information."

Leo leaned close. "But you will do so with me."

His eyes widened, and he slowly nodded. "Yes. But please don't tell him how you found out. I'll lose my job."

"I won't. But know that you will see me again if I discover you're not telling the truth about this afternoon's events."

The man hastily scrawled a name and address on a piece of paper and slid it toward Leo. "Here. Take it. No offense, sir, but I would rather not see you again."

Leo glanced at the paper, then stuffed it in his pocket. He would deal with Mr. Abbott shortly. But not until he made certain Ella would recover. He hated the fact that she'd been hurt. Added to that was the realization of how much worse the "accident" could've been. Protecting Ella and finding her father's journal had just become his top priority.

Chapter Fourteen

E LLA PRESSED A hand to her aching head as Norah and Lena escorted her into the drawing room. Leo had followed them separately in his carriage.

"Are you certain you don't want to retire to your bedroom so you can lay down?" Norah asked.

"I hardly think a bump on the head requires that." Though she had to admit the idea was tempting. "Besides, Marbury wanted to discuss what happened in further detail." The image of him sitting at her bedside was enough to cause a hot flush to flood her entire body. The drawing room was definitely a better choice.

"His questions can wait until you're feeling better." Norah held Ella's arm as she walked to the couch.

In truth, the incident had shaken Ella more than she cared to admit. Had the man she'd been speaking with tipped the shelf onto her? If so, why?

"Nonsense." Ella didn't want to worry her sisters any more than they already were. "I'm fine." Never mind her aching head and nausea that plagued her.

"Let us remove your hat to better see the injury," Lena suggested after Ella was settled on the couch. "Perhaps we should send for a doctor."

"No need." Ella resisted shaking her head given how much it

hurt. "He'll only advise me that I've suffered a blow. It's already stopped bleeding." At least, she thought it had. She nearly shuddered at the idea of stitches.

Lena gently pulled out the pins that held Ella's hat in place and looked closer, moving aside her hair near the wound, which caused Ella to grimace.

"How bad is it?" Ella asked, hoping the bleeding had truly stopped.

"It's a good-sized lump with a cut but no longer bleeding." Lena straightened, her worried gaze holding on Ella. "Sally said she'd return directly with a compress. I'm so sorry I didn't realize something was wrong sooner."

Before Ella could reassure her, Leo strode into the room. "Shouldn't you be resting?" he asked.

He'd been so kind and considerate when he'd found her. His presence had comforted her beyond measure and made her feel as if no further harm could come while he was near. How unsettling to realize how much she was starting to care for him.

Yet it was the sight of the duke directly behind Leo that had Ella blinking in surprise. She started to stand so she could curtsy, only to have him wave a hand to suggest she needn't bother.

Norah and Lena both curtsied though. "Good afternoon, Your Grace."

He dipped his head in acknowledgment even as he continued toward Ella. "Marbury said there was an accident. That you'd been hurt." Based on his frown and the disbelief coloring his tone, he seemed disturbed at the thought.

"Yes, but I will be fine." Ella's cheeks heated. She didn't care to have everyone staring at her.

The duke stopped beside her, along with Leo, while Lena shifted Ella's hair again so they could better see her injury.

Ella bit back a yelp, as she didn't want them to send for a doctor. Hopefully, the suggestion wouldn't arise. To think the duke was concerned was something she'd have to ponder. Did it mean he truly cared about them as Leo had suggested?

She refused to allow her hope to rise until she had further proof.

"Why did you go into the shop?" the duke asked once he seemed satisfied and moved to sit nearby. His thick brows remained furrowed over his eyes, his expression stern.

Ella explained again, annoyed with herself for having allowed trouble to find her so easily. She knew better than to take such risks, especially after Leo had warned her.

"I didn't expect anything untoward to occur. Mr. Conway has always been kind. Perhaps it wasn't him that I saw." She frowned as she thought it through again. The man she'd seen had worn the sort of brightly colored attire that Mr. Conway so often had. But his back had been to her, and he'd worn a hat. The more she thought on it, the more uncertain she became. "But I don't see why that other man with whom I spoke would've tipped the shelf onto me. Perhaps it was just an accident."

"Why indeed?" Luckily, the duke didn't seem to expect her to answer but instead turned toward Leo with a brow raised.

"Excellent question. I intend to make additional inquiries." Leo studied Ella for a moment. "Can you tell us exactly what happened?"

"I called out to see if anyone was there. No one answered, but I could hear voices coming from the rear, so I moved closer."

"Did you hear what they were saying?" Leo asked.

"No." She started to shake her head only to stiffen when the motion caused her head to pound. "I couldn't distinguish any words." She thought it over, trying to remember. "I believe they were both men, but that's all I could say for certain. When one of them came forward, I told him for whom I was looking. That I was a friend of Mr. Conway's. But he insisted he wasn't there. That no one was, yet I knew that wasn't true. I started to leave but turned back, and that's when the shelves fell."

Leo asked her to describe the man, which she did as best she could. Before he could ask more questions, Sally hurried into the room with a tray that contained a basin and a cloth.

"See her to bed," the duke ordered before the maid could set down the tray. "She should rest. Be certain she's not left alone in case she experiences any issues. And keep me apprised."

His tone didn't allow any argument, not that Ella was feeling up to doing so.

"Yes, Your Grace." Sally curtsied as Lena and Norah moved to help Ella rise.

Ella stood, then looked at Leo, filled with gratitude that he'd found her so quickly. "Thank you for everything. Please take care if you happen to speak to that man." She didn't like the thought of him facing danger. Especially not because of her.

"I will." His expression softened as he held her gaze. The concern in his eyes sent tingles of awareness along her skin.

"You'll let me know what you discover?" she asked. If she felt better, she would've insisted on accompanying him.

"Of course."

Yet it only took one look at his face to know how much he told her depended on what he learned. While she appreciated that he was trying to protect her, she would prefer to know who'd hurt her and why.

The idea of the man in the shop not liking her request to see Mr. Conway was concerning. Tipping over the shelf in order to discourage her was even more so. She had to think that meant Mr. Conway had something to do with her father's stolen journal—if it was truly him that she'd seen enter the shop.

The situation could be more dangerous than she'd realized. Knowing Leo would help her get to the bottom of it was reassuring—except for the unsettling way he made her feel.

"Thank you again," she said with as much decorum as possible. Then she allowed her sisters to guide her upstairs to her bedroom, with Sally trailing behind.

However, the memory of Leo's fierce expression when she'd opened her eyes to find him beside her in the shop followed her. As confused as she was about what had happened, that didn't compare to how perplexed she felt about her attraction to him.

She needed to shore up her defenses when it came to the handsome earl. What would her mother have said if she knew of Ella's interest in the son of the man she'd jilted at the altar? Or would she be intrigued by the idea?

The flurry in Ella's stomach made her wonder if her feelings had already taken on a life of their own. Could it be too late to try to halt what she felt for him?

LEO KNOCKED ON Worley's door, hoping his friend was available. Though tempted to go directly to the address the shopkeeper had provided, he'd rather not go alone. He could've easily brought a footman or two but preferred to have Worley at his side.

His anger over what had happened to Ella was clouding his thinking. In his current state, he might not notice everything he should when they called on the man. There was also the possibility the shopkeeper had warned his employer. No matter how he tried to control his thoughts, they continually circled with what if's.

What if Ella had been struck harder?

What if he hadn't found her so quickly?

What if her injuries had been life-threatening?

The last nearly made him shudder. One thing was certain—Ella was in danger. It seemed as if she'd pressed on a nerve by asking for Conway in the shop. Though she remained uncertain whether it had truly been him she'd seen, Leo tended to think she had. Mr. Abbott was going to tell him where Conway was, whether he wanted to or not.

Soon he was striding into Worley's study, relieved to find his friend home.

"What a welcome surprise." Worley rose with a smile from a chair where he'd been reading by the fire. The smile fell away as he studied Leo. "What's happened?"

Leo explained the situation as quickly as possible. "Care to call on the shop owner with me?"

"I would indeed."

"Excellent. Something foul is afoot. Even more so than we first believed."

Worley led the way out, stopping in the entrance hall for his hat and a walking stick.

"I don't remember you carrying one of those," Leo said with a frown.

"It comes in handy when one is outnumbered and needs a form of defense." The somberness in Worley's eyes suggested he'd experienced that firsthand.

Leo detested that his friend was viewed differently by others because of who he chose to love. When he looked at Worley, he saw a loyal friend, a man with a good heart and honorable intentions. Why couldn't everyone see the same?

With a nod, Leo gestured for Worley to precede him out the door. "We'll take my carriage."

It took nearly half an hour to arrive at the address written on the paper, and Leo used the time to review the events in further detail. The timber-framed Tudor house was in a good neighborhood with small, neat gardens and wrought-iron fences lining the street.

"Based on the description of the shop you gave, Mr. Abbott seems to be making a better living than I would've expected," Worley said.

"I think you're right." The house was modest in size, but one couldn't afford such a place in London without a significant income. "Perhaps he is involved in more than the one shop."

"Or something illegal." Worley gestured for Leo to alight, then followed.

"Excellent point." Leo had been so focused on what he intended to ask the man that he hadn't thought further ahead. Money made some people dangerous. Or rather, the risk of losing that money did.

Leo knocked on the door and soon a servant opened it. "Mr. Abbott, please."

"Is he expecting you?"

"I don't believe so." Leo handed him his calling card.

The man's cool manner grew more respectful after he glanced at the card. "If you'll please wait, I'll see if Mr. Abbott is receiving."

"It's amazing what the mention of a title can do, isn't it?" Worley asked wryly as he glanced around with interest at the striped wallpaper and wood columns in the entrance hall.

Within a few minutes, the servant returned to show Leo and Worley to a drawing room where a stout, middle-aged man with pock-marked skin awaited them. His thin, dark hair was combed over his nearly bald head. That, along with pock-marked cheeks, confirmed him as the man Ella had described. He stood when they entered and bowed. "Good afternoon."

"Mr. Abbott?" At the man's nod, Leo continued, "Owner of the antiquities shop on Baker Street?"

"Yes."

If Leo hadn't been watching closely, he might've missed the slight narrowing of his eyes. But was that out of concern or curiosity?

"Are you aware of an altercation at your shop earlier this afternoon?"

"What altercation?" His frown suggested he was puzzled. "I was there earlier, and nothing was amiss other than a shelf toppling over."

"Who were you with?"

"What concern is any of this to you?" He glanced at Worley, then at Leo's card on the table beside him as if trying to make sense of the questions. Or pretending to.

"A lady was injured when the shelves fell. Knocked unconscious." The image of Ella lying on the floor filled him once again. With it came anger.

"What?" His attempt at surprised outrage failed. "How terrible. I have told Jonesby time and again not to stack the shelves so heavily. I'll have to let him go for this."

Leo stepped forward. "You and I both know the fault was not your employee's. You pushed over that shelf."

"I did no such thing," the man sputtered, his body stiffening. Yet his hand trembled on the desk, a sign Leo's questions were unsettling him. "I spoke with the woman briefly. She must've bumped the shelf on her way out."

Leo pointed at the man's cuff where a smudge of dust was visible. Abbott glanced at it and brushed it off. "It's impossible to stay clean in my line of business."

"Why?" Leo pressed, not wanting to hear more lies. "Why did you shove that shelf? Who is Conway to you?"

"Conway?" Abbott's eyes darted about the room as if he was starting to realize Leo couldn't be fooled. "Who is he?"

"Why was he in your shop?"

Abbott waved a hand of dismal. "Customers who frequent my shop are no one's business. Surely you can understand that I would soon be forced to close if I shared such details."

Leo took another step forward as anger took a firmer hold. "A lady was struck and knocked unconscious in your shop. By your hand. She is the Duke of Rothwood's granddaughter. If word spreads of that, you will definitely be out of business."

"The duke's granddaughter?" The shock on Abbott's face this time was genuine. His mouth gaped open as he seemed to comprehend the ramifications.

"You should've clarified with Conway who she was before he told you to get rid of her." Leo paused a moment to see if his guess was correct.

Abbott's gaze dropped to the floor, suggesting he was trying to decide how to respond. His hands lifted and fell. "I don't know Conway that well. He's a newer customer."

"A buyer or a seller?" Worley asked.

"Bit of both. He says he has something of great importance to sell but is still determining its value. He's considering the idea of holding a private auction to sell it and is garnering interest. That was the extent of our brief conversation. Something to do with treasure hunting was all he said."

"He didn't describe it further?" Leo asked.

"Only that it was one of a kind and of great value. That it could provide the path to a fortune."

Leo shared a look with Worley. From his friend's expression, Worley also clearly thought it had to be David Wright's journal. "That was enough to make you hurt someone?"

Abbott shook his head. "I didn't mean to. I only thought to shake the shelf to make her worry about her safety and to convince her to leave. I didn't realize it would fall so easily." He rubbed his forehead, his distress obvious. "Please don't put me out of business. It was an accident. A mistake on my part. Conway suggested he'd give me the first chance at the item if I got rid of the lady. I didn't mean to hurt her. Just scare her so she'd leave because she was being so persistent."

"Where can we find him?" Leo asked.

"I have no idea. He's always the one to contact me."

"Surely you have his address."

"No, I don't." He lifted his hands up, palms out at Leo's obvious disbelief. "He insists on privacy. Overly suspicious, if you ask me."

Leo studied Abbott's expression closely but saw only sincerity. If he was lying, he was good at it.

"Do you know any other shops he works with? Perhaps one of your competitors?"

Abbott named a few but couldn't promise whether they had dealt with Conway. He added that the man had been out of the country for some time and had only recently returned.

"Is the lady all right?" Abbott asked.

"She appears to be." Leo knew Ella was in good hands, but he intended to call on her the following day to see for himself.

"I'm relieved to hear that." Abbott shook his head, one hand pressed to his chest. "I am very sorry. I offer my heartfelt apologies. Obviously, I allowed my curiosity about Conway's item to overshadow my good sense. I won't do so again."

"Does Conway have an interest in pirate treasure?" Worley asked.

"Don't we all?" Abbott shrugged. "Hard to resist the idea of a chest full of gold or silver, isn't it? Who among us wouldn't have wanted to sail with Bluebeard or Captain Kidd? What an adventure that would have been."

Leo had thought the same until he'd better understood the harsh conditions the crew endured. It was not a life for the faint at heart. "If I discover you've led me astray, I will be back." He waited a moment to make certain Abbott understood his meaning.

"I have shared everything I know." Abbott held his gaze without hesitation, making Leo think perhaps he had.

"You have my card," Leo said. "Contact me if you discover anything else or if Conway is in touch again."

He followed Worley outside. "What did you think?"

"I would tend to say he's told us the truth." Worley smoothed a finger over his mustache as if still pondering the conversation.

"I thought the same as well. Though I hesitate to believe he has no way of contacting Conway." Leo stepped into the carriage, and Worley joined him.

"If we can't locate him through the other shops Abbott mentioned, we might have to return for another conversation."

"Agreed." Leo leaned back as the carriage pulled away, noting the flicker of the drapes in Abbott's drawing room, suggesting he watched them leave. "Let us see what we can discover in the coming days."

He reminded himself that what was truly important was that Ella hadn't been hurt worse. But he intended to do all in his power to make certain nothing else happened to her. While he didn't profess to understand his feelings for the lady, neither would he continue to deny them.

Chapter Fifteen

ELLA FELT SLIGHTLY better the following morning, though her head still ached. Her night had been restless, and she'd slept later than usual. Sally and another maid, Nancy, had taken turns watching over her through the night, which was more than likely the reason she hadn't slept soundly. How could she while being observed? That had only been part of the reason for her unrest. She'd gone over the events from the shop too many times to count, wishing she'd done things differently.

"Are you certain you wish to rise, miss?" Nancy asked after she brought Ella a tray of tea and toast for breakfast. "His Grace suggested you remain abed."

Ella smiled at the thought of the duke's concern. "I would prefer to rise soon. If I start feeling poorly, I can rest again." Her answer seemed to satisfy the maid.

However, by the time she'd dressed, and Nancy had pinned her hair in a loose knot, Ella was nearly regretting her decision. Her head was still very tender, and her headache had worsened. Nevertheless, she went down to the drawing room to find her sisters.

"Ella. How are you feeling?" Lena rose from her chair by the fire to greet her, and Norah quickly followed.

"Better. Thank you."

Norah scowled, her stormy blue eyes filled with concern. "I

153

can see you're not. Between the shadows under your eyes and your frown, you're obviously still in pain."

"It does still hurt," Ella admitted. "But that seems to be the case whether I'm resting in bed or here with you. I'd much rather be with you."

"Come and sit with us." Lena took her hand to guide her to the long couch before the fire as if she might collapse before she reached it. "The day is rather dreary, and the fire feels good."

Ella glanced out the window to see it was drizzling. "A good day to stay inside then. Though I hope by tomorrow both the weather and my head will have cleared."

"Why tomorrow?" Norah asked as she retrieved her embroidery and settled in a chair.

"So we can continue our search."

Norah and Lena shared a look that had Ella raising a brow. The pair had obviously discussed this. "What is it?"

"We don't think you—or rather, we—should continue searching," Norah said.

"It's too dangerous." Lena shuddered. "What if something heavier had struck you?"

"If I hadn't been in such a rush to follow Mr. Conway, I would've had both of you with me." The fact that she'd acted so carelessly annoyed her. "As we've discussed, it's highly unlikely anyone would approach the three of us, let alone harm us." Yet concern arose. Was she putting her sisters in danger by having them accompany her on these outings? Maybe she should leave the situation to Leo to investigate.

"Do you truly think Mr. Conway could be involved?" Lena asked. "He seemed so nice on the ship. I simply can't imagine him harming anyone, especially one of us."

"Nor can I." Ella still wondered if she'd been mistaken. "Perhaps it wasn't him I saw enter the shop, after all."

"But why would that man push over the shelf unless he had something to hide? That doesn't make sense either." Norah's solemn expression spoke to the level of her disquiet. Ella hated to think she'd caused it.

"I suppose we don't know what is truly going through someone's mind. Or what motivates them," Ella said.

"True. All the more reason we should leave the search to the Earl of Marbury," Norah said. "He seems more than capable of dealing with it."

"And he appears to have our best interests at heart," Lena added. "I wasn't so sure of that at first, but after seeing his concern for you, I cannot doubt it. Don't you agree?"

Ella nodded slowly, partly because of her aching head and partly because she was thinking.

While she wasn't opposed to having Leo involved—in truth, she was relieved he was—she wanted to have a hand in the search as well. The journal had been taken while under her care. She felt responsible for its loss. Perhaps he could be convinced to allow her to accompany him. After all, she knew what the journal looked like, as well as the basics of what it contained. Someone could easily try to fool him with a copy like the one placed in her reticule.

"Has the earl sent any messages?" she asked. She had no doubt he'd taken immediate action yesterday. Surely he knew something by now.

"Not to our knowledge." As if sensing the turn of Ella's thoughts, Lena added, "I'm certain we'll hear from him soon."

Ella sighed. It wasn't as if she were feeling up to touring more dusty shops or museums at the moment anyway. But she would very much like to hear what he'd discovered thus far. She'd also like to suggest they continue the search together.

The idea held risk when spending more time with him was unwise. Especially since she couldn't deny her attraction to him. Giving into that would be selfish—she hadn't brought her sisters to London so she could indulge her own wants. She'd learned from what her parents had shared how much harm chasing dreams could cause others. Added to that was how much their choices had obviously hurt Leo and his family. Ella had no intention of doing the same. Her sisters came first.

However, he was her only hope of retrieving the journal unless she continued on her own. That clearly wasn't possible. She reached up a hand to touch the lump on her head as if to confirm that truth.

She refused to lie to herself. No point would be served in denying the fact that she looked forward to having an excuse to spend time with him, even if nothing could come of her feelings. If only she could remember that.

⟫⟫✳⟪⟪

LEO HANDED DAVIES his damp coat and hat, then followed the butler to Rothwood's study to provide the duke with an update. The afternoon was early, but he and Worley had spent the remainder of the previous day as well as this morning visiting the shops Abbott had provided for information on Julius Conway to no avail. He knew little more now than he had after the conversation with Abbott.

He cocked his head, hoping to hear the strains of music coming from the music room. The sound of a piano might mean Ella was up and about and feeling better. Much to his disappointment, only silence met his ears.

Had her condition worsened? The concern had him frowning as he greeted the duke.

"How is Miss Wright?" he asked after the usual pleasantries were completed.

"Improving. Still in pain, it seems." The duke gestured for Leo to join him before the fire.

"Have you seen her for yourself?" Leo was growing weary of the duke's reluctance to communicate with his granddaughters. Especially after what had happened to Ella. Rothwood had obviously been concerned yesterday. How could he continue to distance himself from his granddaughters when one, if not all, was in danger?

As Leo expected, the duke bristled at his question. "The maids reported directly to me as soon as she woke and again after luncheon."

"That's hardly the same thing. After what happened, I would've thought you'd want to personally check on her." He certainly did.

"The staff is nothing if not reliable." Despite the denial, Leo could see his comment had affected the older man based on the way he shifted in his seat.

It was almost amusing for Leo to think he was indirectly helping Ella and her sisters in their campaign to soften the duke. If only it wasn't as a result of Ella being hurt.

"What did you discover?" Rothwood folded his hands over his stomach as if prepared for a long story. Leo was about to disappoint him as the story was short.

"Apparently, Julius Conway is a solitary man with few friends in London. No one seems to know much about him or where he is staying."

"How can that be? If Ella has seen him not once but twice, he is obviously milling about."

Leo smothered a sigh. The duke's frustration matched his own. "I will continue to search for him, of course. Worley is helping me as well. But I wanted to provide you with an update and to see Ella." In fact, it had been a challenge to wait this long to visit her. Even hearing of her condition from Rothwood wasn't enough for him.

"What did the shop owner have to say for himself?"

After sharing what little they'd learned, along with further reassurances that they would continue the search, Leo excused himself to seek out Ella.

He took the stairs two at a time, his chest tightening at the sight of her sitting on the couch alone in the drawing room with a woven blanket over her legs and a closed book beside her. Only her profile was visible as she stared into the fire, but even from here, she still looked pale. While pleased she was resting, he worried her idleness meant she still felt poorly.

"Good afternoon, Ella," he said softly, not wanting to startle her.

"Leo." Her smile warmed him, and her blue eyes lit from within. Such a genuine welcome that made it clear how pleased she was to see him. His heartbeat sped at the thought, even as he did his best to dismiss the odd sensation.

She made a movement to rise, but he quickly gestured for her to remain seated. Instead, he sat beside her to study her more closely.

How unusual she was compared to other women he knew, like a refreshing breeze on a warm summer day. Most ladies went out of their way to act coolly. Heaven forbid they allow their emotions to show. He supposed that was true for men as well. Was it any wonder how much of a challenge it was to find a partner in Society when everyone acted as if they didn't care?

"How are you feeling?" he asked, though he could see the answer. Her face had a tightness to it, suggesting her head still hurt. The sight made him angry all over again.

"Better. Thank you." She reached up to touch her head where he knew the bump was. "Still a bit of a goose egg, but it's improving."

"Did you sleep well?" The shadows under her eyes were answer enough.

After a brief hesitation, she sighed. "Not especially. I kept thinking over events, wishing I'd done things differently." She lifted her hand only to let it drop to her lap. "I knew better than to go in there alone, but I only thought to catch Mr. Conway and mention the missing journal." She shook her head. "Not that I'm sure I even saw him. I could've been mistaken."

"You weren't."

Those blue eyes widened. "Truly?"

"The owner of the shop, a Mr. Abbott, was speaking with Conway in the back."

"It was Mr. Abbott with whom I spoke?"

"Yes. He said since you were being so persistent, he shook the shelf with the hope of frightening you so you'd leave."

"He didn't want me to ask about Mr. Conway?"

"Exactly."

Ella's focus held on the fire for a long moment. "Which means Mr. Conway must've suggested he do something to make me leave. How disappointing to think he'd do such a thing after the way he befriended us on the ship."

"I think at this point, we have to assume he has the journal and is contacting a few dealers to try to sell it. He told Abbott he intends to hold a private auction for some item he has. In the meantime, he's trying to generate interest, no doubt to drive up the price." He shared the few other details they had learned, annoyed he knew so little. "I wish I had more to tell you, but I wanted to share our progress and see how you were."

"How kind of you." She smiled. "I have been wondering what was happening and will rest easier now."

"Did you have a chance to see if you remembered Conway mentioning anything on the ship? Family? Friends? Business? Anything that might help us find him?"

"My sisters and I discussed that this morning. None of us remember him saying anything specific. I'm appalled that we didn't realize how vague he was being until now."

"I'm certain you had other things on your mind. Nor would any of you wish to pry."

"I suppose." However, Ella's brow furrowed as if it still bothered her. "I have always thought my instincts were better than that after all our father taught us."

"Such is the life of the daughter of a treasure hunter." Leo hadn't given much thought to what it would be like for the family of one until he met Ella and her sisters.

"He cautioned us when we visited any of the larger towns. It was amazing how often strangers attempted to strike up a conversation with one of us."

"I'm sure it's only natural for them to ask about the progress of the search. People are curious. Especially about such an exciting topic."

Ella scoffed. "Not so exciting after years of it. That's the part most people don't understand."

"Well, most treasure hunters don't spend that long in the same place. I admire your father's persistence."

"Some would call it stubbornness. Mother often did."

Leo chuckled, charmed by the way Ella spoke of her parents with warmth and exasperation. "Do you miss that life?"

She glanced at him briefly before looking back at the fire, quiet for so long that he didn't know if she was going to answer. "I miss them. Not the life. It's not one I would've chosen."

Leo couldn't help but think of her mother. What had made Lady Bethany choose it? Had it lived up to her expectations? Had David Wright fulfilled whatever promises he'd made? Or had she been awash in regret and longing as his father had been? The thought had him looking away from Ella.

Her quiet gasp had him turning back. "I didn't mean to suggest that any of our parents made the wrong choices."

"My father wasn't given a choice. He was left standing at the altar to give excuses on her behalf. That was something from which he never recovered." Though Leo couldn't deny he blamed his father for that. Why hadn't he been able to move forward and let the past go? Why hadn't his wife and son been enough to fill the void left by Lady Bethany?

Memories of his father drinking alone in his study rushed through Leo's mind. Of how his deep unhappiness and unfulfilled longing permeated the house. Permeated Leo's entire childhood.

"I don't have an explanation for why my mother made her choice. Or why she didn't tell your father beforehand. I'm very sorry for the hurt she caused."

Leo reached for her hand. "It's not your fault. Nor is it mine. Yet still, we must live with it." The past was a wedge between them. Not just the events, but those involved who'd been affected by the events. He didn't see how that could be bridged no matter how much he wished otherwise.

"I must be going." He released her hand and stood, suddenly anxious to step away from the situation.

None of it was fair to any involved. Especially to his mother. The thought of her sent a pang of guilt spearing through him, and he couldn't leave fast enough.

"I hope you continue to recover. I will advise you of any developments." With a nod, he departed, wishing the situation was different. Wondering how he should move forward from here.

And why fate had given him this undeniable attraction to the lady he'd just left.

Chapter Sixteen

AFTER THE SECOND day of rest, Ella decided she'd had enough. Though it had been lovely for her sisters to be so kind and considerate toward her, she was starting to feel smothered.

Added to her upset was the fact that the duke had not made an appearance since the day of her injury. While he was no doubt being kept abreast of her progress by the servants, that wasn't the same as checking on her himself. He hadn't dined at home, so they hadn't been able to continue their efforts to converse with him during dinner.

Then there was Leo's noted absence. The way he had left so abruptly after their last conversation concerned her. She told herself it was for the best. She had no intention of even thinking about her own future until after she saw her sisters settled. Only then could she consider what she wanted. She wouldn't place her wishes above others as her parents had. Therefore, she wouldn't—couldn't—see where the attraction between them might lead.

He had stated on more than one occasion that her mother's betrayal had deeply hurt his father. The presence of Ella and her sisters in London would cause gossip. They had already seen a hint of it, and that talk would rekindle past hurts. Ella could only imagine just how much gossip would stir when they attended their first ball.

The most frustrating part was there was nothing Ella could do about the situation. She couldn't stop the talk, nor could she erase the hurt feelings her mother had caused by leaving the way she had. The only thing Ella could do was move forward with her head held high. To see her sisters wed to good men who could provide them with a happy life. Perhaps a few people appreciated that her parents had married for love, an unusual occurrence among the *ton*.

She wasn't bound by the choices her mother and father had made. Instead, she would help guide Norah and Lena toward what was best for them. That was what had brought them to London, and she needed to stay the course.

With that in mind, she sent a message to Lady Havenby to ask what more could be done to prepare them for their first ball. Several of their gowns had arrived and others would soon be ready. The time for their first ball would soon be upon them, and Ella wanted to be ready in every possible way. Thanks to their mother, they knew most of the expectations already, but Ella was certain more could be done to prepare them.

Perhaps another outing to Bond Street, even if they didn't buy anything, would allow them to meet more people. Seeing familiar faces might make attending their first ball easier.

She wouldn't deny that she intended to keep her eye open for Julius Conway. And if she had the chance to visit another shop where he might try to sell the journal, if he truly had it, she would do so with her sisters.

As she considered her plan, another idea came to mind. If people already knew of their past, why not use the fact to their advantage? She could spread word about the missing journal and ask if anyone knew Julius Conway. Sharing the story should make it more difficult for him to sell it.

Lady Havenby replied immediately that she would be happy to accompany them for some additional shopping.

Ella told her sisters of the lady's agreement, and after luncheon, the three joined her in her coach. Norah and Lena were obviously as anxious to get out of the house as she was.

"Tell me what you've been doing these past few days," Lady Havenby said once they were settled in the coach.

Norah and Lena both looked at Ella expectantly, as if waiting to see whether she wanted to share the details of recent events.

"We've had a most unsettling few days," Ella began. "I was injured when someone pushed a shelf onto me while I was looking for our father's stolen journal."

"What?" Lady Havenby was aghast at the news. "Where did this happen?"

Ella shared the story with her sisters adding in details. By the time they reached Bond Street, they'd told her most of the events.

"In broad daylight." The lady shook her head, her dismay obvious. "I never would have expected such a thing. What is our city coming to when something like this can happen?"

"To think Ella was hurt is terrible," Lena added, "but I'm grateful her injury wasn't worse."

"The journal is one of the few pieces we still have of him," Norah said.

Ella hid a smile. Lady Havenby seemed to love gossip, and their story was no exception, based on her enthralled expression. She wouldn't be able to resist spreading the news.

"What will you do now? Is there anything I can do to help?"

"We have to think the more people who know about the missing journal, the better. That will make selling it more difficult for whoever took it." Ella hoped it would help.

"Of course. So clever of you." Lady Havenby nodded with enthusiasm, causing the plume in her hat to bounce alarmingly. "We will soon have everyone talking about what happened and watching out for this Mr. Conway, as well as the journal. You can depend on me to do my part."

"Thank you," Ella said with heartfelt sincerity.

Soon they arrived at Bond Street to window shop. Lady Havenby stopped several times to speak with acquaintances, some of whom she introduced to them, and to even more, she told an abbreviated version of events.

From what little their mother had said, nothing was a secret for long amongst the *ton*. Ella hoped that was the case with this situation. While she didn't care for the extra attention she received for having been injured, perhaps the story would bring more notice to her sisters, as well. That should include the male version, too.

All in all, Ella was happy they'd gained Lady Havenby's assistance to tell more people about the journal and Mr. Conway.

"You look rather pleased with yourself," Norah whispered as they paused to look in a shop window.

"Actually, I am. This isn't the sort of search I had in mind, but it might still be effective, don't you think?"

"Agreed. We have met more people in one afternoon than since we arrived in London. Just don't ask me to remember their names."

Ella smiled. "At least we will see some familiar faces when we attend our first formal function."

"That is true. Let us hope they look kindly upon us." Norah's brow puckered. "I hope the duke isn't opposed to us sharing the details. I worry this news will bring even more attention when Lady Havenby already thinks our presence will stir old gossip. I'm certain His Grace would rather not relive the past."

"Neither would the Earl of Marbury." Ella sighed, realizing she couldn't please everyone. "But we have to proceed as best we can."

Still, her heart squeezed at the idea of hurting either of them.

"I'VE DISCOVERED TWO more places we can search."

Leo looked up from his perusal of an article regarding a potential new discovery in Madagascar to find Worley standing before him. He'd ventured to the Royal Geological Society building with the hope of taking his mind off the search for both Conway and the journal for a time. Neither were bearing fruit, and the situation was beyond frustrating.

"Do tell." Leo pointed toward another chair at the table where he sat.

Worley joined him, glancing briefly at the article. "I would like to read that when you're done. If it's interesting, that is."

"Of course." Leo bit back his impatience. "What is this about other places you've found?"

"Do you remember Professor Lindquist? He taught at Oxford for a time."

"Vaguely, though I don't think I was ever a student of his." Leo frowned as he mulled over the name. "Nor is he a member of the Society."

"True. Though not everyone who collects is. Rumors say that he has been acquiring pirate documents of late."

"What sort of documents?"

"Everything from ships' logs to private letters to and from crew members and their families. Anything else he can get his hands on, really."

"How is it that we haven't heard about his intent until now?" The treasure hunting field was rather small.

"Apparently, his interest is recent and started when he was sorting through a box of old family letters. An ancestor of his supposedly served under Captain Kidd."

"Interesting. I should like to speak with him regardless of whether he knows anything about Conway or the missing journal."

"I assumed so. I arranged for us to call on him at two o'clock this afternoon." Worley gave a satisfied smile.

"Perfect." Leo glanced at the tall clock that stood in the corner. "That gives us an hour to arrive. What else did you find?"

"A shop in Cheapside that specializes in hard-to-find objects. However, its reputation is questionable, as they seem to stop at nothing to gain what their customers seek."

"Sounds a bit unscrupulous. It might be perfect for the likes of Conway." Leo studied Worley. "How on earth did you find out about either of these?"

"One conversation led to another at the club when I stopped there for luncheon. I hate to admit it, but Viscount Ludham is the one who mentioned the shop. I know this comes as no surprise, but he doesn't especially care for you, Marbury."

"The feeling is mutual. The fact that he's the one who told you about this shop is concerning. We shall have to keep our wits about us when we go there. But first, let us see what Professor Lindquist has to tell us." Leo set aside the article and stood.

"From what I gather, he's not fond of visitors."

Leo smiled. "Surely, we can charm our way into his home."

Worley shrugged. "I can, but I'm not certain about you." He glanced at Leo, mirth gleaming in his eyes.

"Why do you think you're coming along?" Leo clapped his hand on Worley's shoulder with a grin.

"You're incorrigible."

"As are you. Now let us go."

It took some time to find Professor Lindquist's exact residence, as it was located on a narrow, crooked street that bordered the East End. Leo's driver jumped down from his seat and opened the door with an apology. "Terribly sorry, my lord. I'm not familiar with this area."

"No worries, John. Nor am I." Leo glanced about, able to see why. The area was rather rundown with crumbling walks and overgrown weeds. The houses were two and three stories tall but narrow. "Wait for us, if you would. We shouldn't be longer than a half-hour at most."

"Of course, my lord."

Leo opened the rusty iron gate and led the way up the front walk. Based on the unkempt look of the garden, the professor spent little time outdoors.

"Not exactly a welcoming entrance," Worley muttered.

"Makes one wonder what the interior holds." Leo was beginning to think the meeting would be less than pleasant.

Worley rapped the tarnished brass knocker. They waited several minutes before footsteps could be heard inside, and the door creaked open.

"Yes?" An elderly servant with a stooped back eyed them warily.

"We're here to see Professor Lindquist." Leo handed the servant his card, though based on the rheumy look of his eyes, wasn't certain he could read it.

"If you'll wait a moment." He closed the door, leaving them standing on the front step.

"I thought we were expected," Leo said with a glance at Worley.

"I sent a message and received a reply. Perhaps the servant wasn't advised of the appointment."

Several minutes passed before he returned and opened the door. "This way, please."

The interior was dark and gloomy, though clean. The faint scent of beeswax lingered in the air, a pleasant surprise. The servant led them through a long corridor to a doorway where he bowed and gestured for them to continue in.

"Good day." A rather jovial-looking man with a round face and a shock of untidy white hair rose from behind a desk, tossing aside his spectacles, then bowed. "To what do I owe the honor of this visit? Were you by chance students of mine?"

"Unfortunately, no." Worley introduced them both. "We are members of the Royal Geological Society and understand you have an interest in pirate-related documents."

"Ah, yes. I certainly do." A satisfied look came over the man's face. "A new interest but one for which I have found a passion."

"You're not alone in your interest," Leo said. "Can you tell us about some of your finds?"

The professor glanced at his desk where several piles of papers were stacked in neat rows. "The ones I find the most interesting are letters from ship crews. Mainly the officers, of course, as many members of the crew were illiterate. My search started quite by accident as so often seems to happen. I was looking for one thing when something else appeared."

"I can certainly relate to that." Leo couldn't count the times it had happened. "A bit like venturing down a rabbit hole."

"Exactly," the professor agreed with enthusiasm. "My uncle passed away several years ago and as his only heir, I received his things, including an old trunk full of papers. Though tempted to toss out the entirety, I thought it prudent to be certain it didn't contain anything of importance."

He looked at Leo and Worley as if to see if they were listening, then clasped his hands behind his back and took several steps forward before turning and doing the same in the opposite direction.

Leo nearly felt as if he were back in a lecture hall at Oxford as he watched Lindquist pacing before them.

"I reviewed well over a dozen letters before finding what appeared to be a rather old one. The script was nearly impossible to decipher. In fact, it took me over a week to read. The challenge was something I couldn't resist, you know."

"Of course." Worley nodded. "A mystery of sorts."

"Exactly." Lindquist seemed to warm to his topic even more as he realized they were both interested. "The man, a distant relative, was a crew member on a sailing vessel. I dug through the chest and found several other letters. He described the voyage in such detail that it provided a fascinating insight into what life was like while living on the ship."

"That must've been quite intriguing." Leo wondered if he'd allow him to look at the letters. But before he broached the subject, he wanted to find out if the professor knew anything about the missing journal.

"The more I read, the more I wanted to discover." Lindquist returned to his pacing. "After some research, which included corresponding with a few other relatives on that side of the family, I discovered they had additional letters from the man.

They sent them to me. Since then, I have found letters from several other sailors from various ships, as well. Of course, some are helpful, while others are not. Wading through them is both a pleasure and a trial."

"As is true for most research," Leo added. He'd experienced his share of both.

"Indeed." The professor went on to describe other documents he'd found. Some, including a ship's log, he'd only been able to copy a few pages of, as the owner wasn't willing to give it to him.

As fascinating as all of this was, Leo wanted to ask the question they'd come here for. Yet the professor hardly stopped to take a breath as he continued. It was obvious the man enjoyed talking about his work and apparently didn't often have the chance to do so.

At last, Lindquist paused to look at them both. "I fear I've let my excitement get the better of me. What was it you wanted to know?"

"A journal from a treasure hunter from Oak Island in Nova Scotia is missing," Leo said. "We wondered if you happened to hear anything about it."

"Oak Island?" The professor's brow furrowed as he searched his mind. "What was his name?"

"David Wright."

"Wright. Hmm. I believe he wrote a few articles on treasure hunting that I read, but they weren't about Oak Island. Isn't that a fascinating story? A possible treasure buried on an island in tunnels set to flood if the digging isn't done in the proper manner. Genius."

"Or perhaps merely a tale."

"Of course. But add in the curse and who could resist taking a look? Isn't it interesting how often curses are associated with treasure?"

"What better way to discourage searchers than with a threat of harm?" Worley asked.

"Or death as the case may be. Back to the missing journal," Leo said with a raised brow directed at the professor.

"Can't say that I heard of his journal."

Though Leo had suspected as much, he was still disappointed.

"Do you know a Julius Conway?" Leo asked, knowing it was unlikely as well.

"No, I don't think so." The professor hesitated. "Although Conway is mentioned somewhere. Let me think." He moved around his desk to page through one of the piles of papers. "Sarah Conway is who I was thinking of. She married someone who was digging for treasure."

Leo glanced at Worley, thinking they should take their leave. It didn't appear as if Lindquist could aid them.

"I remember now." Lindquist nodded as he pulled out a piece of paper. "Conway was the maiden name of the woman who married David Wright's partner."

Leo stilled at the news. "Truly?"

"I'm fairly certain, though I can't seem to find the article that referenced it." He glanced up at Leo. "The fact that both men brought their wives along on the treasure hunt made news at the time. I'm sure her name was Conway, daughter of a wealthy shipping merchant."

While the detail was interesting and possibly tied Conway to the hunt on Oak Island, it didn't provide much else.

"That is helpful." Leo reached to shake the man's hand. "Thank you for your time. If you come across any other information about Conway or the journal, would you please contact us?"

"Of course. I'm sorry to hear the curse is proving true. 'Seven men must die before the treasure is found.' Or so the saying goes." Lindquist shook his head. "It often happens that a wild story proves true."

"Treasure hunting is a dangerous business. Both from the digging itself and from those willing to do anything to discover riches." Leo didn't believe in curses. He was scientific-minded enough to think himself above such things. "Thank you again."

He and Worley hopped into the waiting carriage.

"That was interesting." Worley narrowed his eyes as if thinking over the conversation. "If Conway is related to Wright's partner, I'm surprised Ella Wright and her sisters didn't know it."

"There must be a reason for that. I'll have to ask her." Leo thought the connection intriguing though it didn't help locate Conway.

"Care to visit the shop next?" Worley asked.

"I think we should wait until tomorrow." While Leo didn't believe in curses, he did believe in his instincts. Something about venturing to the shop today didn't feel right. "Let us return to the Royal Geological Society and see if we can find anyone who knows more about David Wright's partner."

"Excellent idea."

Soon, the driver stopped before the building on Saville Row and both men alighted.

"Beg your pardon, my lord," John, the driver, said with a tip of his hat. "But I think we were followed here."

"By whom?" Leo quickly looked around.

"The hansom that's turning the corner." He pointed toward the conveyance just moving out of sight. "I could be mistaken, but it seemed to follow us shortly after the last stop."

"I appreciate you mentioning it. Continue to keep watch and let me know if you notice anything." Leo shared a look with Worley. "Perhaps we're on the right track after all."

"It appears so. I'm pleased you decided to postpone our visit to the shop. We might need to be sure we have assistance when we go." Worley tipped his head toward the building. "Now I'm even more curious about Wright's partner."

"As am I." Leo glanced around one last time but didn't see anything out of sorts. The idea that they were being watched was unnerving. It made him worry about Ella's safety even more. He couldn't bear to think of anything else happening to her.

Chapter Seventeen

"**I**S HIS GRACE dining in this evening?" Ella asked Davies, something she did every night, though it hadn't done any good of late.

"I believe he is." Davies offered a trace of a smile but nothing more.

Ella took that as encouragement. She understood how difficult it must be for the butler. While loyal to the duke, she liked to think he was coming to care for her and her sisters. She certainly didn't want to do anything to jeopardize his job.

Five days had passed since she'd been struck on the head. Her headaches had faded, even if the spot was still a bit sore. She had been careful to keep her sisters close the few times they'd ventured out. The idea of something similar happening to either of them concerned her greatly. As for herself, she liked to think she wouldn't be caught unaware again.

Leo had sent a message, sharing that he'd learned of a possible connection between Mr. Conway and Mr. Peterson's wife, and asking if she knew anything more. That had come as a surprise to Ella and her sisters. The topic of Mrs. Peterson's maiden name had never arisen while they'd lived on Oak Island. Nor did the woman bear any resemblance to Mr. Conway, though that wasn't a requirement for them to be related. Ella had replied with the unfortunate news that they didn't have any additional information to offer. Mrs. Peterson had passed away soon after her mother.

Leo had sent a polite reply, reminding them to be careful, but nothing more. The fact that he hadn't called suggested he had no other news to share.

Now Ella hurried up the stairs from the entrance hall to the drawing room where her sisters were. Her nerves tingled at the thought of dining with the duke again. Or at least, dining with him for part of the meal.

"His Grace is dining in this evening," she announced as she joined Lena and Norah.

"Finally." Norah rose to smooth the skirts of her mourning gown. "I do wish more of our new gowns had arrived. No doubt he's tired of seeing us in black. For which course shall we join him?"

Ella knew Norah was anxious to put away their mourning attire. They all were. It didn't seem as if their new life could begin in full until they shed the dark colors, but Lena's had yet to arrive, and they'd agreed to wait until then.

Lena's lips twisted as she considered the question. "We've already done dessert and the main course. Do we choose the first course or repeat one?"

"I think we should join him for the main course again," Norah advised. "It's the longest."

"What topics shall we discuss this evening?" Ella asked, trying to think of something that might appeal to their grandfather. "How about horses?"

"I don't know much about them." Doubt colored Lena's tone.

"Nor do I. But if he's like most gentlemen, he enjoys speaking of them. Surely the topic will discourage him from simply saying yes or no. Maybe he'll actually share something with us."

"Agreed." Norah nodded once, her eyes shining with determination. "Horses, it is."

The clock struck the dinner hour, and they made their way

downstairs to the dining room only to halt mid-stride as they entered the room.

The duke sat at the head of the table, which was set for four. Ella shared an excited look with her sisters, then continued forward, before pausing to curtsy. "Good evening, Your Grace."

Her sisters each did the same and then took their seats with the help of the footman. Though the duke barely nodded in return, the fact that he was there made up for his lack of greeting.

Silence fell over the room as Davies entered with the first course. Ella smiled at the butler whose eyes crinkled with happiness.

"This is delicious," Lena declared after she'd tasted the cottage soup, comprised of small pieces of meat, bacon, potatoes, rice, turnips, and other vegetables.

"It is indeed," Norah agreed. "This might be my new favorite soup, though all of Cook's dishes are delicious."

Their grandfather's focus remained on his bowl.

Ella decided it best to not press him for conversation, so finished her soup in silence. After Davies cleared the bowls, she drew a deep breath, hoping this went well. "What is the name of your horse, Your Grace? The one you ride so often."

He looked up in surprise. "Apollo. The same as the one before him."

"You give each of your horses the same name?" Lena seemed as puzzled by the idea as Ella.

"Saves me from having to remember." He seemed almost embarrassed as he gave a one-shouldered shrug.

For some reason, his confession warmed Ella. It made him seem more human and less of a duke. More approachable.

"Do you ride every morning?" Norah asked.

"Most days." He frowned as he glanced at each of them. "Do you ride?"

"Not often." Ella hesitated to tell him they'd only ridden on the rare occasion they visited a family friend in Quebec. Those visits had been few and far between.

"Why not? Don't you like to?"

"We had few opportunities to ride and therefore aren't especially accomplished at it." Would he think less of them because of that? Conversing with the duke was a challenge. Ella didn't want to say or do anything that would cause him to withdraw.

His frown deepened. "We must rectify that at the first opportunity. Your mother was an excellent horsewoman." His lips tightened as if the admission had slipped out without his permission.

The fact that he'd mentioned her was a leap forward as far as Ella was concerned. She missed her mother dearly, and though at times it was painful to speak of her, she didn't want to forget her. What better way to remember than shared memories?

"What kind of horse did she ride?" Norah asked.

The duke stared into the distance until Ella started to think he wouldn't answer.

"A dappled grey filly. She named her Apple because she said she was the apple of her eye. She loved that horse and enjoyed riding." His deep voice held a hint of emotion, bringing a lump to Ella's throat.

Davies returned to the room with the next course, allowing them a moment to collect themselves.

"It is important that you all ride," the duke continued. "That's something expected of you, not so different from playing the piano or drawing." He paused and lifted his fork. "I will advise Lady Havenby to extend your trousseau to include riding habits if she hasn't already included them."

Ella could only blink at him in surprise. "We wouldn't want to impose." He didn't seem particularly happy about his directive, which meant she didn't know how to react. Nor did her sisters, based on their confused expressions.

"Hmm. I am weary of always seeing you in black." With that, he began eating in earnest, suggesting he was done talking.

Ella ate the roasted chicken slowly, absorbing what he'd said. She didn't feel especially welcomed, but this was a significant improvement over the way things had been. For now, that was enough. She would continue to take their life here one day at a time, and today had been a good day.

LEO STARED ACROSS the meadow in Hyde Park, amazed at the sight before him. Ella and her sisters were riding together with a groom following behind. The laughter filling the air had caught his notice, and the vision the three sisters made held it.

He'd been proud of himself for keeping his distance from Ella for the past week, even if she was often on his mind. Often? Who was he kidding? Frequently. Always.

Coming upon her unexpectedly breached his defenses.

The hour was early, a time when the park was normally almost empty except for a few other early risers. Most of polite society preferred to ride later in the day when everyone who was anyone could see and be seen.

Ella's fair hair was all the more striking in her navy riding habit and a small, matching hat with a black plume. She looked positively stunning and stole his breath. How was it possible his attraction to her had heightened during their time apart?

He forced himself to note her sisters, as well. It wouldn't do to focus on Ella. Not when he had convinced himself that he could set aside what he felt when they were together.

He told himself manners dictated that he greet them. After all, he was one of their few acquaintances in London. With a sigh at the lie, he kneed his horse into a canter toward them.

"Good morning." Leo managed what he hoped was a relaxed smile as he neared.

"Marbury." Ella's beaming smile only set him further off balance. She glanced at her sisters. "We didn't expect to see you here."

"I ride most every morning." He leaned forward to pat his

horse's neck.

"I can see why. It's lovely." She looked around the park, eyes sparkling, and her face glowing.

He didn't think he'd seen her so happy before this moment. Then again, he supposed she hadn't had much cause to be. She'd met with one battle after another since her arrival in London, and the months before that must have been doubly difficult. There hadn't been many reasons to relax and enjoy herself as she seemed to be doing now.

She should look like this every day.

"I didn't realize you and your sisters enjoyed riding." His gaze swept over Norah and Lena deliberately, hoping to break the connection he felt for Ella.

"We don't have much experience, but Grandfather suggested we do more of it," Ella responded, bringing his attention back to her. "We thought it best to come to the park early to avoid the crowds. At least until we become more accustomed."

"Wise idea. It can be quite the crush later in the day."

"I had no idea how beautiful it is." Ella smiled, as did her sisters. "I think we will be coming more often."

"You mentioned your grandfather." The fact that she'd used the term spoke volumes, making him wonder what had happened to change the situation. Had they managed to win him over at last?

"We've been dining with him the past two evenings and consider it a major improvement in our relations," Norah said with no small measure of satisfaction.

"We still have a long way to go, of course," Ella added.

"But progress all the same." Lena looked equally pleased as she trailed a hand over her horse's mane.

He felt a sudden sympathy for the gentlemen of the *ton*. The three ladies individually were amazing. Together, they were compelling. So compelling that he had no doubt they would draw significant attention, no matter where they were or what they were doing. Their closeness and affection for one another was obvious and very charming.

Ella was clearly the leader of the trio of blonde beauties based on her confident demeanor. As far as he was concerned, she was the prettiest of the three with her sky-blue, intelligent eyes and cautious smile. Norah was slightly more petite in stature, and her blue eyes held a hint of green. Lena was taller with long limbs and more energy, always moving, and blue eyes with a hint of gold.

A line of suitors would form at their door. He wondered if the duke was prepared for the inevitable outcome, even as he ignored the pang of jealousy the thought brought. How ridiculous for him to feel that way.

"That is good news. I hope the progress continues," Leo said. "May I accompany you across the meadow?" The horses were growing restless, and he couldn't resist spending more time with the ladies.

"We would like that." Ella eased her mare forward, and Leo joined her with her sisters following behind.

"I don't suppose there were many opportunities to ride on Oak Island."

"No, there weren't." Ella smiled. "We were lucky to visit mother's friends in Quebec and rode there a few times. But those trips were infrequent."

"You ride well." He was impressed given her lack of experience.

"Thank you. We look forward to doing so more often. It's nice to have the duke's blessing for an activity."

"I'm sure." Leo looked forward to hearing Rothwood's description of this new development.

"I don't suppose you have any news?" Ella glanced at him from out of the corner of her eye.

He had known the question was coming. In fact, he would have raised the topic himself in another moment or two. Still, a wave of guilt for having failed thus far washed over him. He and Worley had gotten no further with their search.

Despite the interesting tie Conway might have with David Wright's partner, they had not been successful in locating any details about Conway himself. No one they had spoken to seemed to have heard of him. The antique dealers Abbott had mentioned knew Conway, but none had a way to contact him. Leo was at a loss as to how to find out more.

The shop Worley had discovered with the questionable reputation had remained closed the past few days. At least it was each time they visited. They had ventured to several other shops but without results.

Leo had been certain he'd be able to claim some success by now. Perhaps he wasn't trying hard enough. Was he allowing his own opinion of David Wright to color his efforts? He liked to think he was beyond that, but his failure to gain information suggested otherwise.

"Unfortunately, we have discovered little else. Nothing that has produced anything helpful."

The disappointment in her eyes bothered him more than it should.

"I am continuing inquiries of course," he added. "I find it odd how few people know Conway."

"I took the liberty of writing to Mr. Peterson to ask if he knows him and if so, whether he could tell me how to contact him. But I suppose it will be some time before I receive a reply."

"How unfortunate that Mrs. Peterson passed away."

"Indeed. Her death caused strife between Father and Mr. Peterson for quite some time."

"Why was that?"

"Mrs. Peterson tended my mother when she was sick and, soon after, caught smallpox as well. Her husband was very angry and blamed us."

"How could you have known what would happen?"

"We didn't ask her to come and help when Mother fell ill. After all, I was there tending her as were my sisters. But she insisted it was too much for us to do on our own. I should have argued more. But I was too distraught about Mother's worsening condition and desperate for someone to help her since nothing I did made a difference."

His sympathy swelled at the emotion in her tone and how

helpless she must've felt. "Mrs. Peterson's actions certainly weren't your responsibility. I hope her husband eventually saw that."

"The situation was never truly resolved to my knowledge. Eventually, they just stopped talking about it."

"Did you know much about Mrs. Peterson?"

"She grew up in England, which created a bond of sorts between her and Mother." Ella scanned the distant horizon as if searching her memory for more. "I think I remember her mentioning that she was an only child until her father remarried later in life. Her stepmother had other children, but they were younger than she. Mrs. Peterson didn't seem to have much of a relationship with them to my knowledge. They never came to visit, and I only know of one trip she made to England, but it is a long and expensive journey."

The silence grew long as Leo mulled over what she had said.

"I don't understand why Mr. Conway didn't mention the connection," Ella added with a frown. "I can't imagine that he had been to Oak Island without us knowing. It's a small community."

"It suggests he's hiding something. I have to think that if we continue inquiries, someone is bound to know something. However, that has yet to prove true."

"It's so frustrating to have more questions than answers despite all our efforts." Her shoulders fell as if she were discouraged by the thought.

"I still have another lead or two to investigate." He wanted to reassure her of that much with the hope that she wouldn't act on her own.

"Thank you. We certainly appreciate your assistance."

Leo didn't care for the hint of despair in her tone and searched for another way to comfort her. "I have no doubt we will uncover something soon." Yet even to his own ears, the statement sounded vague and less than positive.

"I'm sure." She smiled politely.

That didn't sit well with him. He much preferred her to have confidence in his efforts. He drew back on his reins. "May I speak with you privately?"

"Of course."

"Let us stop over there." He gestured to where a small copse of trees stood nearby, then turned to her sisters. "If you'll excuse us, I'd like a moment with your sister."

Norah glanced curiously at Ella. At her nod, Norah's gaze returned to Leo. "Very well. We'll continue our ride." She and Lena moved forward with the groom following behind.

Leo hoped it was only because the servant knew him that kept the groom from protesting. He watched the three for a moment as they rode away before moving to the nearest tree where he dismounted, pulling off his gloves. He tied the reins of his horse to a branch and then moved to Ella's side to help her dismount.

Her waist fit perfectly in his hands, and he lifted her with ease from the sidesaddle. He tied off her reins, then turned to face her, grateful for the low branches around them that offered a small measure of privacy.

"I do hope you realize I am doing all I can," he began, "but this is not the easiest task. There is little information to go on."

"Please don't think I am not appreciative of your efforts. Truly. It's just that I am beginning to lose hope." Her long lashes swept down, hiding her eyes as she studied her clasped hands. "With each day that passes, I can't help but feel the journal is further out of reach. Losing it feels like losing a piece of our father when we have so little to remember him by."

Sympathy filled Leo at the thought of his own father. He was lucky in that most everything reminded him of the late earl. The house he lived in. The study he used and the items in it. Even his mother. While Ella had left her home and most everything behind. It would have been impractical to bring much of it here. Nor would the duke have welcomed anything of David Wright's in his home.

"Ella." When she didn't look up, he brushed a finger along her cheek, appreciating the softness of her smooth skin. "Don't give up on me." He held his breath as her gaze lifted to hold on him.

"I haven't. I won't." Her quiet words sounded like a vow of sorts. One he welcomed and appreciated.

Unable to resist, he eased closer, afraid she would turn away—afraid she wouldn't. When she remained still, to his delight, he kissed those full, pink lips, shocked at the bolt of need that speared through him at the contact. It made him greedy for more. He deepened the kiss, pleased beyond measure when she returned it. His tongue sought the seam of her lips, thrilled when she opened for him. Their tongues swept together, then apart in an erotic dance.

Desire rose within him, but along with it came tenderness and affection. Part of him recognized his feelings were more than simple affection. So much more.

What was it about this woman that drew him? The connection they had was disconcerting. It had nothing to do with their parents, yet everything to do with them.

The thought had him drawing back to stare into her eyes, trying to find the will to step away. He'd already witnessed for himself the pain love could bring. He needed to be practical. Leading with his heart would only bring disaster.

"Leo?"

He shook his head, trying to dispel the way she captivated him.

"Promise me you'll take care." Her quiet plea was nearly his undoing.

This situation was impossible. Too much stood between them.

If only...

He gave himself a mental shake. Wishes were for children. Not for grown men with duties and responsibilities. Finding the missing journal was merely another item in a long list of those. Nothing else. He couldn't allow it or this woman to be anything more. His feelings for Ella were something he needed to ignore.

Unfortunately, he no longer thought that was possible.

Chapter Eighteen

ELLA WORRIED HER lower lip as she watched Leo ride away after he helped her mount her horse. He'd offered to escort her to her sisters, but she'd declined since she could see them just across the meadow. Why was it that each time they had a moment together, one where she was certain they were growing closer, he pulled back? With a sigh, she turned her horse to join her sisters, reminding herself that she already knew the answer—the past.

Yet she wished it wasn't true. That the complications between their parents didn't exist. What might happen between her and Leo if their shared history didn't drive a wedge between them? How ironic that what brought them together also kept them apart.

She cared deeply for Leo but wished she didn't. After drawing a deep breath in an attempt to calm her roiling emotions, she urged her mare into a gallop, focusing on the feel of the cool morning air rushing past. It helped to clear the tangle of her thoughts, so snarled that no purpose would be served in trying to unknot them.

Watching her sisters riding in the meadow ahead reminded her of her purpose. They were the reason she'd come to London. This city was their home now. Leo lived here, too, and was part of their grandfather's life. That meant he was part of hers as well.

She needed to learn to ignore the attraction she felt, and she certainly couldn't allow him to kiss her again. Heaven forbid she return it so ardently as she had just now. What had come over her?

Passion, a little voice inside her head whispered.

She pulled back on the reins, shocked at that insistent voice. Yet how could she deny it? Passion had indeed taken over her good sense along with every inch of her body. Trying to ignore the tingling awareness didn't change it. In fact, she felt that way every time Leo was near.

The mare jerked on the reins, eager to join the others, and Ella eased her tight grip to give the horse its head once more. Somehow, she needed to gather her wits before joining her sisters.

"Miss Wright!"

The call had her slowing the pace to turn and see who had called out.

The gentleman and his steed approached at a trot. It wasn't until he drew nearer that she recognized Viscount Ludham, the man Leo had introduced her to at the bookshop some time ago.

She was surprised he'd recognized her from such a distance, though she'd rather he hadn't. She had no desire to speak with him. Especially not at this moment.

"Good morning, my lord," she said politely when he neared.

"It is indeed." He rode alongside her, his horse keeping pace with hers. "What has you racing across the field so early?"

"I was just catching up with my sisters." She tipped her head in their direction.

"Sisters? How delightful. This is my lucky morning." The black stallion he rode tossed its head. "I hope you'll introduce me."

She didn't care for the man, though she knew she shouldn't be so quick to judge. However, there was something about him that made her uneasy. The fact was all the more notable when she considered how being with Leo made her feel. She intended to keep her wits about her when the viscount was nearby.

Her sisters noted her approach and turned their horses to wait. Ella made the introductions, referring to the viscount as an acquaintance of Leo's. She didn't think Leo counted him as a friend. He hadn't acted particularly fond of Ludham at the bookshop.

"Not one but three beauties." His gaze shifted from one to the next, then back again. "My goodness. Rothwood will have a line at the door once everyone meets you."

Ella smiled politely, hoping it didn't look as forced as it felt. "You're too kind, my lord."

"Not at all. I speak the truth. Now do tell me what ball you're attending so I can make certain to be there. Would you think poorly of me if I requested a dance with each of you now? I am loathe to miss such a golden opportunity."

To Ella's amusement, Norah stared at him as if he might not be of a sound mind. Lena's expression was similar.

As if sensing their puzzled stares, Ludham waved a hand in dismissal. "Pay me no mind. I am merely in awe of so much beauty."

"Do you often ride in the park?" Ella asked, hoping to change the subject. He placed far too much importance on appearance, and it made her uncomfortable. The heart and soul of a person were what mattered.

"Occasionally. I will do so more often now that I know there's a chance of coming upon the three of you."

Ella had enough of his blatant flirting. "It's been a pleasure seeing you again, my lord, but we should be returning home. The duke is expecting us."

"I'll escort you. I would feel terrible if anything untoward occurred." The viscount acted as if the groom wasn't directly behind them.

"No need," Ella said firmly. She didn't want to spend any more time in his company. "We wish you a good day." With that she turned her mare and kneed it into a trot, eager to be away and confident her sisters would follow. They joined her immediately, riding on either side.

"I don't think I care for Viscount Ludham," Lena said. "Is he a good friend of Marbury's?"

"An acquaintance but not a friend from what I could tell." Ella understood even better why the two men weren't close.

"I think we should keep our distance from him when possible. His manner made me uncomfortable." Norah scowled. "Let us discuss something more pleasant. What time do we expect Lady Havenby to call?"

They were attending an outdoor concert with her that afternoon and excited at the prospect.

"She'll be pleased to hear we have spoken with the duke. Or will we tell her?" Lena asked.

"Perhaps not all the details." Ella hadn't shared the full extent of their issues with their grandfather. Nor did she know if they were completely resolved. Two dinners were a start. But they had a long way to go before she'd consider their relationship to be on firm ground. Only time would tell.

As would her association with Leo. She didn't know what would become of it or what she wanted the result to be. How odd that she felt so unsettled even after being in London for this long.

She'd been sure the worst of the trials facing her and her sisters would be behind them once they'd convinced the duke to take them in. It was clear that was far from the end of the challenges they faced.

"Leo, darling, I have given the situation much thought."

Leo studied his mother from across the dining room table, wondering where she was taking the conversation. After his unexpected meeting in Hyde Park with Ella and her sisters that morning, he'd spent much of the day at the Society offices, speaking with any members he hadn't already talked to and asking if they knew Julius Conway or Edward Peterson.

He'd also ventured to the shop Worley had discovered in the morning and again in the afternoon, hoping to find it open.

None of the endeavors had paid dividends, much to his frustration.

After the heated kiss with Ella, he'd felt the need to justify his relationship with her. What better way to do so than finding the blasted journal? Then he could put that—and her—behind him.

He didn't want to subject himself or his mother to more gossip by associating further with Ella Wright. But keeping his distance would be impossible while he was still searching for the journal.

The same guilt that had him pestering every possible member of the Society also had him seeking out his mother for dinner that evening. He hoped whatever was on her mind wouldn't make him regret his decision. Something about her tone and the determined look in her eyes made him reluctant to respond.

Yet what else could he do?

"Oh?" He nodded when the butler offered to fill his wine glass. He had the feeling he would need it. "To what situation are you referring?"

"Rothwood's granddaughters. I should like to meet them."

Leo took a sip of wine as he considered her unsettling request. "Do you truly think that wise?"

"I do. I would prefer to do so in a private setting rather than with the entire *ton* watching." She twirled the stem of her wineglass on the tablecloth, the only sign of her agitation.

"I'm certain that could be arranged." Yet he didn't know whether it was a good idea for any of them.

However, he could hardly deny her request when he had been the one to tell her of their arrival so the news didn't take her by surprise. It was only natural for her to want to take the same preventive measure with meeting them.

Still, concern gave him pause. If he was there, which he felt he should be, would she somehow sense his growing feelings for Ella? The worry had him ignoring the roast beef on his plate for another sip of wine.

"Leo, sometimes you are far too much like your father. If something is on your mind, say it. Don't you think it is better for me to meet them before happening upon them at a ball?"

"I am merely pondering the details of how such a meeting could be arranged," he hedged. "I assume you'd prefer to avoid going to Rothwood's."

"Most definitely." Her lips twisted, hinting at her distaste at the thought. "Nor would I want them to come here."

Her statement had him shifting in his chair and setting down his wine glass as protectiveness stirred. It was as if she were already judging the sisters before she'd met them.

He briefly closed his eyes at the thought. Of course, she was. Just as he had. He only hoped meeting Ella, Norah, and Lena would change her opinion. Yet even if she found them presentable, which was the best he could hope for, what then? It didn't change the past or whose daughters they were.

Nor did it provide a path forward for him and Ella. The passing thought had him catching his breath. Just how deep did his feelings for her run?

The important thing about arranging such a meeting was that it would keep all those involved from creating a public spectacle. Therefore, he would find a way to make it as painless as possible for both parties.

"Why don't I determine an appropriate time and location and then see if it suits your schedule?" He needed to think of a place that would offer some privacy yet wasn't at either residence.

"Thank you, dear. I should like to have it over and done with soon."

"As would I." The words slipped out before he could halt them.

"Whatever do you mean?" She tipped her head as if truly

curious.

"Only that it is better that we arrange it beforehand as you suggested." He took a bite of his roast beef as he waited to see if his answer satisfied her.

"True. Will you be attending Ascot this year?" The horse race, held in June, was attended by the Queen and members of the aristocracy and something his mother always enjoyed.

"I suppose. In truth, I haven't thought that far ahead." He'd been so immersed in the search for the journal that he hadn't considered his schedule beyond the coming days.

The conversation moved on to other topics, including a bit of gossip. He liked the fact that his mother was never mean-spirited when she spoke of others. However, she enjoyed keeping up with who was courting whom, as well as the good and bad that so often accompanied life.

"Do you have any interesting news from the Royal Geological Society?" she asked as dessert was served.

"Very little," he began, only to hesitate. Perhaps it would be best if he told her what had taken so much of his time of late. Before she heard the news from someone else. "Unfortunately, a treasure hunter's journal has been stolen."

"How terrible. Did it belong to someone you know well?"

"It was David Wright's journal. His daughters brought it with them to London."

The sympathy in her eyes immediately chilled. "Haven't you always believed he was looking in the wrong place? If that's true, why would someone bother to steal it?"

"My opinion hasn't changed. However, not everyone agrees with me. Some think there might truly be treasure on Oak Island. In which case, the notes of someone who's been searching for it for some time could be helpful."

His mother's brown eyes narrowed with suspicion. "Allow me to guess. You're attempting to find it."

"Rothwood asked me to help. After all, I'm familiar with most of those who look for pirate treasure. Making inquiries is relatively easy for me."

"And also places you in danger."

"I hardly think asking a few questions could be considered dangerous." He focused on his plate, his mind filled with the image of Ella motionless on the floor of the shop.

"If a thief is involved, it does." She glared at him from across the table. "Leo, I can't say that I care for this. Not at all."

"Rothwood is a friend, and I want to help him. His three granddaughters, especially the eldest, Ella, are extremely upset over the loss."

"Because she thinks it holds value?"

"I believe it's the sentimental value that means the most to them."

"As far as I'm concerned, they should search for it themselves." His mother tossed her napkin on the table near her untouched trifle and pushed back her chair before the footman could step forward to help her.

"They are. But none of us have had success as of yet."

"Why do I have the feeling you aren't telling me everything?" She stood, one hand on the back of her chair.

"There's nothing more to tell." Leo stood as well. Sharing what had happened to Ella would serve no purpose. Worse, it would confirm that the task truly was dangerous. He didn't want his mother to worry. Nor did he want to argue about his involvement in the situation. He'd already made a promise and intended to keep it.

"I hope that's true. Do take care, Leo. I don't like the sound of any of this."

"I will." He watched as his mother quit the room, wishing once again that he was closer to finding the journal. But wishing even more that his mother could let go of the past and meet Ella and her sisters without memories casting such a dark shadow over them all.

>>>><<<<

"I THINK WE should consider doing some charity work," Ella suggested as she and her sisters settled in the drawing room with their embroidery the following afternoon.

"After what we saw yesterday on our way to the concert, I couldn't agree more." Norah sorted through the thread in a basket at her feet.

Their ride to the park where the small concert had been held had taken them past the outskirts of the East End. The view from the carriage window had shocked them.

It had been one thing to note a few roughly dressed people who'd obviously fallen on hard times during their searches in antique shops, but it was another thing entirely to see a glimpse of the truly unfortunate.

"As painful as it is to witness the plight of the poor, little can be done about it," Lady Havenby had said when they remarked how concerned they were.

"Why is that?" Lena had asked, her tone full of disbelief.

"Offering money to them only encourages them to beg."

"Surely that isn't true for everyone." Ella didn't believe it for a moment.

"Those living on the streets should go to the workhouse or one of the other charitable establishments that offer help." Lady Havenby sat back on the seat as if not looking at the situation would make the problem go away. As if they weren't talking about people who might have fallen on hard times and needed help. "Now then, I received word from the dressmaker that more of your gowns are ready for a final fitting. Your first ball is less than a week away. When would you like to have that done?"

Ella had let the conversation continue around her while she'd stared out the window. The sight of men, women, and children with ragged clothes and thin faces sitting along the street had squeezed her heart.

So much so that it had been difficult to enjoy the concert when her thoughts had been on those so obviously in need of assistance. She was certain her sisters felt the same way.

"What do you have in mind?" Lena asked. "There are so many good causes that it will be difficult to choose which ones to help."

Ella smiled at her not-so-subtle suggestion that they should help more than one. "Do you have something in mind?"

"The children caught my attention the most." Lena shook her head, her hands quiet on her lap, suggesting her thoughts were in turmoil. "My heart breaks to think of them cold and hungry. What about you?"

"They have my sympathies as well," Ella agreed. "While I'm certain there are numerous needs, helping children seems as if it might make the biggest difference. If they could be fed, clothed, and offered education, their lives might be changed forever." Ella looked at Norah. "What do you think?"

"Yes, definitely the children."

"Excellent. I'm pleased we're in agreement. Though I confess I don't know how to go about helping." Ella wondered if they could raise the subject with their grandfather. They had no money of their own to give, but surely there was some way they could help.

"We might need to do some research on the topic." Norah pulled out a ball of red thread. "Perhaps Mrs. Enfield would have some suggestions. I'd be happy to sew clothing or blankets."

"As would I." Lena's brow puckered. "I wish we could do more, though I don't know what." Her gaze met Ella's. "It would be helpful if we had the duke's support as well, don't you think?"

Ella nodded. "You're right. Let us start with Mrs. Enfield."

When the housekeeper brought afternoon tea, Ella posed the question.

"A children's charity? That's a fine idea," the housekeeper said as she set the tea tray, which included a plate of cakes and biscuits, before them. "I'm sure they're always in need of warm clothing. Though the temperatures are rising as we move into spring, the nights remain chilly. Especially without a roof over one's head."

"Do you think His Grace would mind if we did something like that?" Ella asked.

"Not at all. I think he'd be proud of you for taking an interest. He gives to several charities regularly, though I couldn't tell you which ones."

"Are there schools for poor children?" Lena asked.

"Yes. Though it seems as if the children unable to attend need help even more. Perhaps there's an orphanage that would welcome assistance."

Ella pondered the issue long after they'd finished tea. She wished she could speak with Leo about the topic to see if he had any suggestions.

The thought made her realize just how much she was coming to count on his presence in her life. But it was more than that. He was an honorable man who would always do the right thing. She admired everything about him, from his intelligence to his interest in exploration to his handsome appearance. One look from him could steal her breath and send her heart pounding.

Thank goodness their first ball was nearly upon them. She obviously needed something to distract her from her spinning emotions. Finding the right gentlemen for her sisters would surely do just that. Then she wouldn't have time to think about her own future.

※》》》《《《※

"Isn't it gorgeous?" Norah asked a few hours later as she smoothed the elongated bodice of her new plum-colored silk gown.

Several of their ball gowns had arrived from the dressmaker along with a few others, and they hadn't been able to resist trying them on again.

"You are what makes it gorgeous," Ella insisted, nearly speechless at the sight of her sister dressed in such a beautiful gown. Her blonde hair was pulled back in a loose knot, leaving strands to frame her heart-shaped face. But it was more than that—it was the glow of excitement shining in her eyes. "Mother and Father would be amazed right now."

"Or appalled," Lena whispered as she stared down at her own lavender ball gown. Her chest heaved, and her eyes were wide as if panic threatened.

"Never that." Ella rushed close to take her hands, dismayed at how chilled her fingers were. But even more concerned by the thoughts going through her head. "Why would you think so?"

Lena looked between her and Norah, her face pale. "They left here for a reason. They put all of this behind them. Society and its trappings. Now it feels as if by coming back, we've undone what they hoped to accomplish."

"I don't believe that for a moment." Ella ignored the hot rush of guilt that flooded her. How often had she worried about something similar? That she had made a mistake by bringing her sisters to London. Yet what other choice had there been?

Lena shook her head as she sniffed, tears filling her eyes. "I'm sorry, but this is suddenly too much. Living with a duke who still seems reluctant to claim us as his family. Moving about in Society where we're looked upon as if we're some sort of oddity. I don't feel as if we belong here. Do you?"

"No," Ella admitted. "I don't." Norah gasped, but Ella had to answer with honesty. "But without Mother or Father, I don't think we belonged on Oak Island either. There was no longer a life for us there. That was their dream, not ours. But I have hope for London. For Grandfather. For the life we might make here. These things take time."

"We've been here nearly a month," Lena said. "Shouldn't it be better by now?"

Lena had always been a sensitive soul. There had been many

times in the past when Ella had comforted her as their parents were often busy with other things. She seemed to feel everything twice as deeply as Ella and Norah. If only Ella knew what to say that might reassure her.

"It is taking longer than I thought as well," Norah admitted as she drew near to place a comforting hand on Lena's shoulder. "Life is so different here."

"True." Ella slowly nodded. "But we have much to be grateful for, and we're making progress. Our first ball will be both exciting and overwhelming." The thought of it was enough to form a knot in the pit of her stomach, but she wasn't going to let that stop her from going. Hopefully, her sisters felt the same. "This is our chance to meet more people and make friends. Doing so will help London feel more like home."

She didn't mention meeting potential husbands, as she didn't want Norah and Lena to feel pressured to marry. She wanted that to be a choice, not a duty, and hoped the duke felt the same way. Norah had already mentioned she was in no hurry to marry and that she wanted time to enjoy their new life. Unfortunately, she still hadn't shared what brought that concerned look to her face so often.

"We should practice dancing, I suppose," Lena said after a long moment, color returning to her cheeks.

Ella drew a relieved breath, pleased to see her sister's worries calming. She didn't want them to be uncomfortable but, she could do little to prevent that, especially in the coming days. They were all bound to feel that way as they navigated the first few events. Without parents to guide them, they only had Lady Havenby. Ella certainly couldn't claim to know what she was doing.

"Lady Havenby has been a tremendous help," Ella said almost to herself. "We may not be able to count on assistance from the duke, but being his granddaughters offers its own form of protection."

"More importantly, we have each other." Lena straightened

and took both Ella and Norah's hands in hers. "That is what truly matters."

"Yes," Norah agreed as her gaze shifted to Ella. "I don't know what we would've done without you, Ella. You are our guiding light."

"That's the perfect description." Lena squeezed Ella's hand with a smile. "I know our journey has been especially difficult for you. Thank you for all you've done."

Ella sniffed and hugged them both, hoping she'd done the right thing by bringing them here. While she didn't know for certain, she was doing the best she could. Perhaps that would be enough.

Chapter Nineteen

LEO STARED INTO the grimy shop window with disbelief late the following afternoon. The establishment was once again dark and the door locked. "How can the place stay in business when it's never open?"

"Perhaps it has closed permanently." Worley rubbed the filthy glass pane, but it did little to improve their view of the interior.

"Or maybe customers are advised when to pick up their merchandise."

"That would explain why they're never open. I wonder how we can discover more."

Leo briefly considered the wisdom of his idea before he suggested it. "Let us check the back to see what we can find."

"Won't it be locked as well?"

"Most likely, but there will be fewer people about to notice if we happen to find a way inside. I've grown weary of waiting. I want a better sense of the type of items they carry so we know whether we should cross the shop off our list."

"Marbury, you shock me. An earl willing to dirty his hands in such a manner?" Worley elbowed Leo. "Lead the way, and I shall gladly follow."

The fact that his friend thought it a good idea was enough to make Leo think twice. This was probably a terrible suggestion, yet what choice did they have? After only a moment's pause, he sighed. "We'll have a look and decide from there."

He counted the number of shops until they reached the street corner, then walked to the alleyway and did the same, which brought them to a sturdy wooden door with peeling paint and no markings.

"At least it doesn't have a bar across it like some of the others." Worley studied the muck-filled alleyway before turning back to the door.

"I suppose we should be grateful for that." Leo tried the knob, but it was locked, as expected.

"Allow me to do the honors," Worley suggested as he reached into his pocket and pulled forth a slim leather case.

"Do not tell me you have a pick." Leo supposed he shouldn't have been surprised but he was.

"Very well, I won't. However, these tools have proven helpful numerous times if I happen to encounter locks when hunting treasure."

Leo only shook his head as he kept watch while his friend bent low to work the lock. "I suppose that's one way to see what a treasure chest holds."

"At times, a man must be creative. I do wish the light was better."

The alleyway was full of shadows but also deserted, much to Leo's relief.

"Here we are." Worley rose, turned the knob, and the door swung open.

Leo looked inside, listening carefully to make certain no one was about. A strong, unpleasant odor drifted toward them.

"Damn, but that smell is atrocious. It smells like death," Worley declared.

"I believe that's because it is." Leo made certain to breathe through his mouth as he took a step inside the shop. One didn't spend months of every year on an estate in the country without encountering a dead animal or two. However, he didn't think it was an animal causing the stench.

Crates were piled on top of one another along the back wall, while another stood open on a table in the center of the room. He listened again, but the silence remained thick.

"You still intend to go inside?" Worley asked with disbelief.

"Whoever is in here can no longer harm us. And based on the smell, the person that did the deed has been gone for several days."

"Shouldn't we contact the police?"

"We will. But first I'd like to look around. We might not have another chance." Leo moved to the table and looked in the crate to find several pieces of pottery. The brightly painted pieces were of no interest.

After a quick glance around the rest of the room, he continued forward, wishing he had a light. Then the sound of a match strike was followed by a flame flickering to life behind him. He turned to see that his friend had pulled a matchbox from his pocket along with a small candlestick. "You are truly indispensable, Worley."

"Most treasure hunters are well prepared. At least, the more successful ones. It pays to be ready for the unexpected."

"I appreciate that more than I can say." Leo drew aside the thick curtain that separated the rear of the shop from the front.

The stench was even stronger and pulled Leo reluctantly forward. He paused to allow Worley to proceed him with the light. They had only taken a few steps before they both spotted a body lying on the floor.

Though Leo had been expecting it, the lifeless form still came as a shock. A sense of dread crept over him, and he glanced at Worley to see that he seemed to have the same feeling.

"Poor bastard," Worley muttered. "Doesn't look as if his death was natural."

"No, it doesn't."

Dried blood stained the scuffed wood floor near the man's head. He was on his back, one arm outstretched as if in protest.

Long, stringy black hair partially obscured his pale face.

"He's not familiar to me," Worley said after leaning over the body to get a better look at his face. Then he shuddered, the situation obviously bothering him as much as it did Leo.

"I don't know him either. Then again, I didn't expect to, given that we haven't ever been in this shop." Leo drew forth his handkerchief to press against his nose and mouth, then squatted to examine the body closer. "Can you bring the flame nearer? I'd like to see if we can tell how he died."

Worley did as he asked, moving the candlestick in a slow circle around the man's head.

"Stop there," Leo directed even as his stomach lurched.

Worley halted, and the flickering light revealed a deep gash on the side of the man's head. The sight made Leo uneasy, as it brought to mind another cut he'd recently seen—on Ella's head.

"Why do you suppose he was killed?" Worley asked.

"I have no idea, but let us see if we can find a reason."

"Could've been a theft. A desperate person looking for money or merchandise to steal. The shopkeeper confronted whoever it was, and it didn't end well."

Leo wished Worley's version of events was true but suspected it wasn't. Based on the location of the injury, the man had looked away from his assailant, perhaps still focused on unpacking the crate when he'd been struck. That suggested he knew who'd hit him. But Leo could be wrong.

He stood and looked at the nearby counter. Another crate sat on the dusty surface with packing material strewn about. The objects inside were much like the ones they'd seen in the back. Certainly nothing that could be considered a valuable antique.

He walked around the shop but didn't see anything that suggested the owner was interested in pirate treasure or books of any sort. It seemed unlikely his death had anything to do with David Wright's journal. The realization was disappointing in many ways but a relief in others.

"I thought for certain we'd see more interesting things in

here," Worley said as walked around the tables of merchandise. "With the reputation it has for finding special items requested by customers, I expected shelves full of the unique and unusual. Or at least items of value."

"As did I. Though I suppose they wouldn't leave those out for just anyone to see. However, there certainly doesn't seem to be anything worth killing for." Leo returned to the crate the man had been unpacking and pulled out one of the clay pots. He peered inside, surprised when something sparkled. He upended the vessel into his hand to reveal a ruby and diamond necklace. "Well, well."

"Damn. That's an interesting way to transport goods. We can assume they're stolen, don't you think?"

"Indeed." Leo left the necklace on the counter beside the pot, hoping the police would choose to investigate the matter further.

"Have you had your fill?" Worley pressed the back of his hand to his nose as if to help ward off the smell. "I should like to step outside and take a breath of fresh air."

"As would I. We'll lock the door, then report this to a policeman." Leo looked around one last time and then led the way to the back of the shop.

"What do you suggest we say so it's not evident we were in here?"

"We'll explain that the shop hasn't been unlocked for several days, and we'll mention the smell. That should be enough to convince the police to take a closer look." While Leo's sympathies were with the dead man, it was growing frustrating to have each potential lead disappear.

After they'd explained their concern to a patrolling policeman, he and Worley returned to his carriage. "Let us go to the club," his friend suggested. "I think we are both in need of a drink after that."

"Agreed."

Worley sighed. "I'm beginning to lose hope that we'll ever find the journal. Perhaps Conway gave up on his plan to hold an auction and has found a private collector instead."

"I like to think that us keeping the topic on everyone's mind has forced him to narrow his list of potential buyers. We should continue to do so," Leo said. "Hopefully, whoever is considering purchasing it will think twice." At this point, it seemed to be the only action they could take.

Yet Leo couldn't help but wonder if there was a connection between the stolen journal and the dead shopkeeper. What if the journal held more than the sentimental value Ella believed? Conway might think Wright's notes had enough detail to leave a clear path for another treasure hunter to continue the search. If that were the case, it would definitely be worth murder to someone, including Conway.

⇒⇒⇒⇐⇐⇐

ELLA FOLLOWED LADY Havenby along a garden path at Bateman House two days later with Norah and Lena a short distance behind. Nerves fluttered in her stomach, but she forced herself to focus on her surroundings, hoping it would distract her from worrying about the meeting to come. "The garden is gorgeous."

Lady Havenby paused to look around as if she'd forgotten to do so. "It is, isn't it? Lord and Lady Bateman take great pleasure in their garden."

Though rather formal in nature for Ella's taste, the numerous sculptures, inviting benches, and floral beds were beautiful. The foliage of the trees along the path on which they walked created a canopy overhead. In one section, different colored pebbles were arranged in swirls resembling ocean waves. The garden seemed to have everything.

"This is impressive," Norah whispered when she and Lena caught up with them. "I'm not certain where to look first."

"Just remember, you don't want to be seen gawking about like a young girl," Lady Havenby advised. "One mustn't act overly impressed by displays like this."

Ella was doing her best not to, but given the lush surroundings with unique flowers in nearly every color of the rainbow, it was impossible not to crane one's neck to take it all in. Better that she stared at the flowers than search for Leo and his mother. The thought of meeting the Countess of Marbury at this small gathering was thoroughly unsettling. They'd agreed to arrive early so fewer people were in attendance.

"What must it be like in the summer?" Lena asked. "It's already so beautiful now."

Violin music floated through the air, lending even more elegance to the scene.

As they rounded an artfully clipped hedgerow, Lady Havenby's attention shifted to a few people standing near a white tent where refreshments were being served. "The Countess of Marbury is the one in green standing just outside the tent."

Her description had Ella following her gaze to see Leo standing beside an attractive, slender woman dressed in emerald green, edged with black fringe. Though the countess must be in her fifth decade, she was stunning with wide brown eyes and smooth skin in an oval-shaped face. Her dark hair was piled high in complicated twists topped by a green hat with black netting. Her posture was perfect, her expression serene. She looked like a picture from a fashion magazine and very much like a countess.

And quite intimidating.

Leo's suggestion they meet his mother this afternoon had come as a surprise. Yet upon further contemplation, Ella had appreciated the idea. She'd rather not have a large crowd observing this particular introduction, which made the intimate garden party an excellent choice.

Lady Havenby said she knew the Countess of Marbury quite well. Her connection to both Ella and Leo's mothers made her the perfect companion for this meeting since she understood the emotions behind it.

Not only were their pasts intertwined, but Ella was also curious about the countess simply because she was Leo's mother. She had no idea what to expect, but she intended to do everything she could to have the meeting go smoothly for everyone's sake, especially Leo's.

"Perfect posture and smiles," Lady Havenby whispered as she straightened, making Ella wonder if she was telling them or herself.

Their chaperone led the way forward. "Lady Marbury, how good to see you."

Leo's mother turned, her dark eyes taking in Lady Havenby before quickly moving to Ella and her sisters. "Good afternoon."

Lady Havenby made the introductions, and Ella and her sisters curtsied. Ella's attention shifted to Leo. As always, her heart lifted at the sight of him. He smiled, though a hint of worry was visible in the depths of his eyes. His brown suit coat and striped waistcoat fit perfectly, his easy grace and confidence appealing as always.

"I hope the day finds you well," he said by way of a greeting, his tone formal.

"It's impossible not to be while viewing such a beautiful garden," Ella responded, forcing herself to look at anything except him.

"It is even more impressive in the summer when the flowers are in full bloom," the countess said.

"I hope we have the opportunity to see it then." Ella studied her again, now able to see the fine lines around her eyes and mouth, a testament to her age. Though Ella searched for some resemblance to her son, she saw little. Did that mean he more closely resembled his father?

"How are you finding London?" Lady Marbury asked, her gaze holding on Ella.

"It is much different than Nova Scotia. I think we are enjoying the more moderate climate," Ella said.

"I miss the quiet and fresh air most," Lena added with a polite smile.

"Yes, the London air is frightful. I suppose the winters in the north must be especially long." Lady Marbury shifted her gaze to Norah and then Lena, studying each in turn as the two replied to her comment.

Ella wondered if she saw their mother when she looked at them, as so many others did. Had Lady Bethany liked the countess? Had they been friends?

"I knew your mother, as you may have guessed." A flicker of pain tightened the countess's face before she shifted her attention to Leo.

Ella bit back the urge to apologize for the past. She was done doing that. After all, it wasn't her mother's fault the late earl hadn't been able to move past the unfortunate incident.

Leo touched his mother's elbow as if to show his support and lend her some of his strength. The tender gesture tightened Ella's heart. He was a good son, and that only made her respect him more.

"We miss both our parents dearly." Ella wasn't going to exclude her father from the conversation.

"Life is a challenge, isn't it?" Lady Marbury held Ella's gaze as if taking her measure. "It's difficult to lose those we love."

"That makes it even more important to enjoy the time we have with them." Only too late did she realize how much her statement applied to the late earl. Had her words offended the countess or Leo?

"True." The lady gestured toward the path that led to another part of the garden. "Why don't you and I enjoy the garden together for a few minutes?" She smiled at Leo, whose brow rose with surprise, then moved down one of the paths.

Ella was so shocked by the suggestion that she had to walk quickly to catch up with the countess. A glance over her shoulder showed Lady Havenby's eyes wide with surprise, along with her sisters'.

They walked together where the path was wide enough to fit both their skirts, and Ella followed in other places when it narrowed.

The countess paused frequently to admire a particular flower or a sculpture, often remarking on it. Ella offered a few comments of her own when it seemed appropriate, waiting to see if there was something specific the countess wanted to say.

"Do you garden, my lady?" Ella asked.

"I dabble with roses. In fact, I have a pink variety that is especially beautiful." She paused before a statue of a young maiden that looked as if it had been imported from Greece. "Why is it that so many of the statues have so few clothes?"

Ella chuckled. "Having been raised in a colder climate, I can't imagine wearing so little. Have you been to Greece?"

"My husband and I ventured there after our wedding. The sites were amazing, but I prefer England. Soon afterward, he decided he didn't particularly enjoy travel."

"It can be tiring," Ella said as they continued along the path. "I always seem to forget something I wish I would've brought."

The countess smiled. "As do I. One more reason to stay home. Though there's nothing like travel to gain a different perspective on the world and to better appreciate home."

Home. The word brought a wistfulness to Ella. She missed their home on Oak Island deeply but being there after her father's death hadn't been the same.

The duke's residence was certainly more than comfortable, but she wouldn't call it home. Staying there was more like being on an extended trip. Then again, in many ways, it was. Would she ever feel the connection and comfort of a true home again?

"You have had more than your fair share of challenges I would venture to guess." The countess paused and turned to look at Ella.

"It has been a difficult year." Ella forced a smile. "But we are grateful to have our grandfather in our lives."

"Hmm. I doubt he welcomed you with open arms but give him time. He's rather stubborn but might come around eventually."

Ella was surprised by her insightfulness. Then again, since Leo was close to the duke, it only made sense that the countess knew the duke fairly well.

"Leo mentioned your father's journal was stolen. I'm sorry to hear that."

"We should very much like it back. His notes are something we hold dear and to have someone take it is upsetting."

"If anyone can help you find it, Leo can." She paused before a prickly bush with glossy leaves, running a gloved finger over the surface.

"He has been kind, and we appreciate it."

The countess shifted her attention to Ella for a long moment, making Ella worry that something in her tone revealed her feelings for Leo. She did her best to keep her expression polite but felt heat creep into her cheeks.

"When is your first ball?" Lady Marbury asked when she finally moved forward.

"In three days. The Benbrook ball." After all this waiting, it was difficult to believe the time was nearly here.

"Lady Havenby's suggestion, I assume, though it's a good one. Not too large but still prestigious."

"I confess the three of us are very nervous." Ella didn't know why she had the urge to share that. According to Lady Havenby, they were supposed to act as if none of this were new to them.

"I would be surprised if you weren't. Balls can be rather overwhelming. My advice would be to do your best to enjoy yourself. Worrying about what everyone else thinks is too exhausting."

"Thank you, my lady. We shall certainly keep that in mind." Ella pondered her words, wondering if she spoke from experience.

They were nearly back to the tent. The crowd there had grown, and several ladies turned to watch their approach with interest.

Just then, the countess's skirts caught on a wrought iron

decorative spike along the path.

"One moment, my lady." Ella reached for her arm to halt her, then bent low to free her gown. She checked to make certain it hadn't torn, then straightened. "There we are. I wouldn't want your beautiful gown to be damaged."

"Nor would I. Thank you." The countess smiled for the first time, making her look much more approachable.

"You're welcome."

They joined the others, and Ella was well aware of the questioning gazes coming from her sisters, Lady Havenby, as well as Leo.

"Leo, darling, will you fetch us something to drink? I find I'm rather parched, and I'm certain Miss Wright is as well."

"Of course." He moved to the table where glasses of lemonade were available and returned with two. "Here you are." He handed one to his mother as she conversed with Ella's sisters, who already had lemonade, and one to Ella.

"Thank you."

"My pleasure. Is all well?" he asked, his voice barely above a whisper.

"I believe so. Though I couldn't say what your mother thinks."

"Based on her smile when you freed her gown from that spike, she might be warming toward you."

"You sound surprised." She narrowed her eyes as she looked at him.

"I think she was prepared to dislike you and your sisters."

"You think she changed her mind because I did a favor for her?"

"Not only that. Because you showed you have a kind heart. You could have easily ignored her gown being caught and allowed her to have a rather embarrassing moment, as well as a torn gown. Instead, you saved both her gown and her pride."

Ella blinked in surprise. How unfortunate to think others might be so unkind. "I hadn't thought of it like that."

"I did, and I have no doubt she did as well."

Ella followed his gaze to where her sisters stood visiting with his mother. They all appeared to be enjoying the conversation. Leo wasn't the only one surprised by the events of the afternoon. She wouldn't have guessed the Countess of Marbury would offer them more than a simple greeting. Could they possibly have found another person willing to aid them in their new life in London?

"Thank you, Leo."

"For what?"

"For being the man you are." Ella held his gaze, even as it felt as if her heart did a slow roll in her chest.

"You are more than welcome."

Her breath caught at the heated look in his eyes and his suggestive tone, making her wonder at his thoughts.

Chapter Twenty

LEO ESCORTED HIS mother into Benbrook House for the ball with no small measure of trepidation. The evening would more than likely be a difficult one. He wished he could spare her, as well as Ella and her sisters, from the gossip that would surely fill the ballroom. All he could do was support them as best he could.

He needed to have his wits about him this evening. If anyone said an unkind word to his mother, Ella, or her sisters, they would quickly be made aware of their mistake. He was determined to do all in his power to make the evening go smoothly.

After the long receiving line to greet Lord and Lady Benbrook, he and his mother entered the ballroom to find it already filled to the brim. He followed as she made her way toward her friends, unwilling to allow her out of his sight.

The ladies she joined gave him an odd look as he normally didn't accompany her this closely, but he ignored them to search the crowd. The Season was in full swing given the number of people in attendance. Though Parliament had been in session for several months, many families remained in the country until the weather was more amenable to travel. As the roads improved, more of the *ton* arrived in London. Leo had chosen to return to London early to attend Parliament sessions, along with some of the Royal Geological Society lectures.

He nodded at acquaintances but made no move to speak with them as he wanted to remain by his mother's side.

A murmur filled the ballroom, and both he and his mother glanced about to see what was causing the chatter. It didn't take long to determine the source.

The crowd parted as if to allow everyone a better view of the new arrivals. The sight of Ella caught his breath. She looked positively stunning—a regal beauty with her head held high. Her shimmering violet gown was embroidered with black flowers and trimmed with black braid. A matching velvet choker circled her neck and white gloves reached to her elbows.

Norah and Lena looked amazing, as well, in shades slightly lighter than Ella's. Both of their gowns were trimmed in black, too, a nod to their continued mourning for their father. The gowns were different yet similar, with Lena's being the palest shade, and marked them as sisters if their blonde-haired beauty didn't already do so.

Ella's expression was calm, her arms gracefully at her sides rather than clasped tightly. No hint of the nerves that surely must be simmering inside her were apparent.

Good, he thought. Acting nervous and worried amidst the *ton* would only make her a target if her notoriety hadn't already done so.

Ella tipped her head to listen to something Lady Havenby said and nodded. The graceful line of her neck was enhanced by her upswept blonde hair with several long curls brushing one shoulder.

Damn, but she was a sight. He could hardly take his gaze from her. The tightening of his chest and pounding of his heart, not to mention his suddenly dry mouth, confirmed not only her beauty but his feelings for her.

Her gaze swept over the crowd and somehow found him, and he stopped breathing for a moment. A connection sizzled between them. How could a simple look cause him to feel so much? He had the sudden urge to march over and take her arm to escort her out so he could have her all to himself.

He tamped down the desire and smiled, hoping to convey how wonderful she looked. That he was proud of her. For the briefest moment, stark emotion showed in her face—a mix of nerves and something else he didn't dare name. More than simple affection shone in her eyes. The realization made his heart thump harder.

Where was his resolve to guard his emotions and set aside his feelings for her?

As her gaze held on him, he knew now was not the time to worry over such things. No matter what happened between them, he wanted to make sure she enjoyed this evening. The crowd surged forward as if many were anxious to meet the three sisters. He had no doubt there would be a line of gentlemen requesting a dance. He needed to claim one with each of them before it was too late.

A hand took his elbow, and he looked down to see his mother staring at the Wright sisters, making him realize he couldn't possibly leave her to greet Ella. Not when she needed him, as evidenced by the tightening of her lips and her hold on his arm. Already he could hear whispers behind them, perhaps from some of her friends who realized the difficulty of the moment.

"We should greet our new friends, don't you think?" She looked up at him and smiled, the strain she must be feeling no longer reflected in her expression.

He couldn't have been prouder. Of course, she understood this was the perfect way to keep the talk at bay—by directly speaking with the sisters before those eager to latch onto a juicy bit of gossip started whispering.

Leo placed his hand over hers and then moved forward. "You are brilliant, Mother. Brilliant and kind."

Her smile became more genuine as she gave a single nod. "Why thank you, dear."

In short order, Leo had elbowed their way through the crowd until they were standing before Ella.

A flash of relief crossed her expression before she dipped into a curtsy. "Good evening, my lady. My lord."

He bowed. "Good evening, Miss Wright. You and your sisters look especially lovely this evening."

"Thank you."

"You do indeed," the countess added.

As if his mother's compliment held more weight than his, Ella's expression relaxed the slightest bit as they continued to exchange pleasantries.

"Will you save a dance for me?" he asked.

"I'd be honored."

The emotions reeling through him as he took in the number of people anxious to meet her and her sisters caught him by surprise. He wanted to push them all away.

Lady Havenby chose who and in what order to introduce them, seeming to have the situation well in hand. Leo was aware of other gentlemen nearby who looked ready to pounce. Rather than snarl at them to be gone, he did his best to reassure the sisters as he requested dances with both Norah and Lena as well. He managed to make them both laugh, which he counted as a win. The pleased look on Ella's face suggested she appreciated his efforts as well.

Worley joined them and was his usual charming self with the ladies and soon escorted Norah to the dance floor.

His mother visited for a time and made several introductions to those she deemed worthy. Not only was her gesture kind, but it declared to everyone who witnessed it that she supported the three sisters. He hoped that smoothed their path forward. No one watching would believe for a moment that their arrival in London had upset the countess.

Now if only he could convince himself they hadn't thrown his own life into turmoil. Yet as he watched Ella, he realized that sometimes change was welcome. Where it would lead, he didn't know.

>>><<<

FROM THE MOMENT Ella entered the ballroom, the evening passed in a blur. She wanted a moment to take it all in. To absorb all that was happening. The sights and sounds were nothing like she had seen before.

The brightly colored gowns against the dark evening attire of the men were a study in contrasts, especially as couples whirled on the dance floor. From the outlandish to the truly beautiful and everything in between, the gowns on display were as stunning as the ladies wearing them.

She liked to think she and her sisters held their own. Their attire was neither too ornate nor too plain but somewhere in between. She hoped their mother would be proud and was looking down upon them with a smile.

Once their initial nerves had worn off, both Norah and Lena seemed to enjoy themselves. They had all agreed the evening would be overwhelming and to take Lady Marbury's advice to do their best to take pleasure in it.

To Ella's surprise, most everyone was friendly, though she knew both Lady Havenby and Lady Marbury had made that possible, along with Leo's help. Without a nod from them, their welcome wouldn't have been quite as warm. Ella and her sisters might be the Duke of Rothwood's granddaughters, but he was nowhere in sight. That made it easy for those in attendance to forget their relationship to him.

She was pleased they'd taken time to practice their steps as they danced more times than she could count. By partnering with many of the same men as Norah and Lena, she had a chance to meet them and judge for herself whether they were worthy of her sisters' interest.

But there was only one dance she truly looked forward to, and that was with Leo.

Several of the gentlemen to whom she spoke seemed nervous, much to her surprise. The realization they had that in common eased her own nerves. She did her best to make polite conversation and hoped she handled herself well. A few gentlemen were obviously rakes or the like as they flirted shamelessly. With a firm tone and a pointed look, she made it clear that sort of behavior was not welcome.

"Thank you," she whispered to Lady Havenby when she'd once again returned to her side after a dance.

"What for, dear?"

"For taking us under your wing. For all of your advice. This evening wouldn't have been possible without you."

The lady blinked rapidly as if filled with emotion, and she pressed a gloved hand to her chest. "The pleasure has been mine. Your mother would be so proud of the three of you. I hope you know that."

"I like to think so, as well."

Before she could say anything more, a throat cleared at her side, and she turned to see another gentleman had arrived to request a dance.

As the evening lengthened, her feet began to hurt but her excitement didn't dim. The sight of her sisters laughing and smiling as they twirled on the dance floor made her heart light.

Yet as time passed and Leo didn't return, her nerves bubbled up again. She couldn't help but search for him, hoping he hadn't forgotten.

"Looking for someone?" His deep voice had her turning quickly to face him with a smile.

"You remembered."

"Of course." He offered his arm and nodded at Lady Havenby, then escorted her to the dance floor. "I would ask how everything is progressing, but I can see for myself the evening is a success."

Ella chuckled. "It's too early to declare it so, though our first ball has gone much better than I hoped."

"Trust me. You can declare it a triumph."

The strains of a waltz began as he drew her into his arms. His hand on her waist as they took the first steps made her forget all else.

Dancing with Leo was more like floating as they twirled to the music. Added to the sensation was the way he looked at her, so steady and sure, yet with a certain hunger in his eyes.

An answering need arose in her. She dearly wanted to kiss him. To have him hold her tight. And to see where that might lead.

"You dance divinely," he murmured, the heat in his hazel eyes burning.

Why was it she felt as if he were saying something else entirely?

Rather than the flirtatious behavior of some of the other gentlemen, Leo made her feel more with one look than all of their outrageous statements combined.

Was this how her mother had felt about her father? As if she couldn't take her next breath if he wasn't at her side? This deep longing to be with him. To touch him. To have him touch her.

She gave herself a mental shake. So much stood between her and Leo. And as nice as his mother had been, that didn't mean the countess would welcome her into the family. Far from it. Dreaming of such a future was dangerous.

"What is it?" he asked, his brow furrowed.

"I only was thinking of how kind you and your mother have been. We appreciate that so much."

For some reason, her response seemed to displease him. As if it wasn't the answer he wanted. But she could give him no other. This was for the best. She was certain that deep down, he understood that as well. The glow of the evening dimmed and suddenly exhaustion took a firm hold.

She forced herself to straighten and smile. At the very least she could enjoy this moment with Leo. She just had to take care that she didn't allow her feelings to grow more than they already had. After all, they were both bound by the past and neither of them could change it.

>>><<<

"I MAY NEVER walk again," Norah declared as she dropped into a chair in Ella's bedroom.

The hour was late, and they were all exhausted. But they weren't quite ready to retire. Not until they'd shared their experiences now that they had a few minutes alone. Lady Havenby had left them on the doorstep and continued home, having declared the evening a "delightful success."

"These shoes felt comfortable earlier." Lena plopped onto the end of the bed, then lifted her skirts to toe-off her shoes. "Now they pinch terribly."

"As do mine." Ella sighed as she, too, sat down. "Balls are incredibly exhausting."

"How many do we have to attend in the next two weeks?" Norah's frown suggested she was concerned by the thought.

She should be. It was far too many. "I'm sure we won't mind the idea come morning," Ella reassured her. "A good night's rest will do wonders to restore us all. Now do tell. What was your favorite part of the evening?"

"Dancing." Lena sighed as she sat back in her chair. "Even after so many, I loved it." She looked at Norah. "What about you?"

"Dancing with Lord Westbrook was especially enjoyable." She wiggled her eyebrows, causing her sisters to giggle. "He was very handsome."

"Which one was he?" Ella asked. All the names and titles ran together in her mind.

"He was tall with dark hair and blue eyes that made you catch your breath."

A vague recollection of the man filled Ella's mind.

"Ah. I remember." Lena nodded. "He is indeed quite handsome."

"And an excellent dancer," Norah added, only to give Ella a stern look. "But don't think I am in any rush to marry."

Ella was thrilled to hear a particular gentleman had caught her sister's eye.

"What of you, Ella?"

Ella hesitated, wondering if she should share the truth. Then she decided to at least share a portion of it. "I enjoyed waltzing with Marbury. It was lovely to dance with someone I didn't feel as if I had to watch every word or struggle to make polite conversation. I could just...enjoy the dance." She hoped neither of them realized how much more she'd felt than the little she'd told them.

"His mother is much nicer than I expected." Norah's eyes narrowed. "It can't have been easy for her to befriend us the way she did. From the bit of gossip I overheard, the former earl remained in love with our mother for a very long time. Even after he married the countess."

"I can't imagine." Lena shook her head. "How terrible to know your husband was in love with someone else."

"I heard someone say the countess truly loved him," Norah continued, "though I suppose that faded after so many years of watching him pine for another."

The idea hurt Ella, as well. She only had to think of how she'd feel if Leo loved another. That sort of pain was nothing she wanted to experience, let alone face each and every day.

"A few remarks I heard suggested it made the current earl's life difficult as well," Norah said.

"Why is it that people enjoy speaking of the bits of life that are going wrong rather than the ones going right?" Lena asked.

"Excellent question, but one to which I don't have the answer," Ella said. She didn't like to think people were mean-spirited but sometimes they were. "Well done, ladies. But I, for one, am ready for bed."

Norah placed a hand over her mouth as she yawned.

"Agreed. We truly do need our beauty sleep after this."

Lena giggled, just as Norah had meant her to. Ella's love for her sisters tightened her throat. They were so lucky to have each other.

Norah rose and bent to kiss Ella's cheek. "Thank you for all you've done for us. I'm pleased you insisted we come to London. I do think we have found our place, even if it doesn't feel like it quite yet. Soon it will."

Perhaps Norah's pensive moments were a result of her feeling torn between enjoying these new experiences and feeling guilty for doing so.

"Yes." Lena kissed her other cheek. "It will soon. For all of us. Thank you, Ella. You are the best sister we could have."

The two sought their rooms, and Ella's maid entered to help her prepare for bed.

"I hope you had a fine time, miss," Sally said as she assisted her with her gown.

"We did. More so than I expected." Ella smiled as memories of the evening drifted through her mind as Sally brushed her hair.

"I'm pleased to hear that. May it be the first of many wonderful evenings to come."

After she'd banked the fire and left, Ella stared at the canopy of her bed, her thoughts circling. So many voices from the evening echoed in her head, so many faces.

But only one held in her mind and in her heart—Leo.

Her feelings for him confused her. But as of this moment, she was too tired to try to sort them out. Instead, she held tight to his handsome image and the memory of their dance as she closed her eyes. It came as no surprise that she dreamed of him.

Chapter Twenty-One

"CONWAY?" THE SHOPKEEPER of Mendenbury Antiques frowned. "Why, yes. He's a customer of ours. Why do you ask?"

Leo stared at the man, doing his best to mask his surprise. After hearing so many no's, a yes left him nearly speechless.

"I'm trying to reach him about a particular item in which he might be interested." Leo could hardly contain his excitement to finally have a chance to locate the man.

"I have his address here somewhere. Only because we had to arrange to pick up some items he sold us, of course." The man paused in his search to stare at Leo over the rim of his smudged spectacles. "I assume I can count on your discretion if I were to give it to you."

"I have no intention of sharing the address with anyone." Other than possibly the authorities, depending on what Conway had to say for himself. But Leo didn't mention that. He shouldn't assume Conway's guilt, even if the little they knew pointed to him.

"Always happy to help a fellow collector." The shopkeeper continued rifling through a stack of papers, leaving Leo in doubt whether he'd be able to find it.

Leo glanced about the shop as he waited, trying to hide his impatience. A variety of antique glassware took up most of the space of the small shop just off Piccadilly, which was one of the reasons he'd doubted the shop could be a lead for Conway. But he was working his way through as many establishments as possible, nearing the last few on his list.

The interior was clean and well organized with the exception of the man's desk. His filing system seemed to comprise of placing papers in various stacks on the wooden surface.

"Here it is." He pulled a paper from the pile with a triumphant flourish. "I believe he lives just off Mincing Lane."

Mincing Lane was near the center of the spice and tea trade. The area surrounding it certainly wasn't one of the finer in London. The location came as a surprise because the way Ella had described Conway, Leo had thought he most likely lived in a more affluent neighborhood.

"Thank you." Leo memorized the address. "May I ask what Conway purchased?"

"Actually, he sold us a collection of nearly two hundred pieces, including decanters, finger bowls, goblets, and more that came from Versailles. Quite the find for us."

"How did he come across it?" And why did someone who had such a collection live in the neighborhood he did?

The shopkeeper chuckled as he adjusted his spectacles. "He wouldn't say. Only that his source preferred not to be identified."

The answer made Leo wonder if he'd stolen the collection as well.

He thanked the shopkeeper, then stepped outside, the sight of Ella and her sisters approaching bringing him to a halt. Two days had passed since the ball—since their dance, which had surely ruined him for all others. Dancing with Ella had taxed all of his senses, leaving him aching for more. He was in over his head with this woman and the way she made him feel.

What to do about it remained unclear.

"Ella. What a pleasant surprise." Except for the fact that he suspected he knew why she was here.

Her eyes went wide, and her lips parted briefly only to close.

Damn, but he wanted to kiss her again. "Good afternoon, my lord. This is indeed unexpected."

From the look on her face, she was truly surprised—and guilty. Her deep blue silk gown matched her eyes, distracting him for a moment until he remembered that guilt.

Based on her glance at the shop from which he'd just emerged and the pink filling her face, she had started making inquiries of her own again.

He greeted her sisters, who looked equally uncomfortable.

"What brings you this way?" he asked, wondering if Ella would tell him the truth.

"Well, we were just... That is to say..." She heaved a sigh as if resigned to giving up the attempt to hide her actions. "We were going to see if this particular shop knew anything of Mr. Conway."

"I thought we agreed you weren't doing such things anymore." Didn't she understand how dangerous it was after what had happened? Now, he almost wished he'd told her about the murdered shopkeeper, though that seemed unfair given that Leo didn't know if the incidents were connected. But perhaps it would've discouraged her from venturing to shops such as this one.

"That is what I told her," Norah said with a glare at her sister.

"We are only visiting establishments in better areas. At least, ones that look presentable from the outside."

"I don't think a shop's appearance can truly serve as a guide to its potential danger." Leo shook his head even as he admired her pluck. Her persistence seemed to match her father's.

"In my defense, I would like to point out that I am not alone." Her brows rose as if she were hopeful he would count that as a mark in her favor.

"Duly noted." He offered his arm, which she took almost reluctantly. It didn't go unnoticed how perfectly she fit against him, or how complete she made him feel. "As it happens, I have just come from that shop and now have Conway's address."

"Truly?" Ella's excitement exceeded his own, and her hand tightened on his arm, which tightened other, unmentionable parts of him. "That is excellent news." She looked over her shoulder at the shop one more time as he escorted her back the way she'd come, her sisters and the maid following. "I wouldn't have guessed they would know him."

"Nor would I."

"Are we going to his residence now?" Her hopeful tone was impossible to ignore. Damn if it didn't make him want to give her anything she asked.

"No, *we* are not." He shook his head. "I am."

"You can't possibly go alone." Her horrified tone warmed his heart. Perhaps she cared about him more than he thought.

"I will bring Worley along in case I need assistance."

"I think it would be best if I joined you as well."

"The viscount and I can manage."

"But neither of you know what Mr. Conway looks like. He could walk past you, and you wouldn't recognize him. Besides, I should very much like to hear what he has to say for himself."

Leo debated the idea, as it wasn't without merit. As long as it had taken to gain Conway's address, Leo didn't want to take the chance of missing him. Yet he couldn't possibly bring Ella and her sisters along. After all, the situation wasn't without risk. "Why don't you describe Conway's appearance to me?"

Those oh-so-kissable lips tightened. "Why don't I just come with you?"

"She has a point, my lord," Lena said with a smile. She leaned a bit closer, blue eyes sparkling with amusement. "If you haven't yet noticed, she can be stubborn at times."

Ella merely raised a brow when his attention returned to her, suggesting she expected him to change his mind. The woman was both incorrigible and beautiful.

"We can't all go." Even as the words left his mouth, he realized he had just acquiesced. What had happened to his negotiating skills?

"Ella, would you prefer that I accompany you?" Norah asked. "Or Sally could, while Lena and I return home."

"Perhaps it would be best if Sally came. Are you certain the two of you don't mind going home without me?"

"Not as long as you promise to tell us everything the moment you return," Norah replied. "I do hope he has the journal and hands it over."

"As do I." Ella frowned as if doubtful.

"I shall have my driver follow your carriage to Rothwood's," Leo said. Having Ella step into his carriage in view of the other shoppers on the street could easily damage her reputation. "We'll leave from there."

"Very well." Ella seemed impatient with the details and nearly pulled him along the street.

"Have you and your sisters been basking in the glow of the success of your first ball?" he asked.

"Heavens, no." Ella shook her head, seemingly further embarrassed by his remark. "I'm just pleased that both Norah and Lena enjoyed themselves."

"But not you?"

"I did as well, but they're the ones who matter."

"You matter, too, Ella." Leo frowned, not liking that she placed herself below them.

She glanced at him from beneath her lashes. "Their happiness is important to me. The last few months have been difficult, and it's wonderful to see them smile."

"I'm sure." They'd have even more reason to smile if he retrieved the journal. However, it was too soon to make any promises. He paused, holding her gaze for a long moment before handing her into the carriage along with her sisters. "I'll see you shortly."

"Promise?" Ella leaned forward to catch his gaze, the hopefulness in her expression squeezing his chest. "You won't go without me?"

"You've convinced me of the wisdom of bringing you along."

Leo shut the door and nodded to the driver.

In short order, he collected Ella and her maid from Rothwood's. He debated the wisdom of finding Worley, but he didn't want to wait that long. Not when this sense of urgency was pressing at him. The driver and a footman accompanied them, and they would have to serve as protection if the need arose.

He also considered seeing if the duke was at home to advise him of their plan but decided against it. If Rothwood wanted detailed information on his progress, he should've stayed involved both with the search for the journal and his granddaughters.

"What if Mr. Conway isn't there?" Ella asked once the carriage rolled away from the duke's residence.

"Then we will return again later."

"What if he is there?" Ella's worried tone suggested that was just as concerning of a possibility.

"Then we shall ask if he has the journal." Leo had to think that the moment Conway saw them, he would guess why they were there. No purpose would be served in pretending they'd called on him for any other reason.

"What if—"

"Ella, we will know what to do when we get there. Trust me." At least, that was his hope.

They traveled through the streets in relative quiet, both seeming focused on the confrontation ahead of them. It took nearly half an hour before they arrived at the address.

Though the area was central to the tea and spice trade, it wasn't long ago that opium had been its focus. Now, many tea merchants had offices there, and the area, in general, had improved, though it still left much to be desired.

Conway's residence was situated on a side street where rows of red brick townhomes were stacked together tightly as if the builder had worried he'd run out of space. From the outside, one had to wonder if the residents could reach out and touch both walls of their homes, as they appeared so narrow.

"Keep watch," Leo advised his driver and the footman when he'd stepped out of the carriage. "We may need your assistance if the situation goes awry."

"Of course, my lord," they agreed.

Leo assisted Ella to alight and escorted her up the steps to the front door, her maid following behind. After knocking, they waited, turning to survey the street, though there was little to see. The houses lacked a garden of any sort and few people walked past.

"Yes?" A man peered through a crack in the door, seemingly reluctant to open it.

Leo glanced at Ella but could tell this wasn't Conway. "We'd like to speak with Julius Conway, please."

"Who's calling?"

"Miss Ella Wright." Ella looked at the man expectantly as if he should let them in.

"I see." As he didn't open the door any wider, it wasn't clear if her name made an impression. "A moment if you please."

He drew back, and Leo was certain he intended to close the door and leave them standing on the step. Leo placed his boot in the way, preventing the door from shutting.

"We are in a rush, so it would be best if we could speak with Mr. Conway straightaway." Leo didn't bother to attempt a smile or to say please. Not when what he really wanted to do was shove open the door and search the place for Conway himself.

"Humph. Very well." The stranger released his hold on the door as if realizing he was no match for Leo, given that he was nearly a foot shorter than Leo's six-foot frame. Then he scowled and drew back as Ella, Leo, and the maid entered. From his attire, he appeared to be a roommate rather than a servant. "Wait here."

"Here" was merely the space behind the now closed front door. There was no true entrance hall. A worn Persian rug on the floor and scuffed walls suggested the home had seen better days. Conway lived modestly, from what Leo could see.

The man stalked down the corridor toward the back of the

house, pausing once to cast a glare over his shoulder as if to make certain they remained where he left them. He entered a room at the far end, and the sound of voices echoed in the house.

Leo was considering escorting Ella down the hall when another man appeared wearing a gold-colored suit coat with a striped waistcoat and pumpkin-colored tie.

He strode toward them, rubbing his hands together as if he were cold—or nervous. "Miss Wright? Is that truly you?"

With dark hair that held a hint of red and a thin build, the man smiled, though it seemed forced, especially when he took in Leo's presence.

"Mr. Conway." Ella's voice held no hint of a warm greeting.

"What a delightful if unexpected surprise." He looked from Ella to Leo, clearly waiting for an introduction.

"This is a friend of ours who is helping my sisters and me search for a missing item." Leo wasn't certain why she chose not to make a true introduction, but he assumed she had a reason.

"It's a pleasure." Conway held out his hand, which Leo chose not to shake. After an awkward moment, Conway dropped his outstretched hand with a frown, his brown eyes chilling.

"We believe you might be in a position to return this missing item." Leo hesitated to outright accuse him of the theft. Especially when he didn't act guilty. The important thing was for the journal to be returned. The rest could be sorted out later.

"I don't see how I can help, though I dearly wish I could. Anything for you, Miss Wright." His second attempt at a charming smile was no better than the first. "What is the item?"

"My father's journal. You may remember me mentioning it on the ship."

"It's missing? Oh, that is terrible. I'm so sorry to hear that. What happened?"

Leo studied Conway's expression with a sinking sensation. Either the man was remarkably good at hiding the truth or he didn't know anything about it. The realization was disconcerting. Leo had been certain he'd be able to tell whether the man was guilty with one look. Normally, he was adept at reading people.

"As you can imagine, my sisters and I are beside ourselves with worry." Ella sniffed delicately and blinked several times.

Leo stared at her with alarm, surprised to think she was so upset. Yet he couldn't hold back his concern that she might cry.

The same feeling apparently flooded Conway, as well, for he took a step forward, his brows crinkling with worry. "What happened to it?"

After watching Ella another moment, Leo began to suspect she was acting with the hope of gaining Conway's sympathy. Leo waited to see what she intended.

"We've searched everywhere, but the truth is clear." She paused for a dramatic moment. "It's been stolen."

"Stolen? Are you sure?" Conway frowned, though he didn't act especially surprised. "I can't imagine such a thing."

"There is no other explanation." She retrieved a small square of embroidered white linen from her reticule and pressed it to her nose. "We are devastated."

"I can imagine." Conway watched her closely. "This is truly terrible news."

Leo was certain the only thing that kept Conway from taking Ella's arm in a show of comfort was his presence.

"In fact, we would do nearly anything to have it returned," Ella continued.

"Oh?" A hint of interest colored the man's tone now.

"Yes," Leo added, trying to think of how he could support Ella's act. "A reward is being offered. Significant enough to convince whoever took the journal to return it."

"I see. Well, I do wish I could help, but I'm not certain how."

"We were advised that you are a collector." Ella watched Conway closely. "In all honesty, I was surprised to learn this, as you never mentioned it on the ship."

"Didn't I?" Conway seemed to ponder that for a moment. "I thought I had. So many of our conversations were positively delightful and riveting."

"I would've remembered." Ella blinked again.

The urge to comfort her, even though he knew she was pretending, nearly overwhelmed Leo. Her performance was remarkable.

"At any rate, we would appreciate help recovering the journal, and as my friend mentioned, are happy to provide a reward to anyone who offers assistance to locate it."

"My dear, Miss Wright, I wish there was some way I could help." He looked into her eyes as if he meant it. Leo had his doubts.

"Perhaps you have acquaintances in the collecting world who might have heard of it," Ella suggested.

"Well, I do know quite a few collectors," Conway admitted with a one-sided smile.

Leo clenched his jaw, hoping to find patience and restraint to keep from wiping the smile off the man's face.

"I'm sure you're being modest," Ella said. "Why, someone like you must know many."

Conway's chest puffed out, his ego seeming to gain the better of him. "I do know quite a few."

"Perfect. Then you'll help us? As I mentioned, the reward would make it worth your while."

"I suppose I could make a few inquiries."

"That would mean the world to me and my sisters," Ella said. "If you could send word if you hear something, we would appreciate it."

"Of course."

They sorted out the details, and soon Leo closed the door behind them, Ella at his side and the maid following. The meeting hadn't gone according to what Leo expected, and he wasn't sure what to make of it.

Based on Ella's stiff form, he had to think she was sorely disappointed they were walking away without the journal. So was he. Leo felt as if he'd failed once again, and he didn't care for it. The danger of caring for someone meant wanting to help them.

While he liked to think he'd been successful in helping his mother, he certainly had never been able to aid his father. He detested settling for anything except success with Ella.

There had to be something more he could do, but what?

ELLA WATCHED LEO as they approached the carriage, his expression unreadable. In truth, she didn't know what had come over her when she'd made the suggestion to Mr. Conway. But instinct insisted that accusing him of stealing the journal would gain them nothing. Then again, she wasn't certain her efforts would either.

"I hope you don't mind that I gave Mr. Conway the chance to return the journal."

"I confess I sorely wanted to shake the truth from him. Though I suppose there is no guarantee of success with that approach." He handed her into the carriage where she sat beside Sally.

"I thought I'd know whether he was guilty the moment he saw me." Ella shook her head. "But I couldn't tell."

"Nor could I. You have given him the opportunity to return it without admitting guilt. That could be the impetus he needs to do so. Especially if he thinks there will be a reward."

"I don't know how I can pay it if he does. It's doubtful Grandfather would be willing to do so."

"I will be happy to take care of that if need be."

"Thank you." Ella was so grateful to have Leo to depend on in this situation. She couldn't imagine dealing with all this without him. "I thought I'd come to know him fairly well on the ship, but now I see that was not the case. I hope that by making it clear how much the journal means to us and how upset we are by its loss that he will feel guilty and be inclined to give it back."

"Few thieves allow guilt to guide their actions, but I suppose it might work. I must admit I was impressed by your performance. I thought for a moment, you were actually going to cry."

His praise and the hint of admiration in his gaze caused her to smile, her heart warming. "I only had to think of how I felt when I first discovered the journal was gone for my emotions to be genuine. While it would have felt more satisfying to show my anger, I couldn't bring myself to when I was so uncertain of his guilt."

After a long moment of silence, Leo turned from watching the passing scenery to look at her. "There might be a way to make returning it even more attractive."

Something about the determined look on his face made Ella wary, her pleasure slowly fading. She had the feeling she wasn't going to like whatever he was about to say.

"We make the reward a greater value than selling," Leo said.

"How?"

"By declaring the journal worthless."

Ella gasped in dismay, unable to believe he'd even say such a thing. "That's a terrible suggestion."

"Conway might be more inclined to return it if doing so gains him more money. And if he isn't the one who took it, this could still improve our chances of getting it back." He seemed to be warming to the idea as he mulled it over based on his pleased expression.

Ella didn't like the idea at all. In fact, she was hurt that he'd suggested it. Doing so would be the same as calling her father's work worthless. That all his years of effort amounted to nothing. What a terrible disservice it would be to his memory.

"As I have some expertise in the field," Leo continued, "by declaring it without value and stating that I believe your father was digging in the wrong place, the reward would be deemed the only option by whoever has it."

"You mean by saying what you have always believed." Ella couldn't hold back what she knew to be true. "It's what you've thought all along."

"I won't deny it. That is what my research has shown."

"Can you honestly say you haven't allowed your personal feelings and the events of the past to color your professional opinion?" She couldn't keep the sarcasm from her tone.

"I have done my best to be objective. However, I am only human. The history of our parents may have played a role in how I feel. But it's substantiated by my research. Surely you can see there is little evidence to prove anything is buried on Oak Island. The fact that your father tried for decades with no success confirms it." His gentle tone only made her angrier.

So angry that her upset nearly choked her.

"While he may not have found a chest of pirate treasure, he did find other things." She hated the helplessness flooding her. "You can't deny that something happened on that island. Someone dug more than one shaft. He found several things that make it clear there could be treasure."

"That doesn't mean the activity was done by a person burying riches. There are other explanations for why numerous shafts were dug. The same is true for the few items he found. While I appreciate that your father had the right to live his life as he saw fit, I don't have to agree with him. Especially when the evidence says otherwise." Leo opened his mouth as if to say more, but Ella held up her hand to stop him. She couldn't bear to hear any more.

"This is obviously something on which we will never agree," she managed, relieved to see the carriage was nearly home. "I won't waste my time trying to convince you otherwise. It's enough to know that I believed in my father and his efforts."

The carriage halted outside the duke's residence, and Ella couldn't leave quickly enough. "If you truly believe declaring the journal worthless will encourage whoever took it to return it, then go ahead. But don't expect me to act as if I agree." She was breathless with hurt and anger. Just when she'd thought the distance between them could be bridged, he created an even bigger gap. The footman opened the door, and Ella quickly alighted followed by Sally.

Leo shifted as if to step out to see them inside, but Ella shook her head. "No need for you to see us to the door."

She forced herself to look at him, wishing circumstances were different. How could this man be someone she adored yet his opinion about her father nearly wiped away all of that? Even worse, she didn't see how it could ever be resolved. Nothing he could say would make her doubt her father. And it appeared as if she would never convince him that her father had been right. This fundamental issue cracked the foundation of their relationship.

The realization was devastating.

"I'm sorry my mother and father hurt your family. But I'm even more sorry that you can't seem to move beyond that. It seems as if you're not so different from your father after all."

"Ella, wait!"

Ella ignored him and strode toward the door, hoping to hold back her tears until she reached her bedroom.

Chapter Twenty-Two

"Care to tell me exactly what you're doing?" Rothwood demanded as he approached Leo where he sat alone in one of the meeting rooms at the Royal Geological Society.

"Can you be more specific, Your Grace?" Leo stood to bow, then gestured toward the papers and maps strewn on the table before him, his mood already black as night. "Do you refer to the research I'm conducting or something else?" He knew he was being deliberately obtuse, but anger drove him.

Anger at himself. Anger at David Wright. Anger at his father. Anger at fate for sending a woman into his life who threatened his tidy, logical plan for the future, which had no place for love. Not when that tender emotion had caused him and his family so much pain over the years.

After leaving Ella at Rothwood House two days ago, he'd returned home and penned an article declaring David Wright's journal nothing more than the meandering thoughts of a failed treasure hunter who refused to accept defeat. The article had been published in the Society's weekly news sheet the following morning.

The fact that there was no turning back from his mission of decreasing the journal's value didn't quiet the voice inside his head that questioned what the hell he was doing.

Yes, he still wanted to find the journal for Ella. But at what cost? Though he'd told himself that she needed to accept the truth about her father, who was he to force her to do so? What if Wright had been about to make a major discovery the day he died in that shaft?

Leo feared he'd made a terrible mistake—one that had cost him Ella. And there was no way to change it.

Perhaps she was right—he was just like his father, dwelling on past events rather than the hope of a bright future.

"You know exactly what I mean." Rothwood's glare would've leveled anyone else, but Leo was immune. Mostly. "You are stirring more talk than I can abide."

"If you're referring to my declaration that David Wright's journal is nothing more than the scribblings of a want-to-be treasure hunter, I merely shared my professional opinion." Strangely enough, it was one of the most difficult things Leo had ever done. All because he knew how much it would hurt Ella and her sisters. Yet he couldn't think of any other way to force whoever had the damned journal to return it.

However, the one person he hadn't thought his efforts would bother was the duke. Not when Rothwood had never liked David Wright. Had his granddaughters made him reconsider?

"To what purpose?" the duke asked as Leo sank into his chair.

"Stating an opinion doesn't need a purpose."

"It does in this case." Rothwood slapped the table as if to emphasize his point. "You are hurting my granddaughters."

His words burned through Leo, tightening the knot in the pit of his stomach. The fact that Ella hadn't told her grandfather his plan was concerning. Still, he did his best to cover his upset. "That was not my intent." Leo leaned close to speak quietly. "I am trying to make the journal less valuable to improve our chances of getting it back."

"Publishing an article that states you think David Wright a fool isn't the best way to go about that. I realize you never believed in his work. However—"

"Nor did you," Leo felt compelled to point out. "Has your

opinion changed?"

Rothwood straightened, obviously considering the question. "I don't know. I have given it much thought of late. Why would an experienced treasure hunter spend decades digging on an island in difficult conditions if he didn't see hints of treasure?"

The duke's question matched many others, including several members of the Royal Geological Society who had already approached Leo with the same question. It was one to which he didn't have an answer.

"The least you could do is be respectful of Wright's efforts," the duke continued, his tone positively chilly. "To give him the benefit of the doubt."

Leo was taken aback by his words, especially when they added to his own guilt. But he appreciated Rothwood's concern for Ella, Norah, and Lena, which seemed to confirm the duke was starting to care for them.

Still, Leo couldn't halt his plan now. He had to forge ahead.

"I am only doing what I think will get the journal returned. The fact that the article matches my opinion makes it believable." Leo gestured toward the papers before him. "However, I'm continuing my research even as we speak. If I find something to change my mind, I will certainly write an article on that as well."

Rothwood's lips thinned. "I don't like it. I'm disappointed in you, Leo." With one last glare, he turned and stalked from the room.

Leo didn't care for how the duke's parting words made him feel. For his entire life, Rothwood had been the grandfather he'd never had. Never before had he expressed doubt in Leo.

He ran a hand over his face, reminding himself of the purpose of this whole endeavor. He was doing his best to get the journal back for Ella and her sisters. At least, he hoped he was. Yet his doubt continued to nag him.

Worley entered the room before Leo had the chance to return to his research, his frown making Leo brace himself for yet another lecture.

"What has Rothwood in such a stir?" his friend asked.

"My latest article in the Society's weekly news sheet."

"I should've known. But you didn't state anything you haven't said in the past. Surely it wasn't a surprise."

"Apparently, it was."

"Because of his granddaughters, I'm sure." Worley pulled back a chair and sat as he glanced at the articles on Oak Island strewn before Leo. "Why don't you tell me what's really going on?"

"How do you mean?" Leo clenched his jaw before forcing himself to look at his friend.

Worley held his gaze for a long moment. "I saw the way you looked at Ella Wright the night of the ball. You are intrigued by her. Don't bother to deny it."

Leo should've known Worley would notice his attraction. Attraction? He nearly scoffed at the term. The word seemed too tame to describe how he felt. "I won't."

"Then why are you doing this? To make certain she detests you?"

"No, I—" His breath caught. Was that what he was doing? By going to such an effort to declare her father's work without merit, he had pushed her away.

He'd promised himself to never permit his feelings to overcome his logic. To never turn into his father and allow love for someone to change him. Or leave him miserable.

From a young age, Leo had watched his father's poor spirits and dissatisfaction with life. How often had he sworn to not repeat his mistake? Love was heartache. Nothing more.

Leo wasn't about to share any of that with Worley. Besides, it was secondary to his true purpose. This was simply a way to get back the journal since none of his other attempts had succeeded.

Yet if that were true, why was he so filled with doubt—and misery?

His swirling emotions couldn't possibly be love. He thrust aside the suspicion, determined to focus on reasoning—not emotions—to resolve the situation. Once the journal had been returned, he'd consider what he felt for Ella.

By then, it will be too late. The voice whispering in his head caused his chest to tighten. Or was that his heart?

"Marbury. What are you about?" Worley's grim expression suggested he wouldn't allow anything but the truth.

Leo glanced around to make certain they were alone before leaning forward. "I am hoping whoever took the journal will either read the article or hear of it and decide to take the reward being offered rather than sell. Perhaps my poor opinion of it will decrease its value and make the reward more attractive."

Worley slowly nodded as he processed the idea. "I suppose it could work."

Leo was relieved his friend agreed with his plan. "Now we watch for anyone who shows interest in the reward."

"Very well." Yet Worley continued to study Leo until he had the urge to shift in his chair.

"What?" Leo asked at length.

"I have to wonder if you're choosing to focus on the wrong treasure."

"What do you mean?"

Worley stood and placed his hand on the back of the chair. "Think on it. You're an intelligent man, and I have no doubt you'll realize you should reconsider your priorities. Some things in life only come around once. I would also like to remind you that you are not your father."

With that, his friend departed, leaving Leo with the unsettling feeling that he was trying to accomplish the right thing the wrong way. Was Worley right and Leo had ruined his future for the sake of a past that wasn't truly his own?

ELLA STOOD IN the drawing room staring out the window later

that afternoon. The dreary, rainy day suited her mood. She couldn't seem to work up the energy to go to the music room to play or work on her embroidery. Nothing she did soothed the ache in her heart.

She'd relived the conversation with Leo more times than she cared to admit. Was she being ridiculous? Perhaps she should disregard the fact that he believed her father a fool. That his life's work was worthless and so was his journal.

Leo's opinion shook her to her very core. She couldn't simply ignore how she felt. How could they move forward? The situation left her listless and unhappy with no idea how to recover.

"Miss Wright?"

Ella turned to see Davies in the doorway. "Yes?"

"His Grace would like to speak with you in his study."

Ella stilled in surprise. She had never been summoned by her grandfather before, nor had she visited his study. They'd had a stilted conversation at dinner the previous evening, though she hadn't shared the events that had unfolded. Why would she when they were only beginning to converse with one another?

She'd only told Norah and Lena an abbreviated version of what happened with Mr. Conway. They'd put her upset down to disappointment at not having reclaimed the journal.

She didn't want His Grace or her sisters to know the extent of her feelings for Leo when he thought so poorly of their father.

Did her grandfather intend to tell her that he agreed with Leo? She already knew he did. Nothing about David Wright pleased him, and she wouldn't bother to try to change his mind. Much like Leo's opinion, that ship had sailed and there was no returning to shore.

That didn't mean she'd allow either man to speak poorly of her father. At least, not in front of her. Regardless of what the duke wanted, she didn't expect it would be a pleasant conversation.

With a sigh, she followed Davies to her grandfather's study.

Stepping over the threshold felt as if she were being allowed into his inner sanctum. It was difficult not to think that something important was going to occur.

Dark wood panels graced one wall while the other was covered in a navy wallpaper with narrow gold stripes. A desk stood near the row of bay windows with bookshelves on either side. Her grandfather sat behind it. Two brown leather wingback chairs sat before the fire, and two other seating arrangements were nestled in the room. A large globe stood on a stand to one side, a testament to his interest in geography.

In truth, the room was cozier than she'd expected. What did that say about her grandfather? Before she could decide, he cleared his throat, drawing her attention back to him.

"Good afternoon, Your Grace." She dipped into a curtsy and remained where she was.

"Ella." His use of her given name surprised her. He stood and walked around the desk to gesture to the chairs before the fire. "Will you join me?"

"Of course." Ella moved forward, uncertainty taking hold. Based on his somber expression, she feared the worst. Yet she couldn't imagine what he had to tell her. She knew her sisters were well. She'd already lost her mother, her father, and her home. Now she feared she'd lost Leo, too. What else could happen?

"It has come to my attention that Marbury has published an article which could cause your father to be discredited." The duke shook his head. "I am sorry for that. I can't imagine what he was thinking. First the stolen journal and now this. It seems like too much for you and your sisters to endure."

"You do realize he did so to discourage whoever stole the journal from selling it?" Why she defended Leo, she didn't know. Especially since he believed everything he'd shared publicly about her father and his search.

She swallowed against the lump in her throat. It didn't matter that in her secret heart of hearts, she wished it wasn't true.

"He mentioned that, but the pain the article causes you isn't worth the slim chance that selling the journal is now less attractive."

"Have you read it?" she asked.

"Yes. Unfortunately, so have many others. As always, Marbury's opinion holds weight, and he's written a compelling argument on the topic." Her grandfather reached out and took her hand to squeeze it in an awkward gesture of support, shocking her to her toes. "But it's only one person's opinion."

Then he sat back, folded his hands over his still relatively flat stomach, and stared into the flames. "Over the years..." He frowned and released a heavy sigh. "That's not quite true. While I have given the matter much thought since your mother left, it's only in the past month that my opinion has shifted."

"Oh?" Ella prompted when he said nothing more.

"Your father must've seen something to convince him of the validity of his pursuit of treasure on Oak Island. His persistence alone confirms it." He paused, then met her gaze. "At any rate, we are all entitled to our dreams. Oak Island was obviously his."

"Are we?" she asked. "Even when those dreams hurt others?"

Her grandfather's expression softened, suggesting he understood why she'd asked. "That is a difficult question. Each person is responsible for their own happiness and pursuing dreams is often part of that. I have come to see how my behavior contributed to your mother making the decision to leave. I didn't want to share the blame for the events that led up to that day or the weeks that followed."

Ella waited, wondering if he'd share more, hoping he would.

"I have many regrets," he said at last. "Losing your mother was a terrible blow. One from which I don't think I'll ever recover. But if I had listened to her and been more open to her opinions, things might have been different. I might not have lost my daughter. I might not have missed out on you and your sisters growing up." The remorse in his tone was impossible to miss. "I have to think Leo's father didn't listen to her either. We all share the blame."

"If only we had such clarity in the moment." She certainly wished she did.

"True," he said with a smile, then heaved a sigh. "It didn't have to be that way. I tend to speak my mind but rarely listen, though I'm determined to change that. I have come to see that Bethany was more like me than I realized. She wanted adventure, too. But I ignored that. While it's too late for me to reconcile with her, I don't want to lose a chance with you and your sisters."

"You haven't." Ella's heart filled at his words.

"Good. I'm pleased to hear that." He nodded, his gaze shifting to the flickering flames again. "Your parents' choices caused heartache, but that wasn't completely their fault. Everyone should have a chance to follow their dreams, wherever they might lead. It's by sharing our desires and listening in turn that we create connections. That we create family and the love that goes along with it. Those things are the true treasure."

"Yes, they are." Ella pondered his words, uncertain what more to say when her thoughts were whirling like a leaf in the wind from all he'd shared. "We are very pleased to have you in our life. I know Mother would be thrilled as well."

"I hope you will consider Rothwood House your home and enjoy your stay here. And I also hope that you find the courage to pursue your own dreams. I only ask that you share them with me. That you allow me into your life if I promise to do the same."

Her dreams? Ella didn't think she had any. She'd done her best to quickly dismiss any before they took hold since she'd been convinced following them would lead to pain and suffering.

Reaching for a goal meant releasing hold of something else. How could she possibly consider that when she had so little left to hold onto?

"You have given me much to consider. Thank you, Your Grace."

"Please. Call me Grandfather."

"Grandfather." Ella couldn't resist rising to hug him. After a moment, he returned her embrace. The feel of his strong arms around her put a lump of emotion in her throat.

He smiled as she drew back. The light in his eyes took years off his appearance. "I waited a long time to hear that. Thank goodness you gave me my wish." He reached out to take her hand. "Don't make the same mistakes I did, Ella. Life should bring joy. I realize you've experienced more than your share of heartache, but I hope that is beginning to change, and I want to help."

"I appreciate that more than I can say." While she didn't know if she was prepared to reach for a dream, her life was certainly changing. Hopefully, it was for the better. "Why don't we both do our best to focus on the joy?"

"Agreed," he said as he squeezed her hand in both of his.

Chapter Twenty-Three

THREE DAYS LATER, Leo sat with Worley in a hansom cab near Mincing Lane, keeping an eye out for Conway. Leo had spent a few hours each day since his conversation with Rothwood watching the man's home and following him on two occasions. He used a hansom cab, as it was unmarked and would draw less notice. Thus far, his efforts had been for naught.

From what little Leo had learned, the man did more selling than buying. How he came upon the items he sold was still a puzzle.

The worst part about keeping an eye on Conway was that it gave Leo far too much time to think. His thoughts constantly circled around Ella. He still doubted whether he'd done the right thing by writing the article about her father. Perhaps there had been a more effective way to convince the thief to return the journal, especially since no one had come forward yet.

Should he have told Ella he didn't mean any of it? But doing so would've been a falsehood, and he refused to lie to her. Then again, he hadn't wanted to hurt her either, though he knew he must have. That was a fact he deeply regretted.

"Is that him?" Worley asked as a man rounded the street corner and strode toward them.

"Yes." Leo frowned in surprise as he'd thought Conway inside. "He's out early this morning."

"How did someone like him come across a glassware collection from Versailles?" Worley scowled. "It makes no sense."

"No, it doesn't. I'm fairly certain he's sold a few things that haven't belonged to him. Whether he stole them himself or is simply willing to overlook how his supplier came to have them remains to be seen."

"I suppose one can pay a lower amount on stolen goods, especially if willing not to ask questions."

"I'm certain you're right."

Worley elbowed his arm. "Say that again. I don't hear it often enough from you."

Leo merely gave his friend a bland look, then returned his focus to Conway.

"Does he walk everywhere he goes?" Worley asked.

"Frequently, from what I've seen. Whether the reason is to pinch pennies or something else, I'm not sure."

"He seems to have numerous idiosyncrasies. Take his brightly colored attire for example."

Leo smiled at the jest as they watched Conway in his saffron-colored suit coat as he hurried up the front steps of his townhouse where he pulled a key from his pocket, unlocked the door, and disappeared inside.

"Perhaps we should have a look around his place next time he leaves," Worley suggested.

"I don't think his roommate would appreciate that. From what little I can tell, the man rarely leaves the house. We will watch a bit longer to see if Conway ventures out again."

Nearly an hour passed before he emerged and walked down the street.

"Thank goodness." Worley shifted on the hard bench seat. "Not that you aren't fine company, but I could use a little excitement to help keep me awake."

"Be careful what you wish for," Leo said. He rapped on the roof of the cab, having already told the driver to follow the man but not too closely.

After a brief delay, no doubt to allow Conway to move ahead, the cab rolled forward. The traffic soon thickened, and Leo wondered how far they'd be able to track him when he was on foot, and they were in the cab.

Conway hadn't gone much farther when he stopped near a muffin man holding a basket of baked goods. Conway purchased one and then stood nearby to eat it.

"I'll return directly," Worley said as he opened the door of the cab.

"Where are you going?" Leo asked.

"To buy some muffins."

Leo could only shake his head but remained where he was. Conway didn't know Worley but would surely recognize Leo. As Worley approached the muffin man, Conway flagged down a lad passing by and had a word with him. Then Conway flipped him a coin, which the boy deftly caught before hurrying away.

Worley, muffins in hand, had also seen the transaction, and with a glance at where Leo sat in the cab, tipped his head toward Conway and followed him.

Leo sighed, realizing that left him to follow the lad. Somehow, he was certain Worley had made the better bargain. Plus, his friend had the added benefit of the muffins. Leo's stomach growled in protest. He dearly hoped his efforts led him to the journal so he could return to Ella. He'd take that outcome over a muffin any day.

"Miss?"

Ella looked up to see Sally in the open doorway of her bedchamber where she'd been reading.

"There's a lad in the kitchen who says he has a message for you. I'm sorry to bother you, but he refused to give it to anyone else. Should I send him away?"

Her heart pounded dully as she considered what the message could be. Surely the boy had word of her father's journal. "I will speak with him. Thank you, Sally."

She rose from her desk, pulled a coin from her reticule, and followed the maid downstairs. She nodded at the cook and the rest of the staff, the kitchen bustling with the activity of cleaning up from breakfast and preparing for luncheon and dinner.

However, no lad was in sight.

"He's just outside the door, miss," the cook said with a gesture of her knife. "Too filthy to wait in here. Do you want one of the footmen to accompany you to speak with him?"

"No need." Ella didn't think a boy delivering a message intended any harm. She looked out the window to see a thin lad shifting from foot to foot, obviously anxious to be on his way. His brown jacket was indeed dirty and too big for his small frame. A cap sat low on his brow, and brown hair curled over his collar. "May I have a slice of buttered bread?" she asked a kitchen maid, who hurried to fetch it.

With the bread in hand, Ella stepped outside and offered it to him. "I understand you have a message for me."

"My thanks, miss." His brown eyes went wide at the sight of the unexpected treat. He took a big bite with relish, making her wonder when his last meal had been. "Indeed, I do." He formed the words while chewing the bread, then wiped his mouth with his coat sleeve. "I'm to tell ye that the item ye desire will be at Burkin and Boyd's shop near Trinity Square. But ye must get there within the hour. And ye must go alone."

Ella's heart raced. "Who sent you?"

"He didn't give a name, miss."

"Did he have brown hair with a slim build?" She held up a hand just above her own head to show how tall Mr. Conway was. "He probably wore a brightly colored suit. Gold or orange perhaps."

"That sounds like him." The lad nodded enthusiastically.

It had to have been Conway. However, she had no idea

where the shop was. "Are you familiar with that place?"

The boy nodded again, still chewing after taking another bite.

She held up the coin she'd brought. "I'd be happy to pay you another if you'd escort me there."

He smiled and pocketed the money. "Be happy to, miss. I'll get ye there straightaway."

"Wait here a moment, please." Ella stepped inside and asked the kitchen maid to give the lad another slice of bread. Then she started upstairs to fetch her cloak and reticule. Did she dare tell her sisters of her errand? That seemed like a terrible idea when she didn't want them to accompany her. There was no purpose in placing all three of them in a potentially dangerous situation. Nor did she have time to argue.

Yet she couldn't go alone. The memory of Leo's tenderness when he'd found her injured at the shop filled her mind as well as his warnings to take care. She'd send him a message to meet her at the shop but take two footmen along in case he wasn't available. She had no intention of listening to Conway's demand to go alone.

Her thoughts fell away as she stepped into the entrance hall, hardly able to believe her eyes.

"Leo?" The weight pressing on her shoulders suddenly lifted, nearly making her dizzy with relief.

"Ella." His hazel eyes held on her as he seemed to drink in her presence. Then urgency tightened his expression. "You're just who I need. There's a lad with a message from Conway—"

"Yes. He's at the servant's entrance."

"What did he say?"

"I'm to go to Burkin and Boyd's shop within the hour. The boy says he can show me the way."

"Excellent." Leo continued to study her, making her wonder what he saw. The traces of sleepless nights? The worry and unhappiness that had plagued her since their last conversation?

All of that would have to wait until after they'd ventured to the shop.

"I have a cab out front," Leo said. "We can take it."

Ella nodded, more relieved than she could say at his calming presence. "Davies, please have the lad brought out front. I'll get my things." She hurried upstairs to fetch her cloak, gloves, and reticule, making sure she had the second coin she'd promised the boy.

Within minutes, she'd rejoined Leo. Davies opened the front door to reveal a footman accompanying the lad to the cab.

"Here now. What's this?" the cab driver demanded as the boy clambered up beside him.

"He's our navigator," Leo advised. "I'll pay extra for the additional passengers."

Ella sat next to Leo on the narrow seat, the hard length of his form beside hers reassuring. His scent wrapped around her like a warm embrace. It was as if being physically together reduced the emotional distance between them. Despite their differences, having him at her side made her feel that everything would be all right. That not only would the meeting with Conway go well, but the issues between them would be resolved, too.

But how?

"Did you truly intend to go there alone?" Leo asked.

"I was about to send you a message to meet me there and take two footmen with me."

"What if I wasn't home?" He sighed, his dissatisfaction with her answer obvious. "I won't bother to tell you that would've been dangerous."

"Good." She turned her head away to look at the passing traffic, the warm feeling fading.

"Ella." The plea in Leo's voice had her turning to look at him. "I don't want anything to happen to you. You are too important."

To him? But she didn't ask as she was uncertain of the answer. "I didn't intend to take unnecessary risks." However, she dearly wanted her father's journal returned. "How did you know about the message?"

"I saw Conway speak to the lad and followed."

"You've been watching Conway?"

He nodded.

That surprised her. In all honesty, it touched her, as well. She thought he'd simply wait to see if anyone came forward to collect the reward rather than taking additional action.

"We have much to talk about when this is done." His quiet words sent a shiver of anticipation tingling along her spine.

Ella nodded, but further conversation would have to wait. Though it wasn't long before they arrived at the shop, her nerves were strung tightly by the time they halted near it.

The boy hopped down and opened the door. "It's just ahead." He pointed to it.

Ella studied the shop across the street, its name neatly painted on a sign above the door. The well-maintained front suggested it was one of the better ones compared to those she'd visited. That did little to reassure her.

The narrow street was busy with coaches, carts, wagons, and riders passing by. A mix of working-class and finely dressed people moved along the walkway.

"Perhaps I should go first and see if he's there," she suggested. "The sight of you might keep him away."

Leo scowled, then nodded reluctantly. "Worley was following Conway but may have lost him on the way here. I'll find a way inside without Conway seeing me. Convince him to show you the journal if possible. Keep him talking."

"About what?"

"Discuss arrangements for paying the reward. Tell him that it may take a day or two to gather the funds."

"And then?"

"By then, I'll be inside."

Ella nodded, struck by the fact that despite everything, she trusted Leo. There was no one she'd rather have at her side in this moment. While it still upset her that he didn't believe in her father's efforts, maybe she could show him the artifacts found on Oak Island, as well as some of the research her father had included in his journal. Perhaps the additional information would allow him to understand why her father had kept searching.

If nothing else, sharing further details might allow them to move beyond their past toward something more.

Knowing Leo would come for her and do all in his power to protect her and retrieve the journal was reassuring. But thinking of a possible future with him caused her heart to hammer so hard that she pressed a hand against her chest. In that instant, she knew exactly how she felt. She loved Leo with all she had within her.

"What is it?" he asked when she hesitated.

"Nothing." She drew a quick breath, trying to gather her wits. Now was not the time for emotion. "I will see you inside." She scooted forward and alighted.

"Ella?"

She paused to look at Leo. "Yes?"

"Take care. Take very good care."

Ella nodded, his concern touching. Then she turned to the lad. As promised, she handed him another coin. "Thank you for your help, sir."

"The name's Sam, miss." He offered a cheeky grin as he pocketed the money. "It's been my pleasure." His brow furrowed beneath his cap as he eyed the shop. "Ye goin' in alone?"

"For now." The sight of Leo's cab moving away left her feeling very much alone. Yet it wouldn't do to have Leo step out in case Conway was watching.

"Hmm. I might hang about a bit. See if ye have any need of me."

"I appreciate that, Sam. But please take care."

"And ye, miss." With another grin and a tug on the brim of his cap, he strode away.

Aware of time quickly passing, she searched for a break in the traffic, then hurried across the street. A variety of items were displayed in the shop window, including a carved wooden box, elegant crystal bowls, and brass candleholders. The place was definitely an improvement over the others she'd seen.

Gathering her courage, she opened the door. A bell heralded her arrival, but no other customers were visible.

"Hello?" She moved slowly forward, aware of every creak of the floor beneath her feet. "Is anybody here?"

The silence sent a chill along her skin and brought to mind what happened the last time she had entered a shop alone.

She walked a little farther, noting the various displays of statues, glassware, and dishes. A few pieces of jewelry were in a locked display case, and a stack of Persian rugs were rolled in a corner. A long wooden counter stood along the opposite side of the room, but no clerk was behind it.

"Miss Wright?"

Ella gave a quiet gasp, a small flutter of fear filling her as Conway emerged from the back of the shop. She no longer considered him harmless despite his friendly demeanor.

"Mr. Conway." She tightened her grip on her reticule as he drew closer, determined to keep her wits about her.

"I'm so pleased you received my message." He smiled as if they were on the friendliest of terms.

His demeanor irritated her, but she bit back a response. Expressing anger before she had the journal would be a mistake. "Do you have news of my father's journal?"

"I do. However, I believe there was mention of a reward."

She studied him, now seeing the sly look on his face and the hard glint in his eyes. It was perplexing to realize how different he was compared to his friendly persona aboard the ship. There seemed to be two sides to him, much like a coin.

"Yes, of course. We will be happy to pay it. But we require the journal to be returned first. I'm sure you understand."

Conway ran a finger along his upper lip as if pondering her words. "That poses a problem, as I need the money before handing over the journal."

"I'm sure you can see why proof is required." Leo's advice echoed in her thoughts, reminding her to keep Conway talking. It was more difficult than she had expected, especially since he appeared to be empty-handed. "We need to make certain that you not only have the journal but that it hasn't been damaged."

"I can assure you it's in fine condition."

"How did you come across it so quickly?" She truly was curious what he'd say, even though chances were he wouldn't tell the truth.

"As you suggested, I have many contacts in the collecting business. It was a matter of reaching out to one or two who had an interest in something of that nature."

"And they agreed to give it to you for a share of the reward rather than sell it?" She had no doubt his "contacts" were imaginary.

Conway frowned. "It seems that its value is now in question. Apparently, a recent article written by an earl who is supposedly an expert seems to have cooled the market for the journal. So much so, it is positively chilly." He chuckled at his jest.

"We seem to be at an impasse. What do you suggest?" she asked. Anything to keep him talking.

"I suggest a different arrangement, as new information has come to light. I recently heard of your association with the Duke of Rothwood. Imagine my surprise when I discovered you and your sisters were his granddaughters. You never mentioned it during our conversations on the ship."

Ella's stomach churned at his words, not liking the direction he was taking the conversation. She should've realized he knew her relation to her grandfather because he'd sent Sam with the message to Rothwood House. "We could hardly claim a relationship when he refused to acknowledge our existence."

"How unfortunate, though I have reason to believe that's been rectified by now." He took another step closer. Too close, in her opinion. Yet she didn't want to show fear by backing away. "I have to believe blood is blood, and he would pay an even prettier price for you."

"No." She stared at him in dismay as he loomed over her.

"Our original agreement stands. Show me the journal, and we will pay you the reward."

"I've decided that is no longer an option." Conway grabbed her arm, holding it painfully.

"Release me at once." Ella attempted to pull free, but he held tight. The man was stronger than he looked. Only the fact that Leo was nearby kept her panic at bay. At least, she hoped he was close. "You will receive the reward for the journal and nothing more."

"We shall see. We're going to send your grandfather a message and then we'll know how much he's willing to pay. Come along."

Ella's thoughts raced as Conway pulled her toward the back. Where was Leo?

⁂

LEO HOPPED OUT of the cab in the alleyway behind the shop. He hated to send Ella in first, but it seemed like the best option if they wanted the journal returned. He looked around one last time, concerned that Worley hadn't made an appearance. Instead of his friend, he saw the lad who'd delivered the message approach.

"Need help?" the boy asked.

"Are you volunteering?" Leo suspected he was more interested in another coin but appreciated his ingenuity. Since there was no sign of Worley, Leo welcomed the assistance.

"Happy to. The lady was kind to me. I'm Sam." He held out a hand which Leo shook.

"I'm Leo." He didn't bother with his title.

"What does the man who gave me the message want?" he asked as he kept pace with Leo.

"Money. He stole something precious from the lady."

Sam shook his head. "That ain't right. We should get it back for her."

"It could be dangerous," Leo warned as he tried to determine which door led to the shop.

"More dangerous than these streets?" Sam grinned. "Have no worries on my account. I've survived worse."

Given that his statement was probably true, Leo didn't bother to argue. Relieved to see a sign with the name of the shop, he turned the doorknob, pleased to feel it move beneath his hand.

He opened the door as quietly as possible and led the way inside, then paused a moment to glance around, listening carefully. The sound of voices from the front of the shop drifted toward him.

He took several steps inside and saw a small man with an apron standing in the doorway that led to the front. As if sensing their presence, he turned and gasped, eyes wide. Leo held a finger to his lips to make it clear he should remain quiet.

The man's mouth gaped open as he looked between Leo and the boy, his indecision obvious as to whether he should warn Conway. Leo narrowed his eyes with the hope his pointed glare made it clear that he should hold his silence.

The man's lips twisted, but he stepped aside to allow Leo to move closer to listen.

"I am not going anywhere with you." Ella's voice rang out clearly, the hint of anger in her tone suggesting Conway was being less than cooperative.

Conway responded, his words muffled. Leo continued forward, wanting a better view. He intended to take Conway by surprise before he did anything to hurt Ella.

"Where is the journal?" Ella demanded.

Anger grabbed hold of Leo at the sight of Conway attempting to pull her to the rear of the shop.

"You'll have it soon enough. But first, you will write a message to your grandfather to request him to send double the reward originally offered."

"I will do no such thing." Ella struggled with little success.

Conway chuckled. "You have nothing with which to bargain. Therefore, you'll have to pay my price. Since your grandfather is a duke, he can certainly afford it. It's only fair that he shares some of his wealth."

Leo's stomach clenched at Conway's words. Was the man truly so bold as to take Ella with the hope of getting more money?

"Release me at once!"

The demand had Leo striding forward, no longer caring about the journal. He only wanted to make certain Ella was safe.

Conway must've heard his approach, for when Leo passed a row of shelving and came into full view, he faced Leo with a glare that showed anger rather than surprise. He gripped Ella's upper arm tighter even as she continued to struggle against him.

"Let go."

"Do as she says, Conway," Leo ordered.

Instead of obeying, he shook Ella angrily. "I should've known you wouldn't come alone as I asked," he told her. Then he glared at Leo as he reached into his pocket. "Do you think I don't know who you are? The Earl of Marbury, the supposed expert on pirate treasure. The very same man who has cost me everything."

"Everything? I hardly think you can accuse me of that." He took another step forward, careful to keep his gaze away from Ella. Seeing her in danger shook him to the core.

Yet the faint gleam of a pistol in Conway's hand threatened to take him to his knees. His entire body stiffened at the fear of losing the woman who meant the world to him.

Chapter Twenty-Four

E LLA WINCED AS Conway tightened his grip on her arm. Yet nothing he did truly worried her now that Leo was here. She knew he'd protect her.

For the first time since her father died, she felt whole. Balanced. Filled with hope. As if the future once again looked bright and held the chance for happiness. Much of that had to do with the man who glared at Conway as if he wanted to rip him apart.

Leo's confidence bolstered her own.

"Release me," she demanded again with a jerk of her arm only to catch her breath as she saw the dull gleam of a pistol in Conway's hand.

The sight of the weapon nearly stopped her heart. Especially when he pointed it at Leo. She held as still as possible, fear threatening to choke her, even as she prayed this moment wouldn't end in disaster.

"Back away," he ordered Leo.

To Ella's horror, Leo took a step closer instead. "You don't want to use the weapon, Conway. A journal is not worth your life."

"This isn't just about the journal. It's about the reward the Duke of Rothwood will offer for the safe return of his newly found granddaughter. It's the least he could do since you ruined my chances of selling Wright's journal for a significant sum."

"Do you admit to taking it?" Leo asked.

Ella wanted to scream. How could Leo speak so calmly while Conway pointed the pistol at his chest? Her mind raced as she tried to think of what she could do or say to convince Conway to drop the gun.

"I admit nothing. But if you want to leave this shop unharmed, you will do as I say. Now back away."

Again, Leo took a step forward. "Killing me won't solve your problems. Just like killing the shopkeeper in Cheapside didn't aid you."

Ella blinked in surprise, even as Conway gasped. The hand holding her arm trembled, suggesting Leo's words had struck their mark.

She didn't know to whom Leo referred, but a glance at Conway's taut expression suggested he hadn't expected Leo to know about the death. To think Conway had killed someone shook her to the bone.

The barrel of the pistol wavered slightly. Ella held her breath as she hoped—prayed—that Leo was getting through to him.

Then Conway tightened his hold on her arm and swung the weapon to point at her temple. Cold fear crept over her, slowing her frantic thoughts to a crawl.

"Perhaps not," Conway said. "But killing Miss Wright might. Stay where you are."

"Doing so will end your life." Yet Leo halted, his gaze shifting to Ella, as if to send her strength, then back to Conway. "You don't want that. She is not to blame for your troubles. I am. Let her go, and take me in her place."

"You aren't listening. Neither of you understand," he insisted, his tone distraught. "I planned it so perfectly, and you've ruined it."

"I would guess your plans began to form soon after Mrs. Peterson died," Leo said.

The cold steel of the barrel pressed against Ella's head as Conway adjusted his hold. She held as still as possible, hardly daring to breathe.

"You know about her?"

"She was your stepsister," Leo answered.

"Yes, but I loved her so much more. She was everything to me. She was my world. I was devastated when she married Peterson and left for Oak Island. She only came to visit once and told me I couldn't go see her. That her husband would be angry if I did. Then she died." He sniffed, his voice catching. "It took some time before I could arrange my affairs to afford the trip to visit her grave and pay my respects." His gaze shifted to Ella. "I was stunned to find you and your sisters on the same steamship for my return home. It was as if fate offered me a new path."

"A path to what? Thievery and murder?" Leo asked.

"A path to a fortune. I am done living so modestly. It is time for me to have my due. To collect and keep rather than sell."

"Selling stolen goods isn't providing you a good wage?"

Was it Ella's imagination or was Leo slowly easing closer to a nearby shelf? Did he intend to use something on it as a weapon? If only he would give her an indication of his plan, she could help. Should she shove Conway? Attempt to knock the pistol from his hand?

One wrong move might see her or Leo shot. Indecision and fear kept her frozen in place.

She caught a movement out of the corner of her eye, but it wasn't Leo. Without turning her head, she couldn't tell for certain what—or who—it was. But surely whoever it was intended to help.

Leo looked at her, his hazel eyes full of a stark emotion she didn't dare name. In that moment, she knew that what stood between them didn't matter. Only the ties that connected them did. Everything else could be overcome.

Her love for Leo was a gift not to be dismissed. Neither Conway nor anyone else could take that away. The love she had for this man was worth fighting for.

Beginning now.

Ella gave a small nod, hoping Leo understood. She shoved the hand that held the pistol, then bent low to ram her shoulder into Conway's side, pushing him off balance.

He yelped as he struggled to keep his feet. Ella pushed him again for good measure as Leo lunged forward, reaching for the gun.

Conway dodged his outstretched hand, the weapon swinging wildly between Ella and Leo as if Conway was undecided who his target should be.

A small form shifted to join the fray. Sam ran forward, grabbed the arm not holding the gun, and pulled on it with all his might.

Leo reached for Conway's other arm, trying to wrest the pistol from his grip. The barrel bounced around the room as the two men fought for control.

Ella ducked when it pointed in her direction again. A loud bang filled the air, along with a flash of light.

She jerked at the sound as she tried to make sense of their flailing limbs, hoping beyond hope that no one had been hurt. "Leo?"

Grunts and a moan could be heard. Leo struck Conway in the jaw, the gun skittering across the floor. Leo hit him again in the stomach before the man fell backward into a shelf. The contents of glassware crashed on him as he slid to the ground.

"Ella?" Leo spun to face her, eyes wild as his gaze swept over her. "Are you all right?"

"Yes. Are you?" She searched his form, relieved to see no obvious sign of an injury.

"Fine." Leo turned, breathing hard, to examine the boy. "What of you, Sam?"

"He missed me by a mile." Yet he rubbed his shoulder as if not completely unscathed.

"Are you certain?" Leo asked as he bent to retrieve the gun, keeping an eye on Conway's still form.

"Nothing but a bruise or two." Sam shook his head. "He's

stronger than he looks."

"Indeed." Leo flexed the hand with which he'd struck Conway as if it hurt. "Thank you for your assistance."

"Happy to help. I'll see if there's some rope in the back to tie him up."

As he walked away, Ella moved close to Leo, looking him over from head to toe again, unable to believe neither of them was hurt. His neckcloth was askew, his suit coat rumpled, and his chest heaved, but he looked so precious to her.

Leo wrapped his arms around her and held tight. "I feared the worst when the gun went off."

"As did I." She returned his embrace, gratitude filling her along with love. "Thank you."

"For what?"

"For saving me."

Leo drew back to look into her eyes, running a gentle finger along her cheek. "You were well on your way to saving yourself."

"Leo, I'm sorry for what I said last time we were together. I should've—"

"Shh." He shook his head. "It's me who should apologize. I'm sorry I rushed to write the article."

Conway moaned, interrupting the conversation.

"We shall talk more after we resolve this matter." Then to Ella's surprise, Leo took her mouth in a heated, if brief, kiss. One so full of promise that she felt it all the way to her toes.

He released her as Sam returned from the back with the shopkeeper, holding a length of twine. As Conway stirred, they bound his hands behind his back. Ella noted a cut on Conway's forehead but had no interest in tending it. The man deserved far worse.

"You might need a repair or two," Sam advised the shopkeeper as he looked at a small hole now in the ceiling.

"I had no idea he intended anyone harm." The shopkeeper shook his head. "He's never done anything like this before."

"Count yourself lucky," Leo said. "One of his other contacts ended up dead."

"Shall I fetch a copper?" Sam asked. At Leo's nod, he was out the door in a flash.

Worley rushed into the shop, his gaze taking in the scene. "It seems I'm too late."

"Where have you been?" Leo asked.

"I lost Conway on the street, so I went to Rothwood's to see if you had gone there. Luckily, the butler knew the name of the shop where you were meeting. What happened?"

Leo explained the details, his arm around Ella. Then with a frown, he bent to pat Conway's clothing and then looked back at her, remorse in his expression. "I'm sorry, but he doesn't seem to have the journal."

"Journal?" The shopkeeper raised a finger. "He handed me something of the sort before you arrived. Told me to keep it safe. Allow me a moment." The man hurried to the back and returned shortly with it.

"Oh!" Tears filled Ella's eyes as she stepped forward to take the journal. "This is it." She turned it over, running her gloved hands over the surface, then paged through it, relieved to find it in good condition.

"Perfect." Leo shared a smile with her. "I'm pleased it's back in your hands."

"As am I." Ella clutched it tight, hardly able to believe she had it back.

A policeman arrived soon after, though Sam seemed to have disappeared. Leo provided the officer with the details of what had occurred, including his suspicions about the murdered shopkeeper in Cheapside, and handed him Conway's gun.

Conway roused as he was being hauled away. "Damn you, Marbury. Damn you to hell."

Leo ignored him, turning his attention to Ella. "Shall I escort you home?"

"Please."

"I'm relieved you're both unharmed," Worley said with a

clap on Leo's shoulder and a nod at Ella. "I'll see you at the club later."

Leo kept his arm around her as they walked out the back to the waiting cab. He assisted her inside and, as soon as the door was closed, drew her into his arms.

"I have so much to say to you," he whispered as he stared into her eyes, his hand cupping her cheek.

"Do you?" Suddenly breathless with her heart pounding madly, Ella waited, scared to hope that whatever he said might match her feelings.

"You have opened my eyes in so many ways. After seeing the misery of my parents, I was convinced love meant heartache. I had no intention of ever losing my heart at the risk of becoming as miserable as they both were. But you made me realize love is none of that. It's more. I love you, Ella. So very much. You bring out the best in me. You've helped me see what's truly important in life."

"Oh, Leo." Ella's heart overflowed with emotion. "I love you, too. I was certain that I needed to focus on my sisters and that dreaming of something more would only hurt others. But you have changed all that."

"Before you came to London, I had dinner with your grandfather. He told me how different he wanted his life to be, but neither of us could have guessed that you and your sisters would soon arrive as if the answer to his wish."

Ella chuckled. "For a time, I rather thought we were his worst nightmare."

"Perhaps you were. Sometimes we need to be thrust into new circumstances to grow and change. I hope you will give him—and me—the chance to show you how much we care."

"I would like that very much," Ella whispered. Then she leaned close to kiss him, pouring all she felt into the moment. She never could've dreamed loving this man was possible. But she already knew she couldn't live without him.

"Ella?" Leo drew back to look into her eyes even as he still held her tight.

"Yes?"

He loosened his embrace and then shifted to face her, still holding her hand. "I intend to speak with the duke, but I want to ask you first. Will you please do me the honor of marrying me? I promise to love and cherish you always."

"Yes." Ella blinked back tears as she nodded. "I should very much like to be your wife." She pulled him back up beside her, and they kissed once again.

As the swaying cab neared Rothwood House, a dose of reality struck Ella. "What of your mother? She won't be pleased."

"I think eventually she will come around. She is already fond of you and your sisters and wants me to be happy. Perhaps our union will heal all of us from previous events."

"I hope that's true. But I don't want to focus on the past. I only want to think of this moment and what the coming days will bring."

"A future with you will be as bright and beautiful as you are. We shall make it so together." He kissed her again only to draw back. "What will your sisters think?"

"I know they'll be happy for me. For us. But I wonder how my grandfather will take the news."

"It might come as a surprise, but I have no doubt he'll be pleased. Especially when he knows I will not take you from him just when he's growing to care for you."

A footman opened the door. Leo stepped out and then helped Ella to alight as she held tight to the journal with one hand and took his offered arm with the other.

"I suppose I never realized he would worry that we'd leave once we married. But, of course, he wouldn't want to risk allowing himself to care only to lose us again."

"I'm certain that's part of it. Let us see if our news helps to convince him otherwise."

Ella grinned. "I hope our union is an answer to his wish."

"As do I. You are certainly the answer to mine."

A WEEK LATER, Leo replaced his pen in the stand on his desk and read the article he'd written one last time to make certain it included everything he intended. Then he read it a third time and made a few final edits. Yes, he decided. It was exactly the message he wanted to share.

David Wright's journal had been different than he'd expected. The fact that Ella had handed it to him with her sisters' blessing the same day she'd gotten it back had only increased his love for her.

"Are you certain?" He'd reluctantly taken it as they visited in the drawing room.

"Yes." Ella nodded. "I'm not trying to change your opinion of my father. But I would like for you to better understand his work. This is only the last of several journals, of course, but I still think it will give you a glimpse into his research."

Norah and Lena had agreed. The three had also shown him the artifacts they'd brought with them.

Those had been interesting, but he'd still been both honored and worried to read the journal, for he feared it truly wouldn't change his opinion. He didn't want to hurt Ella's feelings more than he already had.

If recent events had taught him anything, it was that she mattered more than he could've imagined. He loved her with his whole heart, and he still couldn't believe the happy turn his life had taken.

When he'd returned Ella to Rothwood's, he had spoken to the duke and asked for Ella's hand in marriage. The duke had been stunned by his request but thrilled as well. Her sisters had been much the same, each offering their congratulations.

Leo's mother had been much less astounded than he expected. While pleased, she had seemed reserved, as if still waiting to see how the situation would unfold. But after Ella had spoken with her in private, his mother had been genuinely happy for them.

A formal announcement of their betrothal wouldn't occur for another month as Ella didn't want to take attention away from her sisters during these first few weeks of the Season.

In fact, he would be late for their second ball if he didn't hurry, he realized as he checked the time.

Leo didn't intend to hide his wooing of Ella from anyone paying attention. The more time he spent with her, the more anxious he was for them to begin their life together.

He jotted a quick note to accompany the article and requested a footman to deliver it to the editor of the Royal Geological Society's weekly news sheet. Then he hurried upstairs to his bedchamber and rang for his valet.

In short order, he and his mother were settled in the carriage for the brief ride to the Stallworth ball.

"Shall we host a dinner party when you and Miss Wright are ready to share the happy news of your betrothal?" his mother asked.

Leo looked at her in surprise. "Are you certain you want to?"

"Of course." She smiled. "I do believe your marriage will provide a chance to heal some of the past."

He took his mother's hand. "I am relieved you feel that way. I wouldn't want my love for Ella to cause you hurt."

She turned her hand in his and held tight. "You must know that I only want you to be happy, Leo. That is what I've always wanted."

A tightness in his chest loosened at her words. Never would he have guessed that she would welcome David Wright's daughter into her life with open arms. "Thank you, Mother."

"I will wait to share the news until after the announcement, but that doesn't mean I can't hint at it, does it?"

Leo chuckled as he assisted her to alight and escorted her into the ballroom. He wouldn't tell her not to when he intended to do the same.

"You seem to be in fine spirits," Worley said, having found him directly after Leo left his mother with her friends.

"I am, indeed."

"Because Conway is in custody?" A hint of doubt lingered in Worley's tone.

Conway had been charged with stealing the journal and other items found in his home, along with the murder of the Cheapside shopkeeper. Apparently, the two had an argument about the journal, and Conway had struck him in a fit of rage. Conway's future looked dim, but that was not Leo's concern. The man had chosen the wrong path to follow.

Before Leo could answer, his attention caught on Ella's arrival. She looked so beautiful this evening that his heart squeezed. Then again, it seemed to do that each and every time he saw her. Her lavender silk gown had a grey sheen that shimmered as she moved. The modest bustle and train emphasized her curves. Her honey-colored hair was swept into an elegant coiffure that made her look every inch the duke's granddaughter.

When her gaze found his, he caught his breath at the joy in their depths.

"I am certain your happy mood has nothing to do with Conway," Worley said as he looked between Leo and Ella. "May I guess as to what has put the smitten look upon your face?"

"I can neither confirm nor deny that I am formally courting Miss Ella Wright."

"No need for me to ask if the lady returns your regard." Worley slapped him on the shoulder. "May I be the first to offer congratulations?"

"Thank you." Leo gave a satisfied nod. "Now if you'll excuse me, I would like to dance with her."

Leo made his way to her side, feeling no remorse at elbowing aside the other gentlemen who had immediately crowded around the sisters.

"Good evening, Miss Wright." He took Ella's hand to lift it in his, pressing his lips to it as he bowed.

"My lord." Her graceful curtsy as she smiled sent a pang of desire spearing through him. "How wonderful to see you."

He greeted her sisters, as well as Lady Havenby who stood nearby, positively beaming at the success of her charges. Then he looked back at Ella. "May I have the first and last dance with you?"

Ella chuckled. "Won't that spur gossip as to your intentions?"

"I certainly hope so." He glared at a few of the other men who stood too close to Ella as far as he was concerned. "I do believe the first dance will soon begin. Shall we?"

She took his offered arm, and he tucked her hand possessively under his and moved toward the dance floor. Once again, everything felt right now that she was at his side.

"Have I told you lately that I adore you?" he whispered, delighted when a delicate blush crept up her cheeks. "You look beautiful this evening. Then again, you always do."

"Leo." The censure in her tone only made him grin.

"Yes, my love?"

"Hush." She looked around worriedly. "Someone will hear you."

"Good." He tightened his hold on her arm. "Then the others will keep their distance."

Her gaze met his, and the love shining in her eyes swept all else away. The dance began, and they moved across the floor with ease. She felt so perfect in his arms that he couldn't wait to make her his in every sense of the word. They belonged together. Of that, he had no doubt.

When the dance ended, he guided them to a tiny alcove along the wall, partially hidden by a column. "Ella?"

"Yes?"

"I love you." Then he claimed her mouth, hoping she understood just how much he wanted her. He deepened the kiss, his tongue finding hers as his passion rose.

"Leo." Ella placed her gloved hand along his cheek. "I love you, as well. I confess that waiting to become your wife won't be easy."

"On that, we agree. I intend to take as many moments alone with you as I can."

"Perfect, as I intend to do the same."

He released a low groan as need for her threatened his common sense. "I want to escort you out to the terrace and find a dark corner so that I can have my way with you."

"That sounds terribly exciting," she said with a grin. "But perhaps we should wait until the next ball."

He sighed. "If you insist." Then he took her hand and tucked it against his side and moved to the edge of the dance floor once more. He searched his thoughts for something to distract him from the desire pulsing through him. "I finished your father's journal today."

"You did?" She studied him closely. "And?"

"I thought it very insightful."

Her pleased expression sent a well of emotion through him. "Good."

To his astonishment, she seemed completely satisfied with his answer, as if that was all she hoped for. That only made him love her more.

"I confess that I wrote another article," he said as they slowly made their way back to Lady Havenby. Her sisters were still on the dance floor.

"Oh?" Ella frowned as she looked up at him.

"Upon further research, it has become evident that something intriguing happened on Oak Island. I don't know if Captain Kidd or any other pirates hid treasure there, but someone went to a considerable effort to hide something. Your father's notes make that abundantly clear. I'm very sorry he died in the process of proving it." Leo wondered if the collapse of the shaft David Wright had been digging might have destroyed the chance of finding whatever was buried there.

"You shared that in the article?" Ella's eyes were round with surprise.

"I did. His work shouldn't be forgotten. If I can help make sure it isn't, I will."

"Oh, Leo." Ella blinked rapidly as if about to cry. "That means so much to me."

"I'm glad. I only wrote my true opinion."

"You read the journal. That is all I wanted. Thank you, my love."

"The two of you are drawing far too much interest," Lady Havenby said as she joined them with a worried glance around. "The gossip is already starting."

"Good," Leo's mother said as she drew close. "It's time the *ton* has a new topic to discuss. However, I rather like that it's still in the family."

Lady Havenby's mouth gaped open. "You do?"

Leo shared a look with his mother, then with Ella, and smiled, love filling his heart. He had found a happiness that he hadn't dreamed possible, and it made everything they'd been through worth the price.

Epilogue

Five years later...

"ARE THE CHILDREN asleep?" Ella asked from where she sat at her dressing table as Leo entered her bedchamber. She'd already prepared for bed, wearing a pale blue nightgown with a daring neckline that she was certain would catch Leo's eye.

Evening had fallen at their country estate where they enjoyed the last days of summer. They were due to return to London in two days. Ella looked forward to seeing family and friends, but she adored their time at their home in Lincolnshire. The country was relaxing and so enjoyable, and the children loved it.

"I didn't think Alex would ever close his eyes," Leo said as he shrugged out of his suit coat. "Who knew that a four-year-old could have so much energy?"

Ella chuckled. Leo insisted on seeing the children to bed whenever possible. "And what of Lily?" Though only two years old, she kept up with her brother in fine fashion.

"She was asleep before her head touched the pillow." Leo's smile hinted at his adoration for their daughter.

"Excellent." She met Leo's gaze in the mirror. "That leaves the rest of the evening for us."

"Indeed, it does." He stepped close to rest his hands on her shoulders, his thumb moving back and forth against the bare skin.

Though small, the gesture sent shivers of awareness along her body. "What do you propose we do?"

"I suggest we make love." Already her breasts tingled with anticipation, her nipples tightening from her husband's touch.

Leo smiled, then bent low to kiss her bare shoulder. "I should like that very much." His tongue trailed along her skin as she reached up to grasp one of his hands in hers.

She tipped her head to the side, delighted when he pressed kisses along the length of her neck.

He straightened and pulled the pins from her hair one by one, until it fell along her back, combing the strands with his fingers as his gaze held hers in the mirror. "You are so lovely," he murmured. Then he bent to trail a finger along the daring neckline of her nightgown over the swell of her breasts.

Ella arched in response as liquid heat poured through her. She would never grow weary of this man's touch, nor would her love for him ever falter. She loved him deeply, more with each year that passed. She'd told him that numerous times and, though it crossed her mind to do so again, it would have to wait. All she could think about now was his touch and the ache that pulsed through her.

He reached one finger inside the fabric to caress the tip of her breast and her breath caught.

Anxious for more, she pulled on the ribbon that held the neckline in place to provide him better access. Then she wound an arm around his neck and drew him close to kiss along his strong jaw. His scent, a mix of bergamot and the outdoors, never failed to stir her.

"You are a siren, dear wife," he whispered in her ear, causing her to shiver again.

"Does that mean I can lure you to our bed?"

"Most definitely." Yet instead of taking her in his arms, he once again met her gaze in the mirror. "You grow more precious to me with each year we spend together." He eased the gown down her torso until her breasts were visible, then her stomach.

He shifted to her side and turned her to face him. Then he knelt before her chair and took her nipple in his mouth, licking the tight bud until she could hardly bear it.

The sight of his dark head against her naked skin stirred her more than she could've guessed. Then he eased lower still to kiss her belly, his warm hands roaming over her, and it was all she could do to sit still.

"Leo?" She was breathless with need.

"Yes, my love." He placed a gentle hand on her leg and eased it aside to move between her knees. He kissed her again, his tongue sweeping along hers, bringing her desire even higher.

She tangled her fingers in his hair and then pushed his unbuttoned waistcoat off his shoulders before making quick work of his linen shirt. He drew back long enough to shrug it off, leaving him only in his trousers.

He kissed her again before moving slowly down her body, his tongue trailing a blaze of heat along her fevered flesh. Then he bent low to kiss her very center, his fingers dancing along her thighs. She leaned back, wanting more of his touch.

"Yes." His tongue glided along her center and her hips bucked with need.

"Leo. Please."

"Let go, my love." Then using fingers and tongue, he led her to the edge where her entire world shattered behind her closed lids.

Before she'd settled back to earth, he lifted her to carry her to the bed where the covers were already pulled back. In mere seconds, he'd removed his trousers and settled over her, his hard manhood finding home between her thighs. With one quick, satisfying thrust, he entered her, then stilled as if to savor the moment.

"I love you, Ella."

"And I love you," she whispered, her heart full.

She was still amazed that this wonderful man had come into her life and swept her off her feet. She held him tight, hoping he felt as cherished and loved as she did.

When at last he stiffened with his release, she wrapped her arms around him and followed gladly.

Their world slowly settled, then Leo shifted to the side to gather her into his arms, her head cradled on his shoulder.

"I never thought life could be the blessing I have found with you," he whispered.

"Nor did I. To think it started with my grandfather's wish." Leo had told her the story many times of that evening in her grandfather's study before she and her sisters' arrival.

Leo chuckled. "Once upon a duke's wish. It sounds like a fairytale we can tell our children."

"I already have." Ella leaned up and kissed him once again.

About the Author

Lana Williams is a USA Today Bestselling Author with over 35 historical romances filled with mystery, adventure, and sometimes, a pinch of paranormal to stir things up. Filled with a love of books from an early age, Lana put pen to paper and decided happy endings were a must in any story she created.

Lana writes full time, spending her days in Victorian, Regency, and Medieval times, depending on her mood and current deadline. She lives in the Rocky Mountains with her husband, and a spoiled lab, and loves hearing from readers. Check out her website and say hello.

Website: lanawilliams.net
Facebook: LanaWilliamsBooks
Twitter: LanaWilliams28
Instagram: authorlanawilliams